Lottery and Other Stories

By

Mary-Rose Benton

Published by

MELROSE BOOKS

An Imprint of Melrose Press Limited
St Thomas Place, Ely
Cambridgeshire
CB7 4GG, UK
www.melrosebooks.co.uk

FIRST EDITION

Cover designed by Hannah Belcher

ISBN 978-1-907732-87-4

Printed and bound in Great Britain by:
TJ International Ltd, Padstow, Cornwall

CONTENTS

LOTTERY

Barbara staggered out of bed, yawning. Her cat, Shroedinger, miaowed. "OK, puss, I'll get the sachet. Now then, scissors; where did I put the scissors?" She had better make it quick. She had some much-needed money to pick up. In her haste, plunging her hand into the drawer, she stabbed herself on the scissors. "Aah! Son of a bitch!" More time wasted, as she dashed to the sink and put her hand under the cold tap. She ripped off a square of kitchen tissue and wrapped it round her hand. "I can't miss work today, puss, I have $10,000 to pick up." The cat bumped his silky head against her leg and followed up with his body and tail. "No good you smooching me, animal. If I don't eat, you starve." She had had a spectacular stroke of luck. The office lottery was due to pay out today, and she had won the jackpot, but the winner had to be at the office by nine o'clock, or the win was invalid and the money went on to the next draw.

By the time her hand was bound and the cat was fed, it was a quarter after eight. Well, she would show her face, and the injured hand, then hope for the best. Except that something else intervened. Mr Miller from down the corridor came knocking.

"Barbara, sorry to catch you in your bathrobe like this, only I have a favour to ask of you." Barbara's heart sank, but Mr Miller did many a good turn for her.

"I have to work late this evening, and my brother Martin is coming to stay. Well, we're both getting on, and we might not get to see each other again. Could you take my key and let him in, please? He knows where the drinks are, and he can look after himself."

"Sure, Mr Miller, gladly." Barbara took the key from him as quickly as she decently could, then picked out a light grey suit and a shoulder bag in green leather to match the scarf, chose her favourite red shoes, that she had saved up for, and which now made her life perfect; threw her wallet, cellphone, keys and plastics in her bag; put it, for safety, over her head as well as her shoulder, and made for the door. Most days, she took the local elevators to her office, stopping to chat to friends on the way, but today she would get the express elevators to the one-hundred-and-tenth floor and run down to the ninety-seventh. Just as she was about to leave the front door, the old lady on the ground floor called to her.

"I'm clean out of milk, Barbara; could you let me have a cupful before you go? I can't get out just yet. I still have my nightgown on."

* * *

Barbara usually walked the few blocks from 34th Street, bought the *New York Times* and the British *Guardian* and went on through Vesey Street to West Street, but she decided today to take the subway. It was crowded, and she got jostled and pushed about, as everybody made a dash for the doors. She let the crowd get on before her and waited to get on last. She was about to board the train, when a young man behind her touched her politely on the shoulder and said, casually, "I'll have that," took the bag from her shoulder, wrenching it roughly over her head, and turned and ran quickly back up the steps. Except for her instinctive good sense in not struggling, she had no other time to react, and there was no hope of getting the bag back, nor any other way in which to go. She had to jump on the train.

* * *

Once Barbara was on the train, the enormity of what had happened began to seep its way into her mind, made worse by the fact that even those who did seem interested gave her only an indifferent glance. They were just glad it was her problem, not theirs. However, one woman had sympathy to spare. She passed her tissues and even gave her a few dollars to make phone calls.

She was not aware of getting off the train, nor even of having boarded it, as she walked in a daze southwards. Not usually superstitious, she was aware of a growing fear that an evil conspiracy was at work, trying to stop her in her tracks. By now, she hardly cared what happened to her, as long as she was not too late to pick up the $10,000.

She stopped as usual to buy *The Guardian*; she had an English boss, who drove to work and didn't have the leisure to stop and get it. No point in antagonizing him by leaving it. As she stood at the kiosk, the man in front was fussing over his change. Barbara was too distracted to make it a priority, but was acutely aware of the delay. At last the man was satisfied, and she asked for the paper.

"Sorry, your Limey paper's gone, do you want the London *Times* instead?" Barbara began to get hysterical, gasping as the tears started up again.

"Jeez, lady, it ain't the end of the world. Move on, will ya, I got a living to make."

* * *

It was when Barbara was crossing the last road that the worst happened. A careless driver shot the lights, brushing against her not enough to hurt, but sent her sprawling. When she got up, stumbling to the sidewalk, she realised that one of her shoes had come off and was being mangled by the traffic. Worse than losing the pair, she would have to throw the other one away. She looked at her watch. It was still working and showed the time as eight forty-six. She had only fourteen minutes to get to the ninety-seventh floor, but she was much too far away. It would have taken her a quarter of an hour just to get to the entrance. She could see the famous buildings from where she was. She would surely lose the money now.

"Goddamn it all to hell!" she shouted at the world. "This has got to be the unluckiest day of my life."

It was, in fact, the luckiest. As she looked up at the North Tower of the World Trade Center, at fourteen minutes to nine on September 11th, she saw the Boeing 767 come straight at it out of a mild autumn sky.

ADA MAY

I'm nothing special, me. I like it here; the matron's nice. They're holding a special birthday party for me on Thursday, with just one candle. Well, I don't think I'm up to blowing out a hundred.

I hear a lot of talk in here about 'the good old days'. There was no such thing. And when I remind them how awful life could be, they go, "Ah, but we was happy!" "No, yo' wasn't," I says. "Yo' was bloody miserable." "Ah, but, Ada May," they says, "our hardships have stood us in good stead. It made us what we are today." I don't like to reply to that one, it wouldn't be charitable. Besides, I tell them, if it was so good in the old days, why did anyone want to change it? They've got nothing to say to that one. Some of them are very bitter, but they won't admit that it's because they've been knocked about by life. Not everybody rises above it.

I'm not saying that we didn't have some good times. But you had to snatch at them and mek the most of it. We couldn't afford to go on holiday till about the late 1930s, but we used to go regular to Cannon Hill Park of a weekend. We'd take sandwiches, then come teatime, we'd have a tray with a pot of tea for the four of us. We'd play cricket on the grass, feed the ducks and go in the greenhouse to see the plants from hot countries. That was entertainment for us. Like at home in evening, when we'd play Ludo or read our comics and annuals. Mom and Dad always tried to make Christmas special for us; they'd manage to get some toys from the Church charities: second-hand, but painted up nice; and the British Legion would help out, if your dad had served in the war. We saved up farthings for the turkey, and we put them in a tin on the mantelpiece. Until our kid kept pinching them, to buy marbles with. Mom began to suspect something, because the level didn't go up. Not only that, our kid took to coming down in the middle of the night, saying he had to go out to the lav. So that was when he was tekkin' them.

worcestershire
countycouncil

****
* TICKET NOT VALID **
* FOR ANY TRAVEL **
****

Wed 06 Sep 201[illegible]
13:28

Driver No: 50012
Bus No: 3552
Route No: 16

****

Address

WCC W[illegible]don Depot
Pershore Lane
Warndon
Worcester
WR4 0AA

****
* TICKET NOT VALID **
* FOR ANY TRAVEL **
****

worcestershire
countycouncil

****

** TICKET NOT VALID **

** FOR ANY TRAVEL **

****

Wed 06 Sep 2017

13:28

Driver No: 60012

Bus No: 3552

Route No: 25

****

Address:

WCC [illegible] Depot

Pershore Lane

Warndon

Worcester

WR4 0AA

****

** TICKET NOT VALID **

** FOR ANY TRAVEL **

****

So what our Mom did, she smeared frying fat round the tin. So, come the night time, and our lad goes downstairs as per, reaches up to the mantelpiece and grabs the tin.

Well, it only goes sliding out of his little hands, and the coins all go clattering over the hearth, falling in the coal scuttle, in among the fire irons, and the dog jumps out of his bed and starts barking; thinks it's a game. I hear Mom giggling in the next bedroom, then she goes stomping downstairs, trying to keep a straight face, and I hear her scolding him. "I had to get some marbles, to keep up with the lads at school," he says to her. "I'll give you marbles, you little bugger." "Oh, will you?" he says, "thanks, our Mom," making a run for it to the lav. So she picks up the dish clout and throws it after 'im. She never stayed angry for long, our mother. But she did want to teach him a lesson, so she had to punish him somehow. So she decided not to let him have bread and dripping for his supper. He had to have bread and marge instead. And it wasn't like the nice stuff you have now; God, it was horrible, bright orange, and they called it oleo margarine. Anyway, there's us, sitting at the supper table, with our bread and dripping, and Mom saying, "It's a nice bit of dripping this week, isn't it?" And Dad saying, "Pass us the salt, Mother, I'd like a bit more on my piece, it brings out the flavour lovely." And everyone going, "Um, yes, it's smashing, is there any more to spare?" He never lived that down, our Jackie.

I wouldn't say that life hasn't got me down now and then, but I've fallen on my feet once or twice. But some people get it in the neck from day one. Take the kiddie next door to us in Angelina Street. The dad was alright, but the mom was horrible. She didn't love her kids at all. She left the poker in the fire once, and that must have been deliberate. Then she told the big girl to fetch the eldest lad in at once. But because the girl didn't go straight away, the mom took the poker out the fire and whacked it across the girl's legs. She grew up having to wear lisle stockings to hide her scars. And other gels had got nice rayon or nylons when the Yanks came over. As for the boy, well, she kept trying to kill him; quite blatant, too. The one time, she locked him in the garden coal shed; he kept shouting for the neighbours, and they had to call the police. Then, another time, she came at him with a knife. He was struggling on the landing and the other kids had to tear her off him. He goes off all round the world now, to the most dangerous places. He's only a binman, but he saves up real hard and takes a holiday several times a year to all the danger spots. It's like he's trying to prove how strong he is after all the damage she done.

Anyway, his dad was off sick once, he'd had an accident off his bike, and he was sat on the sofa, not able to move with all the splints and bandages. She'd gone out to get some sugar, *she* says, but really she was off to see her fancy man. And the dad had to look after the babby, who was in his high chair. The kiddie was playing with his porridge and rocking back and forth in his chair, and it overbalanced and he fell in the fire. The dad could only shout and try to get the neighbours in, but they didn't hear him, or they thought it was just another family row. The babby was screaming, too. His little head was right in the fire; the screams must have been terrible. They just went on and on, then they got fainter, and by the time the woman next door come in, he'd stopped. She dashed over to him and did what she could, and someone got the ambulance. But the little lad died on the way to the hospital.

His mother didn't seem all that bothered, but the dad was never the same again. He always was a quiet man, and he would go to his allotments for peace and quiet, but still he couldn't get it out of his head, ever. The little bowl of porridge, the high chair and the kiddie's little head in that terrible fire, and him shouting and shouting for someone to come. It was the way they had to live in those times: the houses, and everyone crammed in. They started falling down, too, in the Fifties; several people got killed. The houses were so rotten, they just fell down round their ears and crushed them.

The son come home from work one day, the one as goes all over the world, and the dad hadn't come in. He asked his mom where his dad was, but she said he was on the allotments, so he could be some time. The son felt something was up, and he couldn't think what, but he said he'd give it another hour, then he'd go and look. Well, as soon as the hour was up, the son went to the allotments. When he got to his dad's plot, he knew something was wrong. The spade and fork and other stuff was still out – his dad was meticulous, as a rule, he put everything tidy before he went. Well, the lad went up the path and the shed door was open. Every time he's told me the story, he's said how his heart thumped.

He didn't hardly dare look in, but he pushed at the door – it was hard to shift. He had to put his shoulder to it. Then he knew something bad had happened. He finally got in and found his dad slumped against the door with his fist held tight against his chest; he tried to wake him and kept shouting "Dad! Dad!" For a long time, but it was too late. Oh well, I mustn't get morbid. I've got a lot to be glad on myself, like living to a hundred, for a start off. And because I was the youngest girl, I had some sort of childhood. I didn't have to look after the other children, like the eldest girls had to in those days. They did get to go to school, of course, not like their aunties and mothers, who were the eldest, but all the same, they didn't get the chances they might have. Anyway, I came in for a lot of teasing from the boys after I left school, because of my name. "Winnie won't, but Ada May," they used to call out. I didn't mind, I was a natural flirt. But I didn't get married. By the time I come of age, most of the young men had been killed off in the war.

Well, like I said, I'm nothing special. Just an ordinary woman, like millions of others, before and after me.

ALL CLEAR

The All Clear lifted its joyful sound to the sky.

"Everyone out of the shelter and back to the house," said Dad, "and if anyone wants to go to the lav, go now, before I lock up." As he walked up the garden path, he disturbed next door's cat, which jumped off the lavatory roof and fled.

Mum swept up the bedclothes and followed Dad up the path into the house, leaving the baby, Billy, till last, in his Moses basket. The older children jumped off their bunks and trudged back up the path. A dog barked non-stop.

"Any minute now," said Dad, "I'm going across to put my boot down that dog's throat."

"Make the kids a cup of cocoa, Jack," Mum said, "while I take these upstairs, then I'll go back and get the baby."

Jack Goodwin got out the cups and the cocoa, while the kettle boiled. The children racketed around, squabbling.

Mum was about to go and get Billy, at the same time as the kettle began to whistle. Something else whistled, too, as an undetected straggler dropped the last of his load. The house was demolished, and everyone in it perished. Baby Billy, now without a family, jumped in his basket, then waited confidently for his mother to come and take him back into the house.

* * *

Professor William Goodwin sat talking with his students. The conversation began in the usual mundane way, when a pupil asked him how people entertained themselves in the home before television.

"Strictly speaking, it had been invented, but very few people could afford it. It was the middle Fifties before we had one."

"They all stood round the piano, thinking, 'I wish someone knew how to play this damn thing,'" said the class wit. Bill Goodwin smiled amid the laughter; it was one of his own favourite gags. "I wish we could go back in time," said one. "It must have been a very vivid time: living while history was being made."

"There's no such thing as time travel," a young man said, "otherwise someone would already have come from the future to tell us about it."

"How do we know they haven't come back, but aren't telling?" said the girl by his side.

"Following the logic of it, we don't know the present has been changed."

"Time travel is riddled with so many paradoxes," said the Professor, "that it's no more than a fascinating diversion. So it's all academic. What's done is done. What's happened has happened." He sighed, collected up his portfolio, shrugged on his sheepskin jacket and bade them all goodnight, as they dispersed.

* * *

The Cosmos shifted slightly, and the gods relented.

* * *

The All Clear sounded, and Dad said, "All right, you lot, back to the house. Go to the lav, you kids, before you go in the house, or I'll lock you out."

Mum got the bedclothes together, as the children stirred sleepily, and a dog barked.

"Can't we stay in the shelter for the night?" the boy mumbled. "I've just got nice and warm."

"Ten minutes," his father told him, "and I'm locking up." He picked up the torch, climbed out of the shelter and made his way up the path. He disturbed next door's cat, who jumped off the lavatory roof.

"Put the kettle on, Jack, and make the children's cocoa," his wife called from the shelter. About halfway along the path, he saw an indistinct shape appear in the dark, which resolved itself into that of a man of some seventy years of age, who was wearing joggers, trainers and a sheepskin jacket. He was saying something, but no sound came.

Jack turned and staggered back towards the shelter.

"What's the hold-up, Jack?" his wife called out. "You should have had the kettle on by now."

"I've just seen a bleedin' ghost, Betty; an old bloke, and the garden's gone all funny."

Betty climbed out of the shelter, leaving the bedclothes behind. She stopped in her tracks. Had she stumbled into someone else's garden? Whoever it belonged to, she didn't think much of it. Where there had been rows of vegetables, there was now an arrangement of gravelled pathway, in a fancy curve, a tiny fountain and a miniature pavilion, with a floor made of wooden slats. Someone had painted the fence blue and purple, or rather, fences, because they were now in sections, placed in a pattern round the garden. How unpatriotic, she thought; instead of digging for victory, someone had lavished all this luxury over precious growing soil. Something else odd had happened, too. The clouds had been scudding across the face of the moon, in a firm breeze. They were now completely still, and the wind had dropped. Next door's cat, who had been in the act of jumping down from the lavatory roof, remained in mid-air, fixed like a frozen still on a film. Even the sounds of the night had ceased; the mundane sounds of war: fire engines, shouts, the artillery on the Hay Mills recreation ground. Even the dog had stopped barking. Betty and Jack stared at each other, then turned back to the apparition. Jack had the strange feeling of having seen him before. His features were a lot like those of Betty, and not unlike his own.

The three of them were all that were moving in the unnatural stillness and quiet. The imitation Rolex watch glittered in the moonlight. The man was waving his arms at them and mouthing: Go back. He pointed at his watch, jabbing at it frantically.

Dazed, they went back. The children were still asleep, and over the boy's face there hovered a feather from his pillow, undisturbed by any breath. Jack whispered, "That figure we just saw – I'm sure I've seen someone like him before. He looked a lot like your dad."

"My dad never wore a flying jacket, nor those athlete's trousers. And what about those tennis shoes – they're sort of chunky, and they've got funny patterns on them. And did you see that fancy watch?"

Jack wasn't listening. He was trying to think where he had seen him before.

"He seemed to know you," Betty said. "Is he one of your Dad's Army mates? He's too old to be called up."

"I'll thank you to refer to it as the Home Guard," Jack said. He was proud to be doing his bit, and the Brummie nickname, The Dads Army, irked him. "He's probably an American." They had just settled back into the shelter when the world came to life again. The breeze got up once more. The clouds raced across the moon, the fire engine bells clanged and the cat completed its jump and skittered away. Even the dog resumed its barking. The bomb whistled down, destroying the house. The inhabitants of the shelter, violently shaken up, automatically ducked, then shook from them the minor debris from the blast of twenty yards away, and questioned each other eagerly if they were all right. Jack shone his torch around his family and was reassured. It came to rest on baby Billy, safe in his mother's arms, and as the unlined child gazed back at his father, Jack realised where he'd seen the old man's face before.

BACKPACK

He felt quite pleased as he made his way through the town. At the age of sixty-five, he was surprised to find himself getting appreciative glances from women. Women of all ages, what was more. From schoolgirls of thirteen, to matrons of his own age and older. As they looked his way, they smiled, and if their line of sight seemed to veer slightly to one side, he put it down to his own faulty vision.

A bachelor, not so much confirmed as circumstantial, he had never craved to have his own offspring, though he got on well in general with children. His own background had brought him to the view that perhaps it would not be wise to reproduce himself, in case he visited on his children the patterns of his own childhood. He had long ago dealt with his early traumas and moved on, but the original instinct had remained. Even animals in the wild, he reasoned, only had young if the conditions were right; in times of dearth and drought they became, simply, subfertile. Nature decided the matter for them. Humans had to use their higher consciousness to tackle the obstacles and hardships, and make adjustments.

He lived alone and, because he didn't care to use the car unless it was absolutely necessary, he walked into the town, every day, with a rucksack on his back to carry the few groceries he needed. He only used the shopping trolley if there was something bulky to take home, so he got used to having a certain weight between his shoulders as he walked briskly along.

He had, today, brought the trolley in with him, and as he consulted his shopping list, he wondered why he had bothered, since they were all small items. He must be getting absentminded. He shrugged. Oh well, maybe he had brought it in case some other purchase occurred to him. He often went into the supermarket, intending to buy just a loaf, only to come out with half the store.

Another young woman smiled his way; the same peripheral glance, and the same sentimental look. I've still got it, he thought. He smiled back and walked on.

It was while he was collecting some items for his niece and her husband, from the baby goods, that he remembered he had to call on them for some reason or other, apart from the disposable nappies. Oh well, it would come to him when he got there. He picked up the pack of disposable nappies and took it, with the rest, to the check-out. He took a plastic bag from the store and carried the purchases in that, rather than bother to take the backpack off to put them in there.

He walked across the park to his niece's house, nodding back happily to the glances. He let himself in and put the goods down. It was only when he went to take the backpack off his back that he remembered what else it was he had to bring his niece. It was his five-month-old great-nephew, Jack, whom his mother had thrust upon her uncle when she went for a swim. Jack, who had been the cause of all those dreamy looks, still fast asleep in the papoose.

BLOCK

Almost the entire writers' circle had writer's block. It spread like a contagion, and took differing forms. Some had plenty of ideas, but lacked a plot to bring them together. One of them had a plot, but couldn't seem to get it moving. The skeleton of the thing just hung there, like a synopsis, with neither dialogue nor the impetus to get the events going. Yet another had his characters fully formed, but they drifted around in hyperspace with nothing to bring them together. They agonised in their different ways.

"I haven't had an original idea for weeks," said Adrian. But then, Adrian would not have recognised originality if it flounced through the door dressed as the Pope in high heels and sat on his lap.

Len, an older member, referred to behind his back as The Great Len, spoke up.

"I don't care what anybody says, you can't beat the old style – a beginning, a middle and an end."

Len had only one story to tell, and though he wrote it well, he wrote it many times. It concerned the Good Old Days, Back To Basics, strict discipline and family values. Len had never been disciplined in his entire childhood, which had been one of complete licence; then, as soon as adult responsibility showed its face, he decided, with a brave toss of the head, that he was a cynic, toughened by life's hard knocks. In other words, a spoilt brat in a sulk.

Miss Hadley, a maiden lady rich in years, who wrote fiercely erotic poetry but led a life of total chastity, was not truly suffering from the block, but her most recent work was so explicit that she had not the heart to embarrass her friends with it. She would, as usual, send it to the gay clubs, to be circulated underground and never get published. Miss Hadley sighed and said nothing.

Phoebe, a young woman who was into anything New Age and Californian, said, "I think we would benefit from a group consciousness-raising session. We should be utterly frank with each other, and try to dig out all the dark stuff holding up the creative flow."

God forbid, thought Miss Hadley, who remembered the early years of the Women's Liberation Movement.

Kevin grunted, tossing his shaven head till all his rings jingled. "I think that kind of stuff comes straight off the stable floor," he snorted. "Just follow your instinct. Write about real life as it happens."

The others smiled. Kevin was twenty-six, took *Flight International* and still lived with his mum. He wrote cartoon strip adventure for small boys and hoped the space comics would one day take his work.

The facilitator brought the meeting to order.

"I know a local author who might help us," she said. "She's had a book published; she hasn't as far as we know got anything else on file, but her book has had glowing references from some very well-known people."

She read them out.

"A classic of its kind … superbly recalls the teen years … a literally stunning evocation of its subject … a piece of social history … will help many people."

(Literally? thought Miss Hadley. Either the reviewer thought the word was a substitute for 'almost' or she really meant that the book, if thrown with sufficient force, would stun whoever it was hurled at.)

The plaudits rolled on.

"An excellent read … appeals to the head as well as to the heart …" and, a little ambiguously: "Fascinating. A remarkable piece of writing."

So Betty Jo Stratford must be good if she could impress four well-known authors, a famous agony aunt, a respected actor and two successful broadcasters.

On a suggestion, they submitted manuscripts for Miss Stratford to cast her expert eye over them, and they looked forward to her visiting them the following week.

When she turned up on the appointed date, she caused quite a stir. A large, good-looking, colourful woman, who swept in wearing a vast black cape, who chain-smoked throughout the evening and evidently had a very good opinion of herself.

She had everyone read excerpts from their latest work and insisted on the rest of the group criticising it in turn. Each piece was at least ten minutes long; the members felt they had to say *something* critical and went on at length about the most nit-picking aspects of each work, (which, in turn, was defended and explained by its author). Some, out of a feeling of charity, and with an eye to their own work being treated kindly, made an effort to find something in each piece to praise. This all meant that not all the work was covered during the meeting, much to the relief of the less forthcoming members.

"I'll listen to what the rest of you have wrote another time," she told them. "Meanwhile, don't be afraid to come to any of my surgeries." (Surgery, in another sense of the word, turned out to be a very apt term.) "By the way," she went on, "I have no time at all for fiction. My own writing is academic. I deal with child development and alternative therapies; this helps others to experience healing from childhood damage. I'm also kept busy as a public speaker."

The throwaway phrase, 'no time for fiction', spoken with contemptuous dismissal, hung in the air. So much for Dickens and the Brontës, then, and Tolstoy need not have bothered. The writers were disconcerted, too, by the Shakespearean grammar the woman used, but the more *avant garde* among them thought perhaps that that was part of her style.

"Speaking as a professional writer," she told them, "I have been quite frank about your little pieces of writing. Don't forget that a manuscript has to be *really* edited before you send it to a publisher. Been there, done that," she added, flicking fag ash off the end of her ciggie for effect. Despite being unfamiliar with any of their work, and unaware of the editing and rewriting they had carried out, she had decided that it needed great chunks to be hacked out of it at random before it was worth considering.

As she rose to go, she handed to everyone reviews of their work.

"Don't read them now. Take them home and give yourself time to absorb it. And don't forget: Read! Read! Read!"

With a swirling of cape and a scattering of ash, Betty Jo was off on her next literary mission.

The members looked at each other. There was something about Miss Stratford's spoken grammar and English usage that gave them reason to wonder how good a writer she was; but then, they had to acknowledge that her work had been accepted by a publisher, which as yet none of them could say of their own writing.

* * *

In the quiet of her bedroom, Phoebe opened her review: 'The writing quite sparkles, but that is not enough, I'm afraid. It needs a good strong plot. This stuff simply drifts.'

Phoebe had written an atmospheric piece: an elegiac stream of consciousness which evoked the softer emotions in anyone prepared to leave themselves open to them. It was *supposed* to drift, and did not need a plot.

Len had put forward his best piece of writing – well structured, with a satisfying number of incidents, detail and telling phrases, and a well-rounded resolution. Miss Stratford's opinion of it read: 'What makes a story interesting is to LEAVE OUT a great deal of detail, and reassemble what's left into bite-sized chunks, so to speak. Always remember – less is more. Don't say it – SHOW it!'

"Silly cow," Len said aloud.

Of Adrian's story for young people, she wrote: 'The characters have no depth. This story is childish.'

Miss Hadley put her reading glasses on and read: 'It's obvious you are a young woman, so I will say nothing of your shallow attitude to the subject. You do seem obsessed by sex. When you are as old as I am, you will see the wisdom of trying to develop the more spiritual side of your nature. I don't like to discourage a budding writer, but it's a hard road, and it would be wrong of me to encourage you falsely.'

The antique Miss Hadley let out a sound between a shriek of joy and a cackle. She would have fun with this one when the chance came.

To Alan, who was sixty-five, Betty Jo had written: 'Thank you for the copy of your autobiography, which I read yesterday. I knew you were a "good writer", but I was afraid you would fall into the usual trap of authors who self-publish and fail to do the necessary ruthless editing which is often all that stands between a *Cider with Rosie* and a rambling, self-indulgent memoir. What we have here is virtually a monologue. If I had been consulted I would have pruned the authorial voice to an absolute minimum, and so kept out any hint of didacticism.'

Alan, whose life story, *A Crusade or Nothing*, was a passionate declamation of Socialist principles, thought: Hang about – it's *supposed* to be didactic; hasn't she noticed?

And so, to each member of the circle, the destructive criticism thumped home in overloaded, badly punctuated, ungrammatical paragraphs of jarring arrhythmia. Tender egos bruised themselves against such phrases as: 'It would be unkind to encourage inferior work and give you false hopes … I could have binned your clever little story and forgot about it … we are here to LEARN or face rejection slips or publication in inferior magazines … sorry, but without strict discipline your talent will be wasted. It's up to you … a pity you didn't have access to a writer in residence to keep you focussed. (Betty Jo was herself a writer in residence.) … it is a pity no one has helped you to see the weaknesses in your work … even an autobiography needs a strong plot. We all, after all, had a childhood.'

So much for Laurie Lee, then.

To them all, she had enclosed a photocopied homily about the trials and satisfactions of publication.

'If family members start throwing writs about or even threatening to do so, as did three generations of my own family, publishers will disappear like snow in summertime. I would suggest you join a GOOD creative writing course if you want to hone your talent. I know the quiet joy of having done a job well.'

When the group turned up for their next meeting, there were some glum faces, a scowl or two and, among the more confident, a glint in the eye.

"I won't ask you to reveal what Betty Jo has written to you, unless you wish to discuss it," said the facilitator, "but I have a copy of her book, *Dust to Dust*. I've read it, and I thought it a good idea for us to read a few sections of it now, to throw some light on what she has said to each of you."

There was an unreadable expression on her face.

"Shall we begin with you, Phoebe?"

Phoebe read the first page. Betty Jo's first sentence included the word 'incredible', a lazy, catch-all adjective that could mean anything from 'splendid' to 'dreadful', and which in consequence has lost its currency.

On the same page, the listeners were cheered to note, the word 'infer' was used where it was clear from the context that she meant 'imply'. Further on, 'the actual fire', was to be found. As opposed to what, one wondered, the *virtual* fire? They all mentally substituted 'the fire itself'.

As they listened to the hackneyed simile, read the quotation and shriek marks, the would-be genteel use of 'I' for 'me', the fatuous emphases, and sentences fizzling out into 'and so ons', 'and so forths' and 'etceteras', looked or listened in vain for the 'appeal to the head' – their faces cleared. It became evident that Betty Jo had no ear for creative writing and had picked up bits and scraps of literary judgement, throwing them around to impress, as she herself had been impressed. She certainly had a good tale to tell, of a disastrous childhood, but she needed a good ghost writer, or at least someone to advise her, to express herself in her own style, since correct English might not be an issue. To encourage her in a little family research, and to elaborate on atmosphere. And certainly to avoid deliberate fiction, which she had imagined gave the story plot, and which had only antagonised her family. She had, it was true, had advice of a sort, but from the same writers in residence as she herself became, who had been given grants for the job, by a council with spare money swilling about.

Phoebe's reddened eyes began to sparkle with relief, the men's anger dwindled into amused contempt, and Miss Hadley mellowed into compassion for poor Betty Jo, cancelling in her mind the cruel phrases she had planned to write to her. Hitting an unworthy opponent was not, after all, her style.

Their writer's block rolled away, to leave the way clear, if not for an immediate flow of ideas, then for the serene realisation that there was someone who wrote more badly than they.

BRIDGEWORK

On a rainy day last week (1946 has been very wet) I crossed the bridge into town. I had decided to go on foot to the dentist's in Bewdley Road. It would be exercise for Lucy, my labrador, and give me time to steel my nerves.

One of my pupils greeted me. "Morning, Mr Jackson; have a nice day." If only. I just wanted to get in there, get on with it, get it over with, and get out. I smiled and walked on. I saw the truck coming and frowned with disapproval at the driver, who had taken his hands off the steering wheel in order to light a cigarette. This image was still in my mind as I was struck sideways, into the ironwork, then I must have lost consciousness.

When I became aware once more of my surroundings, there was a police cordon round the spot where Lucy and I had been walking. Lucy hovered around, uninjured, but whimpering with shock.

"Never mind, old girl," I said, "we're both all right, after all. We'll get back home soon, I'll have a hot cup of coffee and you can have some of my chocolate ration as a treat." But when I went to make a move, I found I could not. Delayed reaction, I thought; I'll tell the policeman who asks me for a statement; he may refer me to the ambulance staff. However, not only did nobody appear interested in my state of health, but they didn't seem to see me. They bustled about, tending to others who were dazed and grazed. Some had been pushed by the impact, or had jumped, into the river Severn. They were soon rescued and taken into the Bridge Inn to be dried out.

"Will someone please take care of my dog?" I shouted to bystanders. No one took the slightest notice of me; but at last, a woman took pity on Lucy.

"The least we can do for him is to look after his dog," she said, as she improvised a leash out of a belt and led her away.

It was this, plus the fact of the body on the stretcher wearing my clothes and bearing a strong resemblance to me, that finally led me to the conclusion I had been trying to ignore.

Then a policeman pulled the blanket over his face, and that settled it.

"Well, at least it was sudden, and I don't appear to have suffered," I thought. I was still reluctant to accept what had happened, because I feared that if I admitted it, I would disappear into oblivion. However, I remained where I was. Dusk fell, and all traces of the accident were removed. People drove, cycled and walked home from work, shopping and school. The Shipley fairground lights came on, and people went for a few hours' recreation at the sideshows and the pubs. Then the chip shops got busy as tipsy youth, grown suddenly ravenous, sought the means to soak up the night's ale. Eventually, the streets became quiet. Nothing happened, except the occasional police car passing through, its bell sounding in short, urgent bursts as it tore across the bridge; the wartime crime wave being alive and kicking still.

The next day came, then the next. Still, I remained in the same place on the bridge, unable to move, while the world moved round me, and through me. As I turned my gaze towards the river, boat trippers took their journey to Worcester, mothers brought their small children to feed the ducks, anglers set up their pitches.

Day after day I remained in the same place. I considered how lucky it was that I had died on such a pleasant spot. It could have been worse. I might have expired in some dark hole and spent eternity there. As it was, my one grief was for Lucy. I missed her and wondered how she was getting on with her new owners. Would she be grieving for me, wandering among her old haunts by the river, looking in places I used to take her? I hoped they would walk her down the river footpath. I might at least see her.

The seasons changed. Summer brought school holidays. Then autumn, and the preparations for Christmas. After this came the worst winter since 1939. Ice floes swept downstream. The pavements vanished under the snow, thawed partially, then froze again, more treacherous than ever. It was nearly April before the thaw came. I listened to what people said, and learned several things about the changing world. With spring came a rise in the school-leaving age to fifteen. Another rainy summer came and went; then in November, the town became bright with flags, bunting and everything in red, white and blue at the least excuse. A pretty princess married a handsome naval officer.

The year 1948 brought more social changes, and I heard people talk about the new National Health Service, and how you could get free teeth and wigs. It was the year the Olympics were held in London; Fanny Blankers-Koen, the magnificent Dutch athlete, who only four years earlier had been starving during the Occupation, was now a gold medal winner.

Three years on, and the half-century celebrated, but mostly for those who could afford to get down to London to see the Dome of Discovery. More bunting and cheap patriotism. 1952, flags again, and a new head on the coins. In 1957, I saw a man-made satellite moving among the stars; 1961, a man in space, which America sturdily refused to believe in. 1962/63, the worst winter for sixteen years. Then the Sixties burst on the world, and the young shook their elders with beads, beards and flowers. In the summer of 1967, disinfectant straw was laid across the bridge and cattle farmers lost their stock. I heard talk of something called a charity shop; Oxfam set up for business in York Street. 1969, two men walked on the moon. America had to believe it this time. It was their men. During the next decade, green hair and Mohican haircuts were the fashion. Elders felt disgruntled – no free teeth or wigs after all.

Halfway through the Seventies, a small south-east Asian state beat America in war. Now I *knew* I must be dreaming. As the Eighties progressed, I began to notice that there was very little snow in winter. The summers brought flash floods, and the local press came to photograph them. In 1991, a war broke out in the Middle East. It was about oil, or it wasn't. It was about imperialism, or it wasn't, depending on who was speaking. At midnight, the 1st January 2000, the sky burst with light and noise, and I felt the world turn. The following year, the bridge was spread with impregnated straw again. In September of that year, the unthinkable happened. America was attacked, and thousands died in Manhattan. 2002 brought more terrorism; in February 2003, despite two million people marching on London, another war in the Gulf; oil, imperialism, colossal weaponry, a moral crusade, take your pick; and the world braced itself for disaster.

As the twenty-first century sped by, the scenery changed. A new boathouse was built. The small cafés vanished, to be taken over by someone called MacDonald. Premises in Bridge Street, shut down for years, were taken over, at first by more charity shops, but then, as the monetary systems changed, these were superseded by exchange and barter centres.

Through the years, other changes came about. It ceased to snow in winter. There were fewer cars, more bikes and buses, but that did not stop the temperature rising. People wore fewer clothes and kept their heads and arms covered against the ultraviolet rays. Some even wore cotton gloves. The river rose higher.

A year came when calamity struck. Fewer people were about. Those there were scurried from place to place, as if avoiding each other. Some had their mouths covered against the plague. From what I could see of the traffic intersecting the two main roads, no buses or trucks came or went through the town. Cars frequently broke down. One did, in fact, break down on the bridge. What few passers-by there were did not bother to try and get it going, but pushed it straight through the crumbling wall, where it fell into the flooded meadow. The fairground lights began to falter, as the bulbs broke, one by one, leaving an unreadable set of spaced-out letters.

Time continued to flash by. Maybe hundreds of years passed, and the people, by now, had deteriorated. Their clothing was now coarse-woven. They pushed their wheelbarrows and carts, loaded with what produce they had managed to raise, in and out of the town, sometimes striking a bargain with someone coming in the opposite direction.

With a depleted world population, the temperature stabilised. In the winters, people wore as many of their rags as they could, as the cold returned. As the years went swiftly by, I saw the town in flames: fires caused by neglect and helplessness. No one bothered to rebuild. The riverside became a dense wood, inhabited by wildlife and surviving farm stock, now turned feral. As I looked over to where the old Civic Centre had been, centuries before, it was all but buried by trees and tangled creepers, like ancient Incan remains amidst the jungle. What was left of the bridge was a precarious, weed-strewn pass; the concrete, steel and tarmac now decayed to the point where it had become necessary to attach a wooden walkway to the remains of the ironwork. A crude ferry operated at a narrower reach upriver.

And still I thought of Lucy, now long dead herself. Even of the dentist who failed to get me in the chair, all those centuries ago. I wondered if humankind, having destroyed civilisation, had destroyed itself, too, or whether this part of the world had fallen into decay in favour of new centres of commerce and traffic.

Then one day I saw a small party making its way along what used to be High Street, but what was now a narrow track through trees and tangled undergrowth, into Bridge Street.

Clothing, by now, had regenerated back to fine weaving, and these people were well shod and equipped. The area was being rediscovered, as the diminished population gathered its strength. These people took measurements and made assessments, with a view to building a new town once more on the river; reverting to the ancient practice of setting up home where there was a natural highway. A way was hacked through the trees. Roads were rebuilt. The town began to come to life again. The speech people used interested me. I realised how volatile a thing dialect is; how mysterious its origins. A dominant individual who talks a lot could influence an entire neighbourhood. As the populace expands, newcomers bring additions and modifications to the language. As I listened, I noted with relief that the glottal stop had died out, and that speakers were once again taking the trouble to engage the tongue with the palate and to bring the lips together occasionally.

As the years passed, more people came to the town. They rebuilt the bridge into something much bigger and more impressive. I wondered what industry had been brought to the area, as the basin was extended and the canals were recut. Might this be part of the new capital, with Worcester as its centre and Stourport the new Wembley? London and the low-lying land around it must surely have been claimed by the sea by now. Old lessons appeared to have been learned. Transportation by river and canal came back to life. Instead of the internal combustion engine, I saw river craft driven once more by sail. By solar panel, too, its power stored in batteries. Road traffic was mostly human driven, but not the bicycle of old. What I saw were ingenious vehicles driven by complex gear systems and dynamos. The horse had been brought back into use, either for riding or draughtwork. From what I could understand of people's speech, I inferred that wind and tide were now major sources of power. The pace of life was slower than it had been in my time.

Now that the river level had steadied in the stabilised climate, a children's play area was once more in place on the meadow. The town was, by now, no longer Stourport, but Wyrebridge. One of those peaceful periods ensued, during which elders tried to impress the young with the way life had been: hard and dramatic, and how it was the making of them, and kids nowadays didn't know they were born. Until, that is, the next disaster, and the next dramatic human achievement, when the young, now middle-aged, boasted about how good life had been. The good old days, the golden era. And how kids nowadays didn't know they were born.

The centuries continued to roll, until, quite suddenly, everything stopped. One afternoon, pedestrians, river craft, road vehicles, all froze. Then, slowly, they came back to life. I, too, felt myself begin to revive, as if oxygen was flooding my lungs. A new consciousness filled my brain, a memory of another existence, something I had been planning to do. What was it? My surroundings faded a little. These thoughts were suddenly pushed to one side, as I noticed what was happening to the traffic. It was moving, all right, but backwards. Supplies were undelivered from riverside pub to brewer's dray; a dropped parcel sprang from the road to nestle under the arm of a man being led by a cart and horse. Rain lifted from the ground and made its way skyward, to form a black cloud. The events from the previous day unspooled and gathered pace, like a film run swiftly backwards. Eventually, the new structures in the town were dismantled. The new basin became once more a stagnant delta to the river. The new bridge vanished and the old wooden walkway materialised against the iron girders. Timbers joined up again; tree-fellers walked backwards and placed them by their roots, where they were lifted by cutters. Sawdust sprang from the air and gathered to become part of the tree again. The woods returned. The survey party walked backwards up Bridge Street into High Street and disappeared into the undergrowth.

The centuries sped back, and global warming and floods returned. Water reappeared in the now overgrown meadow, seeping upwards through the wild grasses, and spilled back into the river proper. Carts and wheelbarrows proceeded the wrong way round back and forth across the bridge. The barter system diminished and came to a halt; money was exchanged once more. The Civic Centre reappeared through the saplings and the ivy, as they grew younger.

Scaffolding fell away from the new boathouse, revealing the old building. Shops reappeared. The fairground lights came back on.

I braced myself to meet the moment of my death once more. I would rejoin my companion, Lucy. Maybe I would cancel my appointment with the dentist. The police cordon rolled up into the policeman's hands again. The rescued pedestrians came back out of the Bridge Inn, climbed backwards from the riverbank into the river, from where they sprang up, their clothes dry as soon as they left the water, and leapt back over the bridge.

I felt myself slip under the truck and, just as I joined my body, I heard a dog bark. It sounded odd, as if it came from indoors, from another room. Then a voice spoke.

"That's a nice bit of bridgework, though I say so myself. Go and sit down in the recovery room for a while, then you can go home; your dog is getting impatient."

I opened my eyes to the figure in the surgical mask and the white coat.

"Make your next appointment before you leave, won't you? And let the receptionist know whether you want nitrous oxide again. I've never had such a quiet patient. You must have had a very peaceful sleep for the half-hour."

I admired her handiwork in the mirror. "I must tell you about all that some time, Miss Wayland, and if it's all the same to you, I'll chance it with the cocaine next time."

I strode back home with Lucy, relishing the rain and the temperate climate, relieved that what I had been through, from Arctic winters, floods, drought, green hair, illicit drugs, farming disaster, global warming and terrorism, had all been only a dream.

BUDGET

Jack the Lad had a good face for radio presentation. (He had been on TV prior to taking the all-night slot, so everyone who read the tabloids knew exactly what he looked like.) Popular, self-assured, a bit of a gabbler, and when he got excited, he got on his high horse and galloped off in all directions. Riding roughshod over the laws of logic, driven by his own excitement, he demolished his opponent's arguments by sheer volume, garrulity and constant interruption as Jack got carried away with his own hypomania. He ran a phone-in programme to which mostly the misguided contributed, fancying that, because Jack spoke with such ease, it was something that anyone could do. He often got callers who had nothing to say and took a long time saying it. "Hallo?" they began. "Hallo," Jack replied. "Hallo," the caller persevered, hoping Jack would help him out. He seldom did, unless it was a young woman, prepared to talk dirty for him. "How are you, Jack?" callers would ask him, to give themselves time to think, to little effect. "My health is not in question," he told them, for the twentieth time in an all-night shift. "If one more person says 'basically' or asks me how I am, I'll cut them off!" he threatened. This only encouraged the mischief seekers, who did it on purpose to annoy him, and it didn't deter the 'basically', 'you know', 'sort of like' brigade. He threatened to cut these off, too, but they just gave a little chuckle to show they knew he was only kidding, which he wasn't. And they knew that. But they hoped either that he would bale them out and start a conversation with them, or do the merciful thing and pull the plug on them.

Jack had no time for the feckless, who he knew for certain had brought it all on themselves. There was no excuse for being unemployed; surely they could go out and sweep the streets, he told them, overlooking the fact that the council already employed machinery to do this, and that the workers themselves would not thank anyone stealing their jobs from them. "People go begging because they like it. It's a pretty good living," he agreed with a like-minded caller, who told him yet again of the beggars with mobiles, a story Jack never tired of and by which he refreshed his indignation each time. "I bet I could live on three pounds fifty a day, easily," he claimed. He claimed this so frequently that he was finally taken up on it, by a caller who happened to be a Channel Four journalist, looking for a ripe plum.

"Let's go to line five," Jack said. "Hallo, Jeremy, from London."

"Hallo, Jack, I'm interested in your claim to live on three pounds fifty a day; can I take you up on it?"

"Nothing to it, Jezzer, just name your terms."

"I suggest you take it over two weeks, so that you can get through what you already have in the house. It will be more realistic that way. Your every move will be recorded. We'll put a security camera over your front porch, and you'll have an escort to and from the supermarket, and you'll have to send your housekeeper on holiday. We'll pay your petrol and telephone expenses – it's essential for your job."

"I'm game, Jeremy. I'll put you on hold now, and get back to you after the show. Many thanks for that; we'll go into the commercials now."

* * *

Channel Four had thought of everything. Jack surrendered his credit cards from day one and rebanked all his spare cash. A trusted friend came to visit and went over all the cupboards, cubbyholes, boxes and drawers, to make sure there was no extra money scrooged away and no hidden rations.

Even before the residual stores were exhausted, Jack began to feel the pinch. He ran out of toilet paper. He had overlooked the fact that not only were there other items besides food to buy, but that for one in his income bracket, food was the cheapest item, even discounting restaurant bills for £65 for a meal. However, because he was still living on the contents of the house, he could afford the *Daily Telegraph*, so he cut this into squares and made use of it in the time-honoured way. Then he found the soap running out, so he stinted himself and washed less often. He had been used to sending his clothes to the laundry, but this was now a luxury and he had to buy detergent. He had no idea how to seek out the cheapest, and used up an entire day's money on a medium-sized box of washing powder.

The inevitable day arrived when he finished up the food remaining in the house and had to buy the cheapest porridge oats, baked beans at 9p a tin, white bread at 30p a loaf, claggy margarine at 50p for 500 grams, a kilo of sugar, lemonade at 15p for two litres and very cheap coffee powder. This was nutritionally sufficient, but for someone who was used to dining out on dainty fare, dressed with piquant sauces to tempt the jaded appetite, it was unspeakable.

The effects soon showed in his temper, never very placid at the best of times. He snapped at callers whom he usually fell over to accommodate, and snarled at those he hated anyway. Too late, he realised that undecaffeinated coffee was making his nerves stand out on stalks. To the jolly characters who asked him cheerily how he was coping on the kind of living that his dearest enemies had to make, that is, the unemployed, the homeless and that monster of anti-social intent, the single mother, he replied with two words, one of which was 'off'.

He also found he was putting on weight. He had assumed that the poor put on weight because they frittered their money away on extra food, and not, as he discovered, the result of having to make their own chips, fried in the cheapest lard, of filling up with sweet and stodgy biscuits and cake, and putting extra milk and sugar in their tea. Having then filled himself in this way, he found he was becoming addicted to stodge and grease.

The final straw came when, within one week, he ran out of toothpaste, shampoo, toilet soap, washing-up liquid, floor cleaner, oven cleaner and scourers. In the week in which he ran out of face tissues, painkillers and antihistamines, he caught a streaming cold. When the kettle broke down, he at last realised that what to a moderately prosperous person is an irritation, is to someone struggling to run a household on less than a hundred pounds a week, a major catastrophe. He would not be chuckling any more at stories of kitchen calamities of the poor. The tale of a broken teapot, filled with the only tea the family would have had that day, no longer gave him the smug feeling of cosy domesticity showing its farcical side. He made the cold the excuse to end the project. He was too ill, he said, missing the point. Then, learning nothing, from this point he screened out all callers critical of his high-handed attitude to the poor, accepting only those who commended him for his fortitude. He soon got his breath back and railed at his enemies: gays, lefties, unmarried couples who lived together and who had the effrontery to raise children with no more and no less success than the married. In short, anyone who did not fall strictly into line with traditions no older than those under which he was brought up. Then, without seeing any contradiction, he turned tail on his firmly held notions of respectability and declared himself to be a maverick, sturdily independent of the nanny state. Naturally, he flourished as before.

COMEUPPANCE

Derek took the early train to Birmingham that day. Although it would be crowded with commuters, it would be quieter than the next one, full of school students until he reached Hagley, and he couldn't be doing with their liveliness, their loud chatter, and the squeals of the girls. They would be giggling loudly and falsely, and the boys would be swaggering and pushing the smaller boys about. What David Attenborough called 'display', he thought. That he had behaved just as badly at their age was beside the point. He had no tolerance for it himself and loudly decried 'young people nowadays', who had no respect for their elders. Quite when they ever had was a favourite fantasy of his. He was heard to declare how, when he was young, they had had their ears clipped.

"How often did you have your ears clipped?" he was asked.

"Oh, many a time; and it did me no harm. It made me what I am today."

"It obviously did no good as a deterrent, then, if you had to have it done more than once," came the response.

His only reply to this was to repeat more forcefully what he had already said, in the belief that a stern voice and brisk manner were indicative of lessons learned and respect earned. The fact was that, as a young boy, he had always been backed up by his mother, who believed her dear son was perfection itself. He was given to shouting insults from his bedroom window or throwing stones at other children from the safety of his front garden, then running to hide behind his mother when his victim came to complain.

"What has my son done to you, that you come banging on my door?"

"Stolen my lunch money, for a start, and disrupted the class for another. But I could give you the rest of the list, if you like."

"Don't be such a big baby, bullying is a fact of life. You should learn to stand on your own two feet."

"Tell that to the hateful little creep hiding behind your skirts." But both mother and son had gone indoors by this time.

Derek now took his seat and took out his *Daily Mail*.

Katrina picked up a copy of *Metro*, put her feet up on the side-facing seat and waited for the train to start. She felt good about herself. Her hair extensions swung seductively around her face, the deep purple eyeshadow gave her that air of adult sophistication that she had longed for since she was fourteen, some four years now, and she had a new face stud, this time at the side of her nose. Best of all, she had that morning given her mother a mouthful of vulgar abuse for reminding her to pick her clothes up off the floor. She had then flounced out, slamming the front door. That would teach the old hag; she would have to treat her like the grown-up she was.

It escaped her notice that she had also trodden in some chewing gum, which was now transferred to the upholstery of the opposite seat; that her hair extensions looked like dirty string; that the eyeshadow made her look like a bewildered rabbit; and the nose stud looked like a skin blemish.

John Cross looked forward to another day at the insurance office in the city. He had just engaged a new junior and was making her life a misery. He particularly enjoyed bawling her out for all the office to hear, for minor mistakes, not always of her making, trying to get her to cry. That really did it for him. It made him feel powerful, as well as having other, less admissible effects. As she stood there, willing the tears not to fall, she knew there was nothing she could do. No one spoke up for her or told Mr Cross to leave her alone. So she knew the departmental boss would not be interested, either.

John sighed contentedly, looking forward to such another day. It was, he admitted to himself, a pity that the more spirited juniors stayed no longer than a few months, and that he had driven out all the good staff and now found himself with inferior workers, but this did mean that he had more fuel for his loud criticism. Besides, pleasure had to be paid for. As long as others did the paying.

Betty was chief cashier at the local swimming pool. She was large and dominant, and went crashing about the office, her voice seldom less than a bellow. She tested everything, and everyone, to destruction, including, eventually, her husband, who sensibly left her for another woman. Although she told newcomers to the job quite sternly that they were not to close the safe with the bolts out, this did not stop Betty herself from deliberately turning the handle so that the sensitive mechanisms were exposed, then smashing them against the front of the safe, before she believed it was fit to be closed. The man from Chubb's was a frequent visitor. Lack of self-knowledge prevented common sense from showing her to be wrong. Like a simple animal, she did whatever felt right to her. All other ways and means were, by definition, wrong. She gossiped freely, saying of one woman whose child, according to Betty, was of dubious fatherhood, "It's a funny thing she never brought that child in here for us to see," mouthing like Les Dawson. Nevertheless she boasted that: "I never talk to them out there," or "I never talk to the manuals." These were the humble creatures who guarded the pool, some of whom she took into her confidence to discuss the private lives of others. When the new manager took over, he interviewed each of the staff privately, telling one of them that, "I want to make it clear that I will not tolerate tittle-tattle, and by the way, I understand you have had slimmers' disease." He had evidently had the benefit of Betty's blabbing tongue and wanted exclusive rights to it.

Betty, by means of the council's ranking system, was an 'Officer', something she firmly impressed on her new colleague. "You're an officer now," she repeatedly told the new woman, who cringed each time.

The only time Betty did not go lunging about the place, smashing doors shut after her, came when someone brought her new baby in. As members of staff came into the staffroom on their coffee breaks, their quietly exhausted demeanour was rewarded with Betty hissing loudly at them: "SSSHH! Jenny's brought her baby in, you've got to be quiet!" Betty was the only person who could whisper loudly.

The world belonged to Betty, although it stubbornly refused to acknowledge the fact, but at least those who inhabited her own little world had better know it. If a member of the public had the impudence to ask politely how far up the queue their child was for swimming lessons, she indignantly put them at the back of the queue. She deeply resented answering questions posed by the public, and puffed and tutted at them as they sought information at the information desk.

Derek, Katrina, John and Betty occupied a corner of the car, three of them facing the way the train was going, and, as the train entered the tunnel on nearing the city, each was occupied with personal thoughts. As was the nervous young man sitting next to Betty, checking something in the backpack he had just taken from his shoulders.

It was in this tunnel that the lights suddenly went out, at the same time as the yellow flash, followed by all the air being sucked out. The impact was felt by everyone, except the subjects of this story. In the sudden quiet following the trauma, the lights came back on, and they stared at each other. They were the only ones in the car now, and looked around at the otherwise empty carriage, baffled, but stunned enough not to work out what was going on. Katrina had the impression that she had just woken up in bed; Derek, too, thought he was still in bed, dreaming; John was so busy with his tumescent fantasy concerning the office junior that he was only dazed; while Betty was merely indignant that something drastic had happened without her permission. The young man with the backpack, however, bore a look of eager expectation.

The train had picked up speed again, rattling and lurching violently from side to side, and appeared to be going downhill, as briefcases, handbags and backpacks slid forward to the door connecting to the next car. They should be in the station by now, but the journey was taking so long that it had the feel of eternity about it.

They felt disinclined to question it, however, as the train continued on its journey through the tunnel. Although the lights had come back on, they bore an eerie green tint, and as the remaining five passengers looked through the windows, expecting to see brick walls and criss-crossing railway tracks, all they could discern was a dull red glow, which grew in intensity as they moved into the station.

As they did so, the name of the station appeared, or rather, bits of it, as they were going too fast to read it properly. They caught glimpses of some of the letters. To some of them, the name seemed mostly to begin with H. HEL … HADE … To others, it read STYX … DAMNA … and PURGA …

Their journey halted abruptly, with a jerk that sent them sprawling. A voice was heard over the intercom: “You will now leave the train, quickly, without fuss or complaint. Move, NOW!”

They stumbled out, into a railway station like none other. Certainly it had neither the modern look of New St Station nor the *Brief Encounter* quaintness of Snow Hill. There were crowds there, certainly, but they seemed more like spectators, come to gaze at the newcomers.

"We had all better go to the information desk," Betty told them, looking around for it. It seemed to appear as soon as she voiced the thought. She strode towards it.

"Bossy cow," Katrina muttered, clip-clopping behind her in her platform soles.

"Never mind that, girl," John ordered her, "just do as you are told." He had been robbed of the initiative and felt he had to assert his authority.

Derek took the option of panic denial and airy dismissal. "There's nothing to worry about, I've known far worse crises than this. Everything will right itself, don't you fret yourselves."

It was true enough that he had seen emergencies, mostly caused by himself. He had once urged a friend, bluffly, to jolly himself out of the heart attack that he was being treated for, Derek's voice booming across the ward. Just as predictably, he had for several years casually denied climate change, and would have continued to do so until the waters lapped round him and his hat floated.

The receptionist at the information desk looked Betty up and down.

"What do you want?"

"We need to know what is going on. Has there been some kind of accident?"

"You are not supposed to question me, go to the back of the queue."

"Queue? There is no queue."

"Don't argue, do as you are told!"

John Cross pushed his way forward.

"Now look here, young woman, don't presume to treat your betters in this manner. Just get this matter sorted out, or I will report you."

She gave a mean little smile.

"Don't think you can bully me like a defenceless junior. Be assured the authorities will think up a suitable punishment for you if you even think about it."

Katrina had a try.

"Look, you ugly mare, you're only a jumped-up servant. Get us to where we ought to be."

"You already are where you ought to be." She shuffled some papers on her desk.

"Right; here are your orders. You, Mr Derek, will take a class of delinquents. You will have your work cut out – they have all been spoilt from birth and will not take orders gladly. They will show their disrespect in the most ingenious ways, tormenting you daily. You will not be allowed to punish them. If you are caught doing so, you will get your ears clipped."

She turned to Katrina.

"You can report to the sanitary department, who will issue you with cleaning materials. You can make a start cleaning the lavatories, then pick up every bit of litter in the station. Mr Cross, there is a group of adolescent schoolgirls in the Ladies' Waiting Room. You will be deputed to look after them." John Cross looked a little hopeful at this. "And by the way, there will be cameras trained on you perpetually, so be very careful to respect these young ladies."

They had, by now, figured out just where they were, but could not quite square it with their traditionally held views of the place. Where were the demons, they wanted to know, with prodding tridents? The lake of eternal fire? The Devil, with his horns and hooves? The receptionist sighed.

"You people make me tired. Just get this: this place is a figment of your imagination. You are being punished by yourself, and will only be free when you have learnt the lessons you refused to take when you were alive. Only then will you be granted oblivion. I'll do you a favour; to save yourself from finding it out the hard way, remember this. The secret is to help each other. You may find this hard, considering the kind of people you had let yourselves become, but it is what mankind has to learn every time, and each individually. You were born with a sense of decency, but got waylaid by selfishness, when things were made too easy for you. You took short cuts to maturity, demanding immediate satisfaction, mistaking sly cleverness for wisdom, as embodied by you, Katrina. You, Mr Cross, found the power nature granted you too pleasurable in itself to direct it to the protection of the weak. Similarly with you, Betty. You, Derek, mistook boldness for bravery, missing the point that you can only be considered courageous if you feel fear. Admit it to yourself, if not to others. The trick is to feel the fear, but do it anyway. If you were not afraid, you would have no need for bravery.

"For all of you, it is the destiny of the foolish, at the best, to be quietly forgotten by the people you have hurt. You were born pure, but you fell into unoriginal sin. And believe me, you have no idea how unoriginal it can be. Now be on your way, I'm busy."

They mooched off, thoughtful, each prepared to make eternity as bearable as they could for themselves.

"It might not be so bad after all," Derek said. "At least it won't be boring. All the best people appear to be here. Look, the place is full of priests, politicians and princes. And look over there, there's a gaggle of World War One generals. I'd like to have a word with them, about my great-grandfather. He was a very courageous man, but that didn't save him from being shot for cowardice. I'll while away many a happy hour making sure that lot are kept awake and punished for dozing off. As for those women with the white feathers…"

Meanwhile, the young man with the backpack looked round with a mixture of bewilderment and disappointment. Where were his seventy-two virgins?

CONFESSIONAL

Mrs Billings drew back the curtain of the confessional and stepped in. In her present mood, she did not feel like kneeling, but since there was no seat, only a hassock, she had to kneel anyway.

She started in straight away.

"Now listen, Father Rhys, I haven't come here to confess and ask forgiveness, I've come to make a complaint. I've always said that, on Judgement Day, it wouldn't be us mortals being judged, it would be Him up There. I'll be waiting with a long list of grievances, starting with gynaecology and going on to reproduction in general. I said as much to my mother, and do you know what she said? 'Well, you'll have to wait in a bloody long queue, then.' I'm fed up with your preaching and pontificating. It doesn't encourage me to be a better person, and what is more, it isn't even necessary. I know the difference between right and wrong, despite all the clever philosophers trying to kid me that even they don't know. I know it's wrong for that blabbermouth next door to tell our neighbours all my personal business and to slander me every chance she gets. I know it was wrong of my husband to think that it would be a waste of his wages to spend them on feeding his children. It was even wrong of him to run away and leave us, though I must say we are glad to see the back of him. I've had more than my fair share of trouble; my children have all deserted me, saying bad things about me. It's all made up. I gave those children the best upbringing they could have wished for. They'll thank me for it later when they realise it was all for their own good.

"And another thing. It's wrong of the supermarkets to behave as they do. Someone in the office gets bored and puts the tape on. If it was soothing music, I wouldn't mind, but it's either some bloke with a voice like a costermonger, or some yowling, yelping female. The checkout staff can't stand it either, but they've become too brainwashed and too apathetic to tell the manager they don't want it. And when I try to talk about it to a man in a suit, he says, 'No one else has complained.' Of course they don't, there's no point. I've written letters to the management and to head office, but they don't bother to reply. I've noted it down on the notebook left out for the customers to make remarks, and still nothing gets done. I've even threatened to fill up the trolley with frozen goods and leave it, if they don't do anything. All to no avail."

Father Rhys appeared to make a small gesture. A light sound escaped his lips. His indigestion had been playing up again. Mrs Billings ignored this and plunged on.

"Do you know what I think is at the bottom of it all? No discipline in the schools. They ought to bring back the strap. Young people nowadays get away with murder. When we misbehaved, we got a good hiding for it. It was the making of us. It's the only deterrent. Every time we caused trouble, we got walloped. Even when we didn't misbehave, we still got beaten. At least once a week. That's what the kids need nowadays, a regular beating. They'd only have to swear or write graffiti, or cheek their parents once, and they'd get a damned good hiding. They wouldn't do it a second time. They'd only need to get one good hitting. That would fix them. I lost count of the punishments I got. But it made me what I am today.

"And as for that Mr Westcott out there, waiting to tell you all about it, I don't think he'll bother to tell you about his fancy woman. Trying to kid us he only gives her a lift to work. There's something going on there that his wife needs telling about. I can tell. He's got that shifty look. You just wait till I get some real evidence.

"So I tell you straight. Don't bother telling me to go in peace and try to sin no more. I've got a clear conscience. And don't believe what they tell you about me and Mr Westcott's car. Someone else scraped those messages on the paintwork. That was a story trumped up by the police. Besides, he needs telling. And those rumours about that middle-aged couple and their teenage daughter. There's no smoke without fire. And they had the cheek to send the social services round to *me*, telling me not to cause trouble. All because I sent them a little letter, giving them some friendly advice. Young people nowadays have too much fun. More than I ever had. Besides, I know what teenagers get up to, I was one myself once. Whatever she's doing, she ought to be stopped at it. With her nose studs and her green hair. And then they wonder why they get pregnant! And it's a funny thing that they left the district after I drew attention to it all, isn't it? Guilty conscience, that was. Trying to kid everyone on they were hounded out." She paused to think.

"And another thing. You should be aware of Mrs Jessop. I see her in the pub regularly every Tuesday, with a man who is not her husband. She lets on he's her brother. She thought that one up on account of they look so alike. They must think we're stupid. I wasn't born yesterday. I can see what the world is up to. So you think about it, and don't be so full of yourself. I've got to be off now; I'm needed at the Moral Vigilance Society. There are one or two people who need checking up on, especially that man who cycles past my house, whistling dirty tunes. And I suspect my cleaning woman has been taking home small quantities of my cleaning fluids, so I will have to take valuable time out of my busy day to give her a long talk about it."

And so she left the confessional, having cleansed herself of a load of bitterness and hate. That is, until she built up another burden of bigotry and bile. Father Rhys didn't say a thing. But then, he had been dead for the last half-hour.

CONNIE GETS A LIFE

My biographer hadn't a clue about women, which was probably why he wrote such a patronising book about me. "Give her a role," he declaimed. Now, it's bad enough being a fictional entity without being held up to the literary world as a model of what it is to be female. In fact, I'm portrayed as being little more than feminine, but I won't enter into debate over the essential difference between those two misapplied words.

David Herbert Lawrence's alter ego, Oliver Mellors, had a yearning need for my dependency. As a free spirit, and one rich enough not to be tied down to my impotent husband, I am described as unhappy, skinny and angular. Then, once my life becomes sanctified by the presence of a potent male, I begin to bloom, my curves round out, I become soft and glowing. Give me a break! Since when have contentment and weight gain been synonymous? Why should happiness make you eat more?

It has never been clear to me why the author was so vindictive towards Sir Clifford. He was rendered disabled by wounds received in the Great War, but it seems his damaged body was grounds enough for Mellors/Lawrence to despise him – rather than for his being a routinely upper-class chancer, keen enough for the continuation of the Chatterley line to turn a blind eye to a randy gamekeeper.

As for the sex; what can I say? What an oaf. When it didn't work for me, he uttered a surly dismissal. He would never have got away with such boorishness in the 1990s. But here was I, stuck in the 1920s, when most men knew flap-all about female anatomy; and those who did know anything declared that the deployment of its non-reproductive bits for her pleasure was at best immature, and at worst, sinister and 'beak-like'. He seemed obsessed with doing things "properly, properly," as he primly spread the blanket. It had to be penetrative or nothing. He even disapproved of women who had the wrong kind of orgasm. It smacked too much of safe sex and nobody getting hurt, for his liking.

The only laughs I got out of our affair arose from his foray into personalised flower arranging. I certainly did not enjoy some of the other activities, illegal until a short while ago. Call me old-fashioned.

Reader, I dumped him. I sent him packing with a cheque for £50. See how he liked being patronised. I then joined the suffragettes. Mellors could go and start the revolution. He had always been banging on about it, but he seemed to confine his ideas to getting working men to wear scarlet trousers to cheer themselves up. Well, that should brighten up their lives while they worked themselves to death.

Leaving Sir Clifford to the ministrations of his housekeeper, I took myself down to London where my money and connections gained me entry into such company as Radclyffe Hall, Ethel Smyth, Marlene Dietrich and Nancy Spain; and a gay old time I had with them, I can tell you.

CONSEQUENCES

Rebecca had been married six months before she found her oyster silk knickers had been put through the wash, when she was certain she had not worn them for weeks. The elastic in them was stretched and slack as well. After this had happened a second time, she became inquisitive. Nerving herself to open his briefcase, she found a midnight blue negligee three sizes too big for herself, a blonde wig and make-up. So much for those promotional courses his firm had sent him on.

She was not so much outraged as resentful. How dare he exclude her from his more particular needs? Did he think she could not have coped with them? Objectively, she did not see why men should not wear silks and satins if that enhanced sensuality for them, though she was puzzled at their seeking out the discomfort of high heels and brassieres; if they had a concomitant need for inflicting suffering on themselves at the same time, then that was all to do with the closed book of male sexuality and its mysteries. The male, she believed, a comparative latecomer to evolution, was still floundering in his attempt to reach the simplicities of the female. Subjectively, however, she was annoyed with herself at having lived a life of conformity; she had never got round to frightening the horses; in a vague, unformed belief that society would reward her in some way, if only with its approval.

She threw her coat on and went out for a midnight walk, her anger fuelling her swiftly striding pace.

By half past midnight, her feelings had mellowed. She looked forward to giving him an earful when he came back from his night out with the boys. Boys? She imagined him sitting with a bunch of blue-chinned blokes in frocks, and smiled, in spite of herself. She dumped in a waste bin the poppies she had ripped out of a neat front garden – had torn up in fury with the orderliness of other people's lives.

That'll teach them, with their neat little lives, and their neat little husbands, and neat little children, she thought with relish, as she let herself in the front door.

* * *

Veronica wondered if she would ever get used to it. The feeling of guilt at losing a child. It must have been something she had done wrong. If she had not let him play football that day, he would not have struck his head against the goalpost. She even blamed herself for his being tall enough to play in goal. Reason had nothing to do with any of this.

Looking around the bedroom as she rose, she found everything still looked as grey as it had been for months now. It was grey, not in the literal sense, but as though the colour and flavour had gone out of life. She no longer took pleasure in even the simplest things, except one. She didn't want to read, listen to music, nor watch television. Even eating was a chore like any other.

Sighing, she decided to give life one more chance to prove its point and drew the curtains back.

She looked, at first, in puzzlement at the wrecked flower beds, thinking the seasons had shifted without her noticing. But she realised that the poppies, the remaining pleasure in her life, had been taken violently from her. That seemed to be the sign she had been looking for.

She went downstairs to the kitchen, closed the windows, locked the kitchen door and placed an old cardigan along the bottom of it. She took some kitchen roll, dampened it and did the same to the living room door. Then she opened the oven door, and turned on all the gas taps.

CONTRASTS

Donna turned the knob on her dream maker and yawned. In this year, 2055, you could choose your own reality for a few hours, before settling back into real life. Technology had reached such a point that you could form a group and make a holiday of it. She, Maggie and Joy had clubbed together to get a machine, with three receivers, and often took time out for a dream. It was the universal therapy; most people had one, just as the poorest person fifty years earlier had a television set, some more sophisticated than others.

Donna looked out her warmest coat. She had to go to the shops, as the pantry was nearly bare. There were a few dry crusts from yesterday, if the mice hadn't eaten them. The wind was howling round the group of hovels that formed what was laughingly called a street. The roadway consisted of the remains of tarmac set down in more prosperous times, and there were so many potholes that, even if anyone had possessed a car, they could not have driven it. There was no longer any pavement. The front gardens were little more than dirt patches, filled with discarded junk and uncollected garbage.

She met Joy and Maggie at the shops. They were dressed as poorly as she; Maggie's teeth had nearly all gone, and Joy weighed far more than she wanted to, on account of the cheap junk food she had eaten when she was young. The flesh had accumulated, and stayed with her even now she was half-starving. Although Donna was nearer the front of the queue than her two friends, she joined them farther back, for the sake of shared grumbles. She flexed her rheumaticky shoulders.

"I wonder what the government is selling us today. All I've had since yesterday was a heap of mash. I managed to get some potatoes from the garden before the blight got them. I put plenty of pepper on them to disguise the taste of mould."

The woman in front of them turned sharply. Pepper? Where had she got pepper from? Some people began to mutter and glared at her.

"It was some I've had in store for years. I had forgotten all about it." She spoke loudly enough for everyone to hear. She didn't want another break-in.

Maggie glared back at her friend's attackers. "I could do with a bit of pepper to rub on my gums. I've got the worst toothache ever. Could you let me have a little of it?"

"Yes, of course. There's just enough left in the container." That should discourage the disgruntled listeners from bothering to try to steal it.

When they reached the head of the queue, there were only half a dozen bread rolls left. The shopkeeper let them have two each.

Donna invited them all back to her place. She got a fire going with one of her few remaining matches, some dried-out grass from the summer's mowings and some twigs and branches set by for the same purpose. They huddled round it, each with their two rolls.

"Who would have thought that global warming would result in this?" Joy said. "I mean, fifty years ago it was just assumed that the world would get hotter, not colder."

Maggie felt she was more on the ball in these things. "You have had it explained several times by now. The Gulf Stream was affected by the melting ice caps; it just shrivelled away to nothing. Now we get the cold stuff straight off the Atlantic in the autumn and winter, and extra-hot weather and drought in the summer."

"Anyone for tea?" Donna suggested. The other two glanced at each other swiftly and away again. Donna had had only one tea bag left for the past three days, and it was almost exhausted. But, too polite to choose instead the dangers of tap water, Joy accepted on behalf of them both.

"Just what we could do with. And I've got a few ginger biscuits to eat with them." They always saved up little treats for when they met up.

The kettle took five minutes to boil, on what little gas was coming through. When Donna's guests tasted the tea, from the motley mugs and cracked cups, they made an effort not to pull a face. They had long become used to managing without milk or sugar, but they had difficulty in doing without tea itself, as they had always known it: the real thing, from India or China. Usually, they made do with their own concoction of garden herbs: mint, rosemary or sage. This latest crisis in world crops had come upon them so abruptly, the same crisis in which all three women had lost their young husbands in a pointless war, that people in general had not had time to develop the more homely methods of food production. One hundred years of prosperity had softened the rich countries, who were now no longer rich. They were now as poor as those countries that were once known as undeveloped. It would have been even worse, had not the population dropped from the result of pandemic, flood and general poor health, combined with a failing health system.

They sipped their tea in a thoughtful silence, broken at length by their hostess.

"The woman next door is still managing to look well fed, and I hear she gives sweets to the delivery boy who brings her newspapers. The rumour is that she saw the crisis coming some five years ago and began stockpiling. She must have put by hundreds of tins and packets. It should all be coming through the bedroom floor by now, considering the state of the buildings round here." She paused, then lowering her voice, "I have heard that some neighbours have been putting about the story that she's a witch." Maggie nodded. "I've heard stories. The government is threatening to search everyone's house and to commandeer supplies. The excuse is that it should by rights be redistributed, but we all know where it would land up. In the garden shed of the spivs who would resell it."

Donna finished her tea, and took care to eat every crumb that fell from her bread rolls. "My gran used to tell me what her mother told her about the black market in World War Two. It wasn't all about heroism."

"You can't blame your neighbour for putting food stocks by," Joy pointed out. "Calmly building up a stockpile is much more sensible than waiting until the emergency, then making a mad dash round the stores, emptying the shelves."

They all agreed that it was a blessing that they had not had children yet. It was harrowing to see the state some families reached. The adults jealous of the extra rations allowed for children, and the deliberate starving of their less favoured children. One heard the worst of stories – about some parents, in extremes, who had killed and eaten their own children. Something they thought only happened in those parts of the world destroyed by earthquake and tsunami. Though some heroically upheld the principles of protecting the weak and of fair play, humanity in general had quickly discarded its aspirations and descended to primitive desperation.

Corruption of the law and of monetary practice, never far below the surface, had been the first casualty.

Maggie sighed. "At least we know the worst about people. Nothing can surprise us now, though we're still shocked."

"How is your toothache, Maggie?" Donna asked her. "Would you like to try the pepper I suggested?"

"Thanks all the same, but on second thoughts, it would be a waste of good seasoning. After all, the toothache is going to come back again. I'll just have to hope that the tooth gets so rotten that it falls out." The state of dentistry, and lack of anaesthetics, did not bear thinking about. She had had an offer from a dentist to pull it out for her, without a pain killer, the old-fashioned way, but it was just a broken stump now, and he would have to cut through the gum. And then there was the matter of removing the nerve.

She sighed. "What do you say we turn the knob on the dream machine?" She looked round at them. They all looked tiredly at each other and nodded.

* * *

A mild spring day. They were off on a picnic. Their husbands had all gone to the gym and the children were at school, so they took Joy's car and made for the countryside. They had a selection of their favourite tapes under the dashboard and chattered as they went. Maggie, like the other two, had a mouthful of perfect white teeth, and she was looking forward to getting them stuck into the crisp salad she had put together, with salmon in the cool box and the lemon meringue pie to follow. There was mineral water for the abstemious and a light white wine for whoever wanted it. The mode of dress was a light summer frock for Joy, now a size twelve, with long slender legs; a tee shirt and pedal pushers for Donna; and jeans and a check shirt for Maggie, the tomboy.

Joy lay down under an oak tree and stretched, watching the clouds in an impossibly blue sky.

"You can't beat the Midlands for scenery."

Donna laughed. "Lying back like that, you can't see it. You're just looking at the clouds."

"I don't care; besides, it will still be there when I sit up. As long as

Maggie doesn't get the machine stuck again."

"That's not fair, you would insist we buy a second-hand model."

Joy intervened. "OK, you two, it's too nice a day to spoil. More wine, anyone?"

They all remembered with a shudder how they had spent two weeks in a blizzard, stuck in Joy's poky little house, without electricity or gas and with only some stale cereals to eat. When they got thirsty, they had to go outside and eat snow. At night they had huddled together in one bed, for warmth. Maggie was not going to be allowed to forget it.

But for now there was the afternoon to enjoy, as they lazed it away, talking about their children and about how they would prove to be a comfort in their old age.

Maggie was the hard-headed one. "Doesn't always work out that way, of course. My gran thought her children would make her proud and look after her, but she was disappointed in every one of them. She used to say how all the girls should get married off young, before they knew what they were missing, and that the boys ought to get themselves good careers and marry later. The middle boy did well enough, but he left home as fast as he decently could, and the other two boys drifted about, then they got their girlfriends pregnant. Then one boy deserted his girl, and the other married hastily, and made a disastrous marriage. As for the two girls: well, their mother was so desperate that they shouldn't be made a fool of by men that she hardly let them out of her sight. So they didn't get to make boyfriends and became old maids. That was a worse disgrace in the long run than having a child out of wedlock. It meant she had failed as a woman. At least the unmarried mother could claim to have fulfilled her feminine destiny."

Joy finished her glass of wine. "My mother got teased by her younger brothers. They warned her that if she didn't get married by the time she was forty, she would go mad." She paused, beginning to doze.

Donna couldn't bear the suspense. "So? What did she do?"

"She married the wrong man, and went mad at twenty."

The other two shouted with laughter.

"Brothers, eh?" Maggie helped herself to more lemon meringue. "Did she smack their silly heads?"

"Oh, they got plenty of that. It didn't make the little buggers any better behaved."

It amused them to reminisce about the bad old days, now safely in the past, and they continued in this way until it was time to turn the dial on the dream machine.

* * *

It was just as Maggie was putting on her pyjamas that night that she found the lumps in her breasts. She froze, brought up short, and glanced round at the miserable room. At the bare boards, the broken furniture, the rags at the window, the once stylish curtains. She considered the dirty crocks in the sink and the daily battle against vermin and disease. She thought of the drudgery she went through to meet the challenge of everyday life. The starving winters, the fierce heat of the summers. And now this. Would it be such a bad idea to walk away from it all? She lifted the telephone and left a message.

"Joy, let Donna know I've had enough. I'm unplugging my receiver from the dream machine. It was only ever a pose, making believe we knew what the hard life was. I realise now it is an insult to our grand-parents, who really had to live like that, for us then to play-act at having to struggle. I suddenly knew that I should instead rise to the challenge of coping with the boredom of the Utopia that is our real life, instead of playing at being poor, like some grand lady of the eighteenth century; those silly rich tarts who dressed up as shepherdesses, but returned to their pampered lives when it suited them.

"Don't misunderstand me. I won't think any differently of you if you prefer to put yourselves through artificial misery – to give your lives the contrast we all need to keep our senses alert. This all struck me when this damned machine inflicted the notion of breast cancer onto my imagination. So I'm switching it off, and I look forward to a long life, free of those hideous, outdated carcinomas. I will construct my own meaning and purpose, not have them manufactured by some theatrical producer selling nightmares. I'll see you around in the real life. Love you both."

She unplugged the machine. The imaginary street of hovels vanished, and the neat pavements, the modern street lighting, casting the minimum of light pollution, the colourful front gardens and the modest houses, with their real everyday joys and comforts, returned.

FAMILY MATTERS

Oh yes, I know my own children. You don't bring up two boys and two girls without knowing every little quirk of their characters.

Take Rose, 'the first and the worst'. Our little joke, though she never laughs at it. Pretends it's not sophisticated enough for her. She's a lot like me, I think. She had a lovely white wedding. She said she didn't want a fuss, but she came round to the idea eventually. Children sometimes have to be pushed into knowing what they really want. I think she loved it really. She's an old-fashioned romantic at heart, like all true women. When she married, it was for keeps. Well, she intended it that way, which is the important thing.

She'd been a bit of a tearaway when she was very young, but only in the schoolgirl sense. Silly things, like teasing other girls. But they made too much fuss about it; pretending to be upset, little drama queens. Anyway, they were little nobodies, their parents hadn't two ha'pennies to rub together. Or they looked silly, they had funny-shaped faces, or they were too big or too skinny. There was one kid who was bald! Well, I mean, she could expect to be teased about it, the gormless article. Anyway, her school attendance record wasn't very good; she came less and less to school; then we heard no more about her. It was about this time that Rosie was excluded from the school.

My Rosie was a fighter! Well, you can expect a girl with spirit to get into scrapes. The head teacher kicked up too much fuss about it. Said Rosie should at least pick on someone her own size. She actually accused her of being on the look-out for someone to bully! What's wrong with a girl fighting her own battles? The other kids should have taken an example from her.

My elder son, John, he's the quiet one. He got ahead and made it to grammar school. I always knew he would do well. That was my doing. I prodded him on. Told him to pull his socks up and stand on his own two feet. He was always the clever, hard-working one, but it doesn't do to let them know that. A bit of nagging doesn't come amiss. I used to let on to him that he was a bit simple, to keep him from getting above himself. Well, I'm entitled. I gave birth to him, he should never forget that. If it wasn't for me, he wouldn't have had a life to be clever in. A child should always be reminded of how his mother looked after him as a baby, especially in company; just to make a joke of it, to show you're not being unkind. But they should always be made to be grateful. Well, like I said, I pride myself on him having done so well. He's been married fifteen years now. I haven't seen the children yet, because he went to live in Australia as soon as he could afford it.

My younger daughter, Maureen, comes to see me now and then. She hasn't got married yet, but she'll get round to it. She just hasn't found the right one yet. Well, she won't, dressing the way she does. She's got her hair cut so short, it's nearly shaven. Doesn't wear make-up or pretty clothes either.

"Maureen," I used to say to her, "you'll never attract a nice man if you go striding around in slacks and clumpy shoes. And those tattoos! I mean, a butterfly on the shoulder or a little chain round the ankle, yes, but not a huge great snake down your arm." Mind you, I tend not to argue with Maureen, she's very much her own person. She's quite popular, too. Always seen around with smart women. Pretty women, too, they are. She brought two of them over to stay for Christmas. I was worried about there not being enough beds, but she brushed that aside. "No, don't worry," she said, "we'll all scrunch down in the big bed in the front bedroom." She's very thoughtful like that. In fact, before John left, she used to sleep in the tiny back room; didn't fuss about having it done up to look pretty – not even a dressing table, and only a few pictures on the wall. Rather dull ones, I thought, of earnest-looking women. Suffragettes wearing trilbies, I think. But some modern ones, too. A rock singer who had her name in small letters. k.d. something, and Martina whatsit, the tennis player. "You do have some dull-looking role models," I told her. Except for the one of Marlene Dietrich, that is. An old-fashioned girl, really, my Maureen, always was.

Anyway, she and her friends seemed to enjoy themselves. I heard them giggling and laughing half the night. Then they'd go quiet for a while; then start giggling again. All girls together. It's nice when they can be so normal.

I used to worry about Brian, my youngest. I admit I tried to make a bit of a mummy's boy of him. And I took his part against his father's discipline. More so than I did for the others. Well, a mother needs a favourite, it keeps the others on their toes. Besides, he was the pretty one of the family, with his floppy blond hair and his big brown eyes. He didn't do so well at school though, I must admit, too busy drawing pictures of women's clothes, but he did surprisingly well once he'd made the right friends. He was very popular with influential men; he's the personal assistant to a dress designer. My husband wasn't happy about him being so much into the arts. He used to say to me, "You know, I think there's something a bit effeminate about our Brian."

"Oh no," I told him. "He's very much a man's man. Besides, now he's lost his boyhood prettiness, he's grown that big moustache, he's got that crew cut and he's always down at the gym. It's like he's changed roles. And what kind of cissy boy would spend most of his time building up his muscles?"

He's the only one who hasn't left home yet, but a lot of grown-up children are staying on at home nowadays, it's the economy. Besides, he takes no looking after at all. He dresses beautifully, keeps himself clean and smart, and I don't have to clean his room at all. Just collect up his washing and his old magazines for recycling. And they are all men's stuff. Some of them have even got men on the cover. I saw him hiding some of them when he came out of his room once, but I'm very broad-minded. It's none of my business what girly mags he reads. Effeminate, my Brian? He's very fond of the ladies. You should see the pictures on his walls. All of them women. Opera divas, film stars, Princess Di, that president's wife with all the shoes. It shows he appreciates the old values, a respect for glamour of the old school; though I must say, if he's looking for a girl who looks like Dusty Springfield, he won't find one nowadays. "It's just a bit of camp, Mother," he explained to me. But I can't think what pitching tents in a field has to do with it.

Well, Rosie is settling down very nicely with her fourth husband. This is *it*, this time. She's really committed to this marriage. No one's perfect, and at least she gets married, not like these fly-by-nights and their so-called partners. They don't know what commitment means, those people. I know of one pair who have been together for twenty years now, and still they haven't taken the plunge into marriage. She says that marriage was invented for the protection of children, which they never had. What twaddle. "You pin him down in marriage," I told her, "make sure he doesn't run off." "What, like Rosie's husbands?" she said. "Besides, my chap is nearly sixty. Who else would have him?" I can't follow her logic at all, she's too clever for her own good.

John phones me regularly, every Christmas, and he's promised to send me a photo of the children. I insisted on that, I'm happy he's successful, but I think he might share it with his mother.

Maureen is planning to set up house with one of her lady friends. I do hope she doesn't turn into a lonely old spinster. Maybe if they go out together, it will be easier for them to find husbands.

Brian will be leaving me for a while. He's going to live in San Francisco for six months with one of his gentleman friends, so I won't even have the baby of the family to keep me company. There's still my husband, Frank, to look after, of course, but I'll need to fill my time in. I may volunteer to work for Relate; give them the benefit of my long experience in raising a family. After all, I really know my children.

FIREWORKS

It would be Bonfire Night soon, and Jackie, at seven, knew that he would have to go to bed three times before it arrived. He tended not to think in terms of days, but of bedtimes, when the Universe closed down until it became light again. He wondered what would happen to the day if he was kept awake all night. Like most small children, he felt the world depended on his reactions to it before it could make its own decisions.

He thought about Bonfire Night of the previous year, the swooshing rockets, a pause, then the blossoming into a chrysanthemum of coloured sparks. Jumping Jacks that skittered at random. Catherine wheels spinning on their pins. He thought about his dog, Rags, terrified by the noise, crawling under the bath and getting wedged tight. Rags was eased out and was put in the lobby under the stairs, from where the sound came muffled. Jackie went in there with him to comfort him, refusing to come out until it was all over.

But this year was to be different. There were to be no fireworks for anyone. No bonfires after dark, and no street lighting. Even the grand stores in the city were in darkness, and people stumbled to the dimly lit buses. If you went outside at night, you had to switch the light off until the door was shut again, and your windows had to be blacked out. Jackie was not afraid of the dark, he told everyone, and whistled loudly to display his nonchalance. Nevertheless, he tended not to go out to the lavatory after dark and used the pot under his bed instead. His mother put cold water in each pot after she emptied it, a mysterious rite that Jackie thought was meant to keep away the witches, but the mundane reality of which was to avoid the ceramic becoming encrusted with uric acid.

Right now he was grumpy about there being no fireworks. No bonfire, no baked potatoes raked out from the embers. They didn't taste the same from the oven. It was too tame for Jackie, there was no adventure in it; no ashes on the fingers to give it flavour. No standing at the bonfire, your face and arms glowing with the heat, and the cold November night on your back. He would miss sharing the light and noise with his neighbours and making up the guy from old sacking and a battered hat. Certainly not with old clothes now; these would be subjected to Make Do and Mend for several years yet.

His father was not around now, to play football with him when he came home from the factory or to tell him stories at bedtime. He did come home once, for two weeks. Embarkation leave, his mother told him. Jackie loved big words, and this one sounded important. It had a good rumbling sound to it. He rolled the phrase about and thought it had something to do with dogs. He had also learned another phrase, which he did not like. Identity card. It reminded him of the dentist. "Identity card," he said aloud, casting it from him with some force and disapproval. Then he rewarded himself by announcing with pomp and grandeur, "Embarkation leave." He practised it, for when he would teach it to the other boys at school and lord it over them with his special knowledge. It did not cross his mind that they too might have heard it. Another word came within his hearing, but it was whispered and didn't seem to have much to do with him, but concerned only boring, grown-up matters. 'Evacuation' would have nothing to do with children, he thought.

His disappointment over the fireworks was mollified somewhat by the purchase of a box of indoor fireworks, and the evening of November the Fifth was passed in the fascination of playful chemistry. He was even allowed to light some of them. The small stub of material that was lit and grew into a brown snake which coiled and writhed on the saucer. He thought it looked like poo, but did not say so. He didn't want to spoil his mother's pleasure. The little Japanese petals floating on the dish of water, which bloomed into flowers. The cellophane fish, which you placed on the palm of your hand to see which way it curled. It was supposed to tell you something rather personal about your nature, but the grown-ups glossed over that one. And of course there were the sparklers, when the light was switched off and they all held them above their heads, watching the sparks as they fell. He was allowed to stay up, in his pyjamas, playing Snakes and Ladders with his auntie. Then later, sitting on the settee, listening to the grown-ups talking, intrigued at the clever way they talked, with such knowledge of the way the world was run; looking at them each in turn, as a point was made with vehemence or reasoning. Until their voices became distant, the words becoming like a background noise with no meaning, fading and returning suddenly when his head jerked back as someone laughed loudly or the kettle whistled. Then he knew no more, and his uncle carried him over his shoulder, up to bed.

By the time the next Bonfire Night came round, he was familiar with noise and light falling from the sky. He would discover, too, that he could, after all, go for a whole night without sleeping and that the next day went relentlessly on without waiting for him to catch up on his slumbers. Every night, sleeping fitfully in the lobby with Rags, as the terrible racket went on overhead; the whistling, the crump, then the explosion; the ack-ack guns in the local park, and the distinctive sound of the Bofors gun, like a book being slammed shut, as the sinister fireworks fell round them, targeting the docks in London's East End.

GREEN WEDDING

Joanna's grandmother, Josephine, was determined that Joanna would have a romantic wedding. She said as much to the girl's great-nana, Ivy. There were four generations present: Ivy, in her eighties; her daughter, Josie, pushing sixty; Belinda, just reconciled to the big four-o; and Joanna, at twenty-two. Also present, as a tolerated afterthought, was the girl's grandfather.

"There's a sad lack of romance these days," Grandma Josie announced. "Not like in the good old days. Women knew how to be feminine then, and they saved themselves for a white wedding. Which is more than some have done." She paused, to glance over at Joanna's mother, Belinda. "Some people have no self-control over their appetites," she continued, in a raised voice. Belinda ignored her. This was an old dialogue, monologue almost, as her mother continued in her self-congratulatory diatribe.

"Premarital sex was strictly forbidden," Josie went on. It was her favourite phrase, so she straightened her spine and treated herself to a repetition. "Strictly forbidden, and if anyone breached the moral code, she was made to suffer for it. She could be put away for life and have her baby taken away for adoption. It was a great deterrent to immoral behaviour."

Didn't seem to deter some young women, apparently, thought Belinda, recalling the whispered conversations she had overheard in her youth about girls some twenty years earlier than that, who had had to get married in green. Besides, if it happened anyway, it can't have been all that strictly forbidden.

"The world is more civilised about these things now," Belinda said, "there never was any need to wreck someone's life just for being stupid." Josephine glared. There was no point in wasting her breath, she decided, having wasted a great deal of it. She was slightly mollified by the thought that there was a current fad for young couples to wear a chastity ring, to indicate that they would wait until marriage before they had sex. It was notable that they were the youngest of couples; still young enough to believe that sexual compatibility was a foregone conclusion.

Joanna's granddad muttered behind his newspaper.

"If they want to wear a ring to prove they're not having sex, why don't they just get married, like the rest of us?" He hoped his wife, Josephine, had not heard him.

It was going to be expensive. It would all cost her father a good £25,000, which was considered average in the current climate of borrowing.

"Weddings are getting out of control," Granddad said now, on his way to the garden. "They don't even make do with a hen night and a stag night; the girls take a whole weekend, and the lads go off for a week, abroad, in some cases. And another thing, proposals are getting out of hand, too. They hang them from sheets on public buildings, spell them out in lights and go down on their knees in public; there was even one proposal pulled by a light aeroplane across the sky. It was on the telly. They make a big thing of swearing to stay together forever. Funny how these are usually the ones that don't last."

Josephine sniffed. "I see nothing wrong in the old certainties: in tradition and romance."

When Josephine was young, she had read the trashy love stories and knew that, ideally, the girl and boy met accidentally, disliked each other on sight, and in the accepted formula, they finally realised that they had been in love with each other all along, and the reader was supposed to die of surprise.

Belinda cut some cotton off the reel and rearranged her daughter's wedding gown on the table.

"There are no certainties. There never were. You've simply taken a model from a particular time, and a particular class. It's always been different according to whichever social status you held. There never was just one best way of doing things. Besides, if you are going to talk about tradition, how about this one? It goes back several hundred years. When a peasant girl and boy got together behind the haystack, they took a purely practical point of view. Once the girl was safely pregnant, or better still, safely delivered, they were able to arrange the wedding. The really hazardous thing was the marriage. If either had proved to be sterile, it was a disaster for the family. They were not allowed to divorce, unlike the grand people. Besides, you can't arrange romance. By definition, it's spontaneous. It doesn't wait on respectability."

Josephine was having none of this. "We should go back to some of the old ways. If a young woman was pregnant, she had to get married in a green wedding gown, then everyone at least knew that much about her."

"You mean that as long as she managed not to get pregnant, she could get married in white; and if she had a period just before her wedding, she could breathe a sigh of relief."

"Don't be so vulgar; you know very well what I mean."

"I certainly do. Your own mother and father knew next to nothing before marriage, and precious little after it. It's a wonder they ever got around to conceiving you. Isn't that right, Nana?" She looked across at Ivy, who wisely had her head in a book, ignoring the bickering.

Ivy had a great fondness for Belinda. Rebellion had skipped a generation, and she had looked to her granddaughter to start the revolution. Do it for me, she had often urged her, remembering the distressing first night, traumatic for both of them. She had given Josie a good childhood, only to find that the child took it all for granted, thinking that she had earned it, and that everyone had had the same chances. Those who didn't, Josie assumed, must have brought it on themselves. She dearly wished to impose upon everyone else the exact pattern of her own existence. After all, she was loved and was made much of; it followed that this was because she was worth it. Anyone who found themselves unloved and neglected had only themselves to blame. If all this was followed by the disgrace of a green wedding, it only confirmed Josie's strictures about self-control.

"Do you know what?" Joanna spoke up. "I think I'll have a green wedding."

"WHAT?!" Nana Josie shouted. "After all the trouble your mother has gone to, to make over her own wedding dress? You'll have a white wedding, my girl, and no nonsense."

The girl laughed. "No, Nana, that's not what I mean. I'm talking about an environmentally green wedding. Flower petals instead of paper confetti; they'll degrade nicely on the driveway. Home cooking instead of catering, and as few air miles on it as possible. As for the hen night, we'll get dressed up to fool around, but everything must be bought from charity shops. We can buy a mini marquee from the Co-op for thirty quid, and the guests can rough it on the lawn. We don't have to hire a band. I'll borrow Great-nana's old records from the Forties. We'll play them on her old wind-up gramophone – we won't even need the electricity for cassette recordings. And if anyone absolutely must get bladdered, it must be on English cider."

"Won't you even have a bottle of champagne on the wedding day?" Granddad wanted to know, as he came in from the garden.

"Well, you know me. I can take it or leave it. I don't need alcohol to make me act daft. I prefer high spirits to potent." Even Josie found herself approving of the girl.

"But I hoped you would have a big, romantic wedding," Josie said now. She never learned.

"You're missing the point, Nana. For romance, I couldn't hope to outdo Great-nana and Great-granddad."

"But they had to get married while they were on leave, and there were no coupons to spare for a wedding gown. Then back home for Spam sandwiches and a cardboard cake."

The girl's face glowed. "Oh yes. Don't you get it? Married in uniform; one day taken out from fighting for their country. Then a few days' honeymoon in Manston before he took off again. I could only dream of anything so heroic."

They sighed and shook their heads. All except Ivy, who looked across at Joanna and winked.

IN CAMERA

Tony was not happy. For some time now his parents had not been at ease with each other, and it was spoiling his holiday. He loved Aberystwyth, and each year looked forward to the funicular ride that took him to the top of the cliff where the camera obscura stood. He never tired of the novelty of seeing the image of the bay, as the fitment of lens and mirrors at the top of the building was turned slowly round.

As they made their way to the funicular railway that took them there, he strode ahead several times and waited for them to catch up. His mother and father were talking urgently together in quiet tones, and as they caught up with their nine-year-old son, they quickly changed the subject.

Now his mother said to him, in a voice just a little too bright, "How would you like to stay here for a few weeks more with Granny Evans? Daddy and I have something we must discuss. Then you can come back home when it's all sorted out. You won't understand, but it will all turn out for the best."

The boy stared at her, somehow disinclined to question their plans for him. He was a thoughtful child, and he sensed that these grown-up matters contained a disturbing element, something beyond his powers to influence. His father had turned away and was gazing at the sea.

* * *

Tony Fraser walked up the cliff path, taking the long way, from the camp site. Aberystwyth was still his favourite place. A quiet town, its clamour confined to the sea, which even on the mildest day threw itself impatiently against the sea wall when the tide was in.

Now, as he made his way up, he reflected on the holidays he spent here as a boy, and how he loved to see the view from the camera obscura, to him a constant wonder of technology. He remembered, too, the holiday in which he was left here with his Granny Evans, when his parents had split up, for years afterwards thinking it must have been his own fault. This had cast a gloom on an otherwise amiable childhood, taking the shine off it.

* * *

The boy looked from one parent to the other as they walked on. A shadow had fallen over the bright day. He had heard about children who had been sent away, and it was always because they were in disgrace. He was suddenly alarmed at the possibility that they might send him away for ever.

He sat in the cable car, no longer savouring the excitement.

"Straighten your face out, Tony," his mother urged, "this is your favourite treat. Don't tell me you've become too grand and grown-up for it."

He tried to balance her motherly demand for childlike simplicity against her expectation of mature acceptance, and forced a smile.

* * *

Fraser paused for breath as he neared the top, and as he looked across the wild shrubbery sloping steeply towards the sheer face of the cliff, he thought back across the years. An average life, thankfully, with manageable tragedies and small triumphs, he would not have changed it in any major way. Except perhaps for one thing.

* * *

The cable car rattled to a stop at the top of the cliff. Mrs Fraser made a decision and braced herself.

"Wait a while, Tony, we won't go in yet. There's something I have to tell you." They sat on a bench while the rest of the visitors went into the small building on the summit. Then she turned to her son.

"The fact is that Daddy and I are going to get a divorce. You know what a divorce is, don't you?"

He nodded.

"You'll be all right; you can see Daddy at weekends, and any other time when you're both free, but he won't be living with us any more."

Tony fought for a way of saying he was sorry and asking how he could put things right, then finally found it in him to ask, "But why can't we carry on living together in the same house?"

"I can't explain why just yet, but Daddy will be living with another lady."

As they sat there in the awkward silence, people came out of the building, and his father made an attempt at jocularity.

"Here, son," he said, handing him a ten-shilling note, "go and buy yourself something from the shop. Then go into the dark room; we'll wave to you when the lens comes round."

* * *

Fraser reached the summit and sat down at one of the picnic tables, enjoying the view and the warm August day. After a few minutes, he went into the building, and as he walked through the souvenir shop, he passed a group of young people, all in jeans, some with dreadlocks, others with their baseball caps on back to front, and the girls with their hair long and straight. They moved towards the entrance, taking their cheerful noise with them. He paid his fee and went through to the dome. Leaning idly against the railing round the viewing disc, he scanned it, expecting to see the young people appear on it as they left the building.

Instead, he saw a youngish couple and a boy on a bench. The woman wore a pleated skirt with a box jacket; the man had his hair parted and slicked back with Brylcreem, and the boy was wearing short trousers and a V-necked jumper. As the boy got off the bench and walked towards the building, his features came into view. Their startling familiarity made Fraser stare, not believing the thought that was forming in his mind.

Another shock hit him. The people leaving the shop and walking out onto the summit were not the same crowd he had seen a few moments ago. Instead of tank tops and jeans, the women wore circular skirts and bolero jackets. Their hair was bubble-cut or Marcel permed. The men wore slacks and check shirts, and had their hair styled in an Elvis quiff or a DA cut.

He dashed out of the dark room and into the sunshine, where he saw once again the young crowd, the jeans and the dreadlocks, the nose rings and the pierced eyebrows, as they left, chattering and laughing.

The couple on the bench were gone, and in their place were the picnic tables once more.

* * *

Tony looked at the array of brightly coloured models, ball games and seaside toys without pleasure. They seemed suddenly to belong to another, lost world, to which he was no longer entitled. He turned from them, paid his entrance fee and went through into the dome. He looked at the image on the disc, at his parents on the bench and saw them wave. He loved them both and didn't want them to part. He sensed that his father had done something wrong, but they were civilised people, who never raised their voices in anger or bitterness, only ever in mild irritation with himself when he was lazy or untidy. Their very stability rendered the break-up all the more shocking to him; and now, as he saw them wave to him, his eyes stung, his nose prickled and he began to gasp with distress. He became dimly aware of a man entering the dome.

As Fraser's eyes grew accustomed to the dark, he saw that the boy in the V-necked jumper was on the other side of the disc and was crying.

"What's wrong, son?"

The boy looked across at the man. It was like looking in a mirror. Green eyes looked across at green eyes; the full, wide mouth of the boy an unformed version of that of the man. Fraser felt reality shifting beneath him, then it settled. The realisation was complete.

"My dad's got to go away, and we can't live all together any more and my holiday has all gone wrong." It came out in a rush of injustice and hurt.

"I know how you feel," Fraser found himself saying, distantly, "but it will be all right later on, I promise you."

"How do you know? You don't know me."

"I know you better than you think, and I can tell you that this is as bad as it will get." He paused, uncertain how to explain that he would absorb the misery and make it part of his personal history.

"Look at it this way: life is an adventure, with scars, and when you are grown up, you'll discover that people find different ways of being happy."

He paused again, unwilling to tell his younger self how difficult it would be to get used to the stepfather who would in time usurp his father's place, and with whom he would eventually declare a truce; of the sibling rivalry that would arise between himself and his half-sister; and the tedious journey of reconciling himself to his new life. He decided to be positive.

"By the time you reach adulthood, you'll see that it has made you a more understanding person."

"It's my fault, isn't it? It's something I've done wrong."

"You can take my word for it that it's not your fault. You see, I know everything about you. I know your father has just given you a ten-shilling note to buy a toy, and about your dislocated shoulder when you fell off the sea wall last year." Fraser flexed his right shoulder now. On damp days he still felt it.

"I know everything that will happen to you, too, and I know you will cope with it all. And, incidentally, what toy you will buy in two minutes' time." He paused to think, and then had an inspiration. "And I know your parents are planning to buy a television set. You'll be the first boy in your class to have one." The boy's face began to clear at the prospect of the simple pleasure ahead.

The companionable silence was suddenly broken when a technician opened the door, letting in a shaft of light. He found only a middle-aged man in the room.

"I thought there was someone else in here with you," he said, "I heard voices."

Tony Fraser smiled pleasantly.

"Just talking to myself."

IN MY DAY –
(History Made Silly)

"Things have gone downhill since my day." John the Twenty-Seventh sighed and shook his head sadly.

"Young people nowadays want it all their own way. They've no respect for their elders, and they waste the natural resources of the planet. If it wasn't for the older generation, I don't know how they would manage. After all, who thought up the slogan: 'Save Energy, Burn Calories'?"

"Young George Bush the Tenth, dear," said his wife.

"Yes, yes, I concede the work done by the King of the Remaining Americas. But the Low Countries had gone under the sea by then, and if it hadn't been for President Windsor, dear old William the Republican, that little group of islands to the north-west of Europe would have been lost to the US. They were going to use it as a prison colony." He panted a little in the Siberian heat, as he gazed out at the Steppes, flourishing now with tropical fruit trees.

"If you've finished the history lesson, dear, we might plan our holiday for 2123. How about the Bering Straits again? It will be cool enough to sit in the sun, come January. Or shall we take the refrigeration ship for Shackleton Base, for a change?"

* * *

"It's not like it was in my day," complained Millennia, the ancient matriarch. She had acquired her name at conception. Her parents had made love on exactly the correct day in March 1999, hoping the baby would be the first in their time zone to raise its cry as the fireworks went off.

"Children have too much given them, and don't want to work for it. Everyone wants to write a book, and you can't get servants any more."

* * *

"Things were different when I was a kid," the old man said. "Television was a new thing, and only in black and white, but your modern stuff isn't a patch on *Hancock's Half Hour*. They wrote better music, too. Where's your Beatles and your Stones of 2004?" He sighed. "They don't write them like they used to."

"I know," said his middle-aged daughter, "and you had to cross the room to change the channel; oh, but I forgot, you only had the one channel till 1957. Don't be such a stick-in-the-mud, Dad. The Seventies produced some very tuneful songs. Unlike now, of course."

"You don't know you're born, either of you," her grandma said. "We had to be contented with going to the pictures once a week. We didn't need luxuries like the telly. Mostly, we made our own entertainment."

"So I heard," her granddaughter chipped in. "Isn't that how Dad came to be born?"

"That's enough from you. There's a child present."

But the child wasn't paying attention. Pop music went to the dogs the day the Spice Girls broke up. Life would never be the same, if she lived to be sixteen.

* * *

Auntie Dolly straightened up from the ironing.

"Can't you turn that wireless off for five minutes? You'll run the accumulator down. It's all rubbish nowadays, anyway. In my day, we had real tunes, not this jazzy stuff."

"It's all the go nowadays," said her niece, Queenie, arranging her kiss curls. "You're just jealous because you couldn't be a flapper in your day."

"You're not going out like that!" her father shouted. "We can see your knees in that skirt. And you can wash all that muck off your face, too." Dad thought fondly back to the days when girls contented themselves with a little rouge, when he went courting in his blazer and straw boater.

* * *

"You want the vote? Whatever for?"

"To make a difference, Mother, and maybe influence policy."

"I never heard such nonsense. I've always let your father worry about that sort of thing. Get married; that should keep you busy enough."

"There are plenty of women to keep the world populated, Mother. I intend to have a career."

"And that's another thing. Women never went out to work in my day."

"Of course they did. Who do you think worked in the factories and mills? The shops and libraries, the schools and hospitals …"

"You know I'm not talking about the lower classes. They don't count. They were born to do the work …"

"And make the profits for us to live on."

"Now that really is enough! I wonder you don't start up your own political party, and have done with it."

Sounds like a good idea, thought Emmeline.

* * *

"Do you mean to tell me, sir, that we are meant to dance together, through the entire dance, with the gentleman's arm around the lady's waist?" Miss Penelope was startled. She had only ever been accustomed to taking the gentleman's hand, as they crossed, walked or skipped together down the line.

"The Waltz is considered quite genteel in Austria, Miss Penny," replied Sir George, "besides, the gentleman places the back of his hand against the lady's back so that no offending warmth is transferred thereby."

"Oh, I see. Austria. A respectable country. Had it originated from France, I could not possibly have agreed to it. I accept your invitation to the dance."

They swirled away onto the floor, under the disapproving gaze of Penelope's mama, who would never have been allowed to be so familiar, in her day, and did not see why her daughter should have the freedoms she had not herself enjoyed.

* * *

"James! What are you up to now? And where is my kettle?"

"I've had a splendid idea. I can make a machine that works without the help of wind, water, horse or hand. It works by pressurised steam. Just think, it goes by itself. We shall be able to manage without horses."

"What on earth is the good of a carriage without a horse? And by the way, I have to inform you that, since you've ruined my kettle, you'll have to have cold milk for your supper."

* * *

"This is going to be a bad year, Master Pepys. There are three sixes in it."

"That's just superstition. Numbers mean nothing."

"I'm sorry to sound old-fashioned, but I believe in Fate. It's an unexplainable force, and we might as well surrender to it."

"Oh, I see, so if you stand under a tree in a thunderstorm or climb a church steeple while the lightning flashes around you, you'll only come to harm if Fate has already decided. In other words, it's nothing to do with personal responsibility."

"You can talk clever if you like, but I know what I know."

"What's the point of arguing? Anyway, I've had a lot of ale; I quite fancy a meat pie."

"How kind of you to treat me. There's a nice little shop in Pudding Lane. Let's go there."

They wandered off, arm in arm.

"It's gone quite warm, have you noticed?" said Samuel.

* * *

"If I see you writing with your left hand again, my girl, I'm taking you straight to the priest, to have the devil exorcised from you."

"Father, the priest himself writes with his left hand," the girl said.

"May you be plagued with boils for saying so," her grandmother raved. She turned to her son.

"I told you no good would come of letting her learn to read. 'Tis the devil's work. It gives them ideas above their station. They should be content to live in ignorance, to fear God and keep his commandments. They didn't allow book-learning in my day."

She remembered only too bitterly how she had longed to tell her elders that she had learned to read on the sly, watching while her elder brother struggled with the words that she found so easy to decipher. She never did let on; she would have been whipped for it.

"The priest doesn't really write with his left hand, does he?" she asked her son.

* * *

William tried to explain his idea very simply.

"If you spread the ink onto the blocks of words, then place the sheet of paper underneath, all you have to do then is to turn the screw that works the press, and the words are instantly applied to the paper, a page at a time. It will be much quicker than writing it all out with a quill."

His friend was sceptical. "Is there any money in it?"

"Indeed. It may in time give rise to a new industry."

"And what would you call this new industry? Would you name it after your cumbersome machine – this Screw thing of yours?"

"I suppose so. Though I haven't decided what to call the machine. It's part Screw, and part Press. Which sounds more impressive – 'My son is working for the Press' or 'He has a career in the Screw'?

His friend narrowed his eyes.

"I think on reflection, Master Caxton, that 'Press' sounds better."

* * *

"You see, Your Holiness, it's like this. The earth moves round the sun, not the other way about. The earth is round, like the moon and the sun, so there is a precedent. It is not as if there was nothing in nature that shape already. The earth is not flat, as we thought."

"Of course it's flat. You can see it is."

"No, no, sire, it is round, like my head."

THWACK!

"It is FLAT, like your head!"

"The Greeks were right, Holy Father, and very clever with it …"

"Bunch of pagans, what would they know?"

"They were better at their sums than we are, and they proved that the earth moves round the sun …"

"Guards! Get the faggots; light the fire!"

"All right, all right. I'll sign … There, now can I go?"

"Push off then, and no more of this modern nonsense."

"Nevertheless, it moves."

"And stop muttering!"

* * *

"Livia, tell the boy to come in this minute; his tutor has arrived."

"Leave him to his games for a while longer, Publius, and offer the tutor a drink of wine. All work and no play makes Lucius a dull boy, you know."

"If I had defied my father like that boy does, he would have taken his belt to me."

"Things have changed since your day. Besides, what kind of example is it to the natives? I saw young Britannicus give you such a look of scorn when you whipped the donkey. You know how much these people worship their animals."

"I didn't come across a foreign, rough sea to these chilly islands to impress a bunch of blue-painted savages, you know. Besides, I'm not sure I'm going to stay here. It's cold and damp, nothing but forest and bog, rain and wind."

"Well, we are the immigrants round here."

"Not for long, the place is ours now; we plundered it."

Britannicus turned to his wife.

"These soft southerners: they come over here, marry our women and throw their weight about. The only reason he wears a belt under his toga is to keep up the breeches he has to wear because he can't stand the cold. Things aren't like they were in the good old days before they came."

* * *

Starwatcher threw another bone on the fire. "What's that you're playing at now, woman?" he demanded of his mate, as he picked at his teeth with a hedgehog's spine.

"It's my new invention."

"What, another one? We've already got fire, and these sharp things to cut our meat with. Any more of these new-fangled gadgets and we'll become dependent on them. It's flying in the face of nature, mark my words."

"This has nothing to do with food, dear. It's for carrying things in."

"You already carry things, that's your job."

"Exactly; that's why we send you on ahead with the spears. But we won't have to hold things in our arms once I get these two round things together. They move across the ground by rolling along, you see. I've just got to put a piece of wood between them, fit a container between the handles and you just pull it along."

"What nonsense, woman. It'll never catch on. We never had such things in my day."

* * *

The dinosaur sat trying to crack a nut; it kept slipping about his mouth, as his old teeth sought to get a grip. He looked over at an infant member of the group, and with his failing sight, noticed that the youngster had a heavy stone in its prehistoric paws. The juvenile was dropping it onto one nut at a time, cracking each of them open. He had quite a pile ready to eat.

Smart arse, the older one thought; the young have no respect for the old ways any more.

* * *

The horseshoe crab turned to her mother and said, "Isn't it time we left the ocean and tried our luck on dry land?"

"Tsk! You perishing kids. We haven't been around for more than five hundred million years and already you want to try another place. What is this mad craze for novelty?"

* * *

"You know," said the X chromosome to her clone, "self-reproduction is all very well, but I think what the world needs is a second sex. It would strengthen the species. What do you say we break off a piece of ourselves and make a Y chromosome?"

"You've just invented sex, you little troublemaker."

JOURNEY TO LONDON

When the fourth poll tax was considered in 1989, most people did not recognise it as such. Those with a smattering of history thought of it as the second poll tax, but most, simply as The Poll Tax.

When I discussed it on the phone with my brother, Billy promised to let me know when the demo from Birmingham would be organised. I looked out a black tee shirt and began to paint the slogan WAT TYLER LIVES! across the back, in white oil paint. I came late to rebellion. When I was the proper age for it, I could not afford to revolt. Now that I had the means, I was going to make up for lost time. In fact, the only demo I had previously joined was in 1965, at an anti-Vietnam war rally. I was living in a bedsit in Victoria, was on my own in the city and keen to join the rest of the world. I also joined the Communist Party, though not out of any sense of rebellion, more a desire to conform to a family tradition. My mother and brothers had been, or still were, party members. In 1990, I looked out my flask and rucksack.

The Uprising began on the 31st May 1381, in the village of Fobbing in Essex, where a poll tax collector was beheaded by the villagers and the local justices sent packing. Hereon, it spread rapidly, with other villages following their example. So it was that the peasants made their way to the strategically important town of Rochester, no doubt taking victuals: cheese, salted meat and skinsful of beer. Bread would last only a day or so, and they would have to rely on the loyalty of the villagers they called on, as they gathered supporters.

Even the police departments admitted that the number of people who made their way to the trains, the coach stations and the pick-up points for private coaches numbered over 100,000. This time, flasks of hot coffee, sandwiches and face tissues were packed. Not just men this time. Young, old, black, white, mums with pushchairs, fringe groups with pamphlets, long-haired hippy throwbacks, opportunist The End Is Nigh preachers, street performers taking the advantage of a chance gig and union members from the sober North, their best suits and polished shoes making some of us, in our comfortable travelling clothes and marching trainers, look like slobs. The optimistic mood held as we swung into Spaghetti Junction and on to the motorway.

The feudal lord derived his income from the fines and taxes which he imposed on the peasant tenants. The lord had the right to the family's best ox, after the death of the head of the household, the Church taking the second best. The privileges of the fold, where the peasant had to graze his livestock on the lord's land, so fertilising it at the expense of his own; marriage fines; tallage; tithes to the Church; and royal tax; so that taxes accounted for as much as 50 per cent of the peasant's gross annual product. Apart from rents and labour services, often paid to the peasant in kind, the lords enforced other dues, including the obligation to grind his corn in the lord's mill, bake his bread in the lord's oven and brew his beer in the lord's brewery. If he didn't brew any beer, he would usually find some poured over his roof, along with the bill. If a peasant's son wanted to leave the estate, then the father would have to pay a tax, and if he wanted his children to receive an education, then he would have to obtain permission from the lord, and pay another tax. If his daughter wanted to get married, he had to pay a fine called merchet. He also had to pay for a licence to sell his livestock. If the serf died, he was fined again, while the heir also had to pay a fine to take over the tenancy, sometimes as much as a year's rent. The earth's riches, produced by the peasantry, were creamed off by those who already had more wealth than they knew what to do with. With the rise of the towns, the feudal lords became more and more obsessed with wealth and luxury, and so were less inclined to forego their lifestyle in order to provide the necessary investment needed to modernise agricultural methods. When faced with a fall in income, they increased the burden of rent on the serfs, so further depreciating the wealth-creating commodity – labour.

As we sat in the coaches, some with toilets, some without, we looked out on to the motorway to see coach after coach pouring down from the North. As they swept past us in the overtaking lane, their occupants looked remarkably fresh and lively as they shouted across to us, considering that they must have started out at dawn, and those from Scotland, in the middle of the night. Those from the London suburbs came by Tube and bus. Others, living in the bedsit lands of Pimlico, walked it all the way, to Hyde Park, then back on the route to Trafalgar Square. By mid-morning, there would be hundreds of coaches parked along the Embankment, from beyond the Tate Gallery to well past Blackfriars Bridge. Before setting off, the coach steward took phone numbers, in case we got lost, hospitalised, arrested or missed the coach for more mundane reasons. On the single front seat, a young woman with a great sense of her own importance picked a political argument with the driver. "Leave him alone," she was told, "we'd like to get there. Besides, you'll be the first through the windscreen." A group of young people, probably history students, had entered into the Medieval mood by changing into hessian tunics. They put make-up on to look like dirt, scruffed up their hair, and some had already taken off their shoes. Billy disapproved of this silliness. Revolution was always a serious matter with him. But I thought then, as I do now, that if you can't have a good laugh while bringing down the State, what was the point? Besides, the ordinary bobby on the beat was as anxious as most of us to keep the atmosphere good-natured; it was only the dog-handlers and the mounted police, with their faces hidden and their identifying numbers missing, who played up to the hotheads, sometimes setting them off. Those concerned with the proper treatment of animals were particularly angry with these specialist police. Anyone who made use of animals to attack people deserved anything they got.

Billy pointed out the usual bunch of Trots on the back seat. I took his word for it. I wish to be spared the complexities and the schisms. I'm a follower of John Ball – a primitive Communist. I wouldn't recognise a Trotskyite if he had an ice pick buried in his skull.

Whitehall was blocked off, as was Downing Street, since a pair of iron gates had been illegally placed at the entrance to this otherwise public highway, so we had to go via the Embankment. From where the coach was parked, we had only to walk from somewhere to the west of the Houses of Parliament, along the Embankment and up through Northumberland Avenue, which took us directly into Trafalgar Square. When we got to the top of the avenue, we found the square to be full and noisy, so we stayed where we were. Like Wat Tyler, we had come to ask, in a well-mannered way, for Parliament to think up some other means of gathering revenue. Like – tax the grossly rich. Blessed are the meek, for they shall see where it gets them. Some who were not so meek were already mixing it with the mounted police in the square, but from where we were, slightly downhill, we had no idea of the fighting going on. It was the smallest minority of protesters whom the tabloids and TV stations picked out for attention. Thus it was that the overwhelming majority of us came peacefully and went away peacefully, not knowing otherwise until we saw it on the television that evening.

The rebels marched on to Canterbury, where they sacked the Archbishop's palace, but Tyler forbade looting, telling his followers that they were, "Seekers for truth and justice, not thieves and robbers." Indeed, when they reached the Savoy Palace, it was systematically destroyed, but not looted – one man who stole a goblet was executed on the spot by Tyler's men. It was soon realised that the sacking of manors and burning of records could not by themselves change the system, so they decided to march to London to demand from the King their freedom. At St Albans, the local Abbot considered the town merely an extension of his own private property and had stolen the people's millstones, using them to pave his dining room. When the Uprising broke out, the leader of the St Albans rebels, William Grindcobbe, told the Abbot that they were joining the rebellion in London, and if he resisted, he promised that Tyler would flatten the abbey to the ground. At the Uprising, rebels broke into the Abbot's house and tore the stolen millstones from the floor 'like breaking bread in Church', each keeping a piece as a symbolic souvenir of their freedom.

At Southwark, they were met by Alderman Horne, who told them that when they entered London, they would be welcomed as comrades by Londoners, who would join in their struggle to a man and would be happy to feed them. This hospitality was later echoed in the hunger marches in the early twentieth century.

Lunch was sandwiches and coffee on the Embankment, in the shadow of Boudicca, watching the river traffic. Drinking coffee on a demo brings another problem. The loos just below Boudicca's statue had queues for both sexes, but an especially long one for the women's. Some bold women walked into the men's loos. Later on, the massive crowds caused this all to fall apart. I glanced at the rows of men at the railings, with their backs to us and their heads cast down, and thought, that's how it must have been six hundred years ago. It was straight out of Chaucer, as were the smell and the puddles underfoot. Some young men, with their faces to a wall, elicited shrieks of merriment from young women and cries of "Higher!" and "Write yer name!"

When Richard met Tyler face to face at Mile End and heard the demands of the rebels, he replied: "I grant it." He then ordered thirty clerks to begin drawing up freedom charters, bearing his seal. Many of them left London with their charters, but Tyler, Ball and Straw remained suspicious. It was eventually agreed that the King would meet Tyler at Smithfield, where the maximum demands were put by the rebels. The King agreed to them. The Mayor, William Walworth, on orders by the King, then provoked Wat into drawing his sword, then stabbed him, fatally. The rebels then prepared to wipe out the King's Council, but the King rode forward and asked, "Sirs, will you slay your King? I am your chief and captain; you shall have from me what you seek." Once the rebels had dispersed, the King's Council finally felt safe enough to institute the counter-revolution with bands of nobles and liveried thugs, arresting and hanging suspected rebels. Ball and the other leaders were captured and executed, but none of them pleaded for mercy or retracted anything that they had said or done. Ball was hung, drawn and quartered. Many of the better-off rebels got off with a fine or a short prison sentence, demonstrating that the Uprising had not been entirely disapproved in higher circles. It was, after all, part of the process which paved the way to capitalism and free trade.

Free trade flourished in 1990, in the form of souvenir shops, selling mainly fatuous junk. We bought some. I pointed out to Billy a key fob in the form of a road mender's pick. "Take it for one of your Trotskyite comrades," I told him. "It wasn't that kind of pick," he said. "It was a small, dagger-like thing for breaking up ice for drinks." And there was I, for years thinking it was something you hacked your way up a glacier with, when Stalin sent the boys round to Trotsky.

As the afternoon wore on, and the time came to pick up the coach again, we went to a café next to the souvenir shop. We sat immediately opposite Big Ben, looking down on the colourful crowds, tiring now, like the police officers on overtime, gasping for a cup of tea; and no one desirous of removing heads, let alone sticking them on a spike. Speechless with fatigue, we sat staring into space, gathering strength.

At Waltham, Richard declared that the rebel's charters were null and void, as they had been given under duress. This, to working men who had lived their entire lives under duress.

The King had this to say: "O most vile and odious by land and sea, you who are not worthy to live when compared with the lords whom you have attacked ... You were and are serfs, and shall remain in bondage; not that of old, but one infinitely worse, more vile without comparison. We shall attempt ... to make such an example of offence to the heirs of your servitude as that they may have you before their eyes as in a mirror, that you may supply them with a perpetual ground for cursing and fearing you, and fear to commit the like."

We've all heard of a sore loser, but a sore *winner*?

Walworth was rewarded for his murder of Tyler, by receiving a knighthood, while Richard used the Uprising to consolidate his power, until he was removed by a coup-de-force, led by his cousin. Not one worker, peasant, merchant or baron rallied to his support, such was the general hatred for him, and he was eventually murdered in a dungeon. The Uprising of 1381 was not, of course, just an isolated incident, but the focal point of a continental revolutionary movement against feudalism. One insurgent cobbler protested at the time that: "The seigneurs would take from you, if they could, even your share of daylight!" Indeed, in England, with the implementation of the window tax, that is exactly what happened.

I had got it into my head that our coach was somewhere parallel to Whitehall, and insisted on us walking almost to Blackfriars, despite Billy telling me that it was the other side of the Houses of Parliament. Thus it was, as the hours went by, and we searched coach after coach, that we finally conceded that we had missed it. We set our tired feet for Victoria Coach Station, where it cost me £24 for two tickets back to Birmingham. I didn't bother to phone home, either from London or Birmingham, since I didn't think there had been anything to worry about at the demo. I parted company with Billy at Digbeth and took a train to Kidderminster, then a taxi back home.

When I got in, some time after midnight, Him Indoors was sitting up, with a face like a bag of spanners. "I've been worried out of my mind about you," he said. "I had a phone call from the coach steward, giving me the phone number of Cannon Row Police Station, and three hospitals." "Whatever for?" I said. "Because of the riots, of course." "Riots! What riots?" "Well, you were there, you must have seen them." "Well, no, it was pretty peaceful, and we were just off the edge of Trafalgar Square." I switched on the television, to see the late news. I couldn't believe my eyes.

JUST REWARDS

Stephanie decided, this morning, as she got on the Tube at Victoria, to go anti-clockwise round the Circle Line, to her job at the British Museum. It would give her a change of faces to look at. The car was crowded, but this did not displease her. Most of those standing crushed up against her were well-dressed young businessmen, smelling pleasantly of clean skin and aftershave. Stephanie was woman enough not to mind being pressed so close to them, and they in their turn had no objection to jostling among the secretaries on their way to work. The young man in chinos and dark blue tee shirt at her side felt very much the same as Stephanie, only he had deliberately chosen the rush hour for this very purpose. He did not have to go out to work. He ran a small antiques shop with his partner, and was at ease with the stereotype that constituted their lifestyle.

Otherwise, the crowd bore that deliberately cultivated lack of expression, the closed look that ensured the only privacy available in the circumstances. In place of the portcullis or the picket fence, there was the downcast or middle-distance gaze that said, my private space is still here, in my head.

This morning, Stephanie planned to change at King's Cross to the Piccadilly Line, instead of walking the rest of the way to Russell Square. This was usually her only chance of exercise, but for some inexplicable reason she felt compelled to stay with the Tube. She often did things for reasons not apparent to herself, and the reason revealed itself in due course. She planned, this lunchtime, to indulge her one extravagance, and buy herself another book.

Michael, the young man, was also bound for the museum. Even on his day off, he liked to do a little research.

Across the car, a woman in her sixties was on her way to a shopping expedition in Oxford Street. She planned to buy something stylish to wear for the dinner date she and her husband would have that evening, in celebration of their fortieth wedding anniversary. Most of the time, Pamela slobbed around in jeans and a baggy shirt, but when she put her mind to it, she quite surprised herself. She was dressed now in a full green skirt; it was easier that way to try a trouser suit on without first having to remove the skirt.

Sitting next to her was a man in his eighties, but well-looking. The artificial poppy he wore at all times in his buttonhole was not only for November. He wore it in memory of his fallen comrades of seventy years ago. He was bound for the National Gallery, and planned to get off at the Embankment and take the Bakerloo to Charing Cross. An RAF navigator in his younger days, his life nevertheless had not revolved around World War Two. Although it had defined his life, he was aware of how easy it was to bore the young on the subject; they had their own lives to arrange, and he kept himself young by getting involved in the lives of his children and grandchildren. He would, as usual, take a rest in the quiet of the Portrait Gallery, before going next door and battling through a million tourists to immerse himself in the Dutch Masters. Holland had a special place in his heart for several reasons. He now tried to settle himself in his seat in a way that was less painful for his rheumaticky shoulder.

Only a few got out at St James Park, and even fewer got on. They lumbered on to Westminster, where the usual press of parliamentary workers got off, and as many tourists took their place. As they picked up speed once more, the silver-haired veteran began to get himself ready to alight and change trains. As he did so, the lights went out and everything went quiet. The swift change from the hurtling train and its noise to this eerie silence was all the more strange as the passengers still felt they were moving. Almost immediately, the lights came back on again, and with them, the noise returned. Stephanie, Michael, Pamela and Alfred stared around them. From being solidly packed, the train now contained only themselves and three others. A Buddhist monk, a young Muslim man, and a ragged man, with a headache and a hangover. Except that he no longer had a headache, and his hangover had lifted. He now looked up in surprise, fresh and alert. The suddenness of the removal of fifty-odd passengers had resulted in Michael's falling precipitately against a steel bar, knocking his elbow rather sharply, but to his surprise, he did not feel any pain. Likewise, Alfred's rheumaticky shoulder no longer twinged at his every move.

"Was that the Embankment?" Stephanie asked of everyone else.

"I suppose it was," said Pamela, "but what in Heaven's name is going on?"

"Blessed if I know," Alfred said, "I was supposed to get off there."

"Well, everyone else seems to have done so," Michael said.

As the train rattled on, lighter now by several hundred passengers, the occupants talked among themselves. Then they became aware that the train was running on a rising gradient. The empty straps swung backwards slightly, as they felt themselves ascending.

"How can that be?" Alfred asked. "The Tube runs on the flat, on whichever level it takes."

"That's not all that's odd about it," Michael observed. "Have you noticed how light it is becoming in the tunnel?" True enough, instead of the usual blackness through the windows lit only by the passing lights of the trains, there was an ever increasing brightness, which grew in intensity in the distance.

By now, his alcoholic confusion dissipated, the derelict was holding an intense, though mainly one-sided, conversation with the Muslim, who listened politely.

"You see, although we know what time *does*, we cannot explain what it *is*. We just repeat the terms we use for it, and the nearest we get to defining it is to say that it is the sequence in which events take place." He paused, relishing his newly regained intellectual faculties.

"So time is pretty much the same as the events which take place within it," the Muslim said, wishing to rise to the other man's enthusiasm.

"Quite so," said the one-time professor of quantum physics. "You can't separate time and event. They have to be the same thing. Time only began at the point when the Universe began. Before that … well, there was no 'Before'. It's not so much that there was no time, as that there was no need for it. If nothing is happening, there is no need for a sequence of events, because there are no events." He sighed happily. He felt he was back in the lecture hall, impressing the young.

"How do you define eternity, in that case?"

"Ah, that's the difficult one. Eternity is something we do not experience. We consider it to be an extension of time, going on forever, whatever we mean by that – just continuing, without ever stopping. Then again, we oppose the notion of time *against* that of eternity. So that to imagine eternity, we have to call a halt to time. Time has a stop, according to Shakespeare. So we either think of eternity as time forever or time stopped. It's a paradox. It both is, and it is not. Something our Buddhist friend here might accept." He nodded sociably to the man in the saffron robes, who nodded back, pleased to have his beliefs acknowledged by an otherwise Unenlightened one.

The professor was back to his old pre-alcoholic self, as they all sat back and let themselves be borne on to their destiny, for another few minutes, without talking.

"What's wrong with our clothes?" Alfred suddenly remarked. "They've faded. I was wearing a dark blue lounge suit when I got on, but the colour seems to be going from it."

They all looked down at their clothing. Pamela's green skirt was now almost white, as were Michael's smart casual clothes. Stephanie's plum-coloured trouser suit was by now pale pink, and as they looked down the car to the tramp and the Buddhist, the saffron robes had by now turned to dazzling white, and the professor's rags were now off-white.

The train continued to run, picking up speed and rising more steeply.

"We've been going for a good quarter of an hour since the lights went out," Stephanie said. "What in hell is going on?" For some reason, she felt that last phrase was not appropriate.

"Somehow I don't really care," Michael remarked. "I find this rather soothing: the swaying of the train, and the light growing stronger in the tunnel. I could go on like this forever."

Not only was the light brighter, but it was of the incandescent sort, that does not dazzle, keeping the viewers' gaze on it, serenely.

At last, the train began to lose speed. They turned to look through the windows. A station came into view.

"It should be Paddington, by now," Stephanie said, "but somehow I don't think it is."

They looked for the name of the station, but they were still travelling too fast to make out the letters.

"It looks like 'Meadow' or something," Pamela said.

"No, it begins V-A-L," the old airman told her, "and there's an H in it somewhere."

"You're both wrong," spoke up the Buddhist. "It reads N-I-R-V …" but he was interrupted by a voice over the public address.

"All passengers alight here, please," the voice requested them politely, "and take your places on the escalator." The doors opened with an electronic sigh. As they stepped from the train, they were greeted by the strains of serene music.

"Oh, how nice!" Pamela exclaimed. "I love Strauss waltzes."

"No, that's Dusty Springfield at her best," said Michael, as the escalator ascended.

"No, that's a Gregorian chant," said the Muslim, an admirer of Christian sacred music. To the professor, it sounded exactly like 'Sailing By', just before you got the shipping forecast. His musical tastes, despite his intellectual talents, tended towards the cheap and potent.

"All I can hear," observed Alfred, "is a lone bugler." He noted with approval that they had got it right with 'The Last Post', and not 'Taps', with which it was so often confused.

Stephanie heard the electronic strains of Vangelis, playing something ethereal, and the Buddhist heard the tinkling of bells and tiny cymbals.

The moving staircase brought them finally to the top. Waving a cheerful goodbye to each other, they all took their separate roads: Pamela to her summer meadow, Alfred to his place, above the salt at the Warriors' feast, Michael stepping out onto a yellow brick road to join Dusty, Judy, Imelda and the rest of the girls, and Stephanie to what looked like a cross between the main street of Hay-on-Wye and Charing Cross Road. She made her way eagerly to the nearest bookshop café, the aroma of real coffee and good cigars already wafting her way. As the former derelict strode briskly to his lecture hall, the Muslim gentleman smiled at the prospect of an eternity of erotic pleasures, and the Buddhist, the weary cycle of birth and death broken at last, went forward to his just reward of blissful oblivion.

Meanwhile, the several hundred passengers who had so rapidly vanished from the train stumbled, dazed and weeping, from the wreckage.

LOVE STORY

David realised he had met the love of his life at one glance. The soft, luminous eyes across the library counter. The shy smile, the husky voice. As David handed in his library books, he thought quickly, employing delaying tactics, thinking up excuses. Anything but tear himself away from those brown eyes. He could have drowned in them forever.

"Is there a Readers' Group?"

"Yes, every third Friday in the month – two fifteen to three thirty."

"Who leads the meetings?"

"My colleague here …"

David didn't hear the name, he had already lost interest and was on to the next questions: the book being studied; which part of the building the meeting was held.

"Can I book a computer for half an hour, please?"

"Yes, of course, if you'll just give me a few details."

As his quarry bent over the booking list, David took in a few details on his own account: the glossy chestnut hair falling across the brow; the mouth with its pretty pout; the woody overtones of the cologne; the lithe figure as it moved about the small space, bending this way and that between other members of staff.

Seated at the computer, David pretended to be absorbed by the information he had raised via the Internet, someone selling antique doorknobs or something, he didn't know, his senses were elsewhere. Out of the corner of his eye he saw the slender figure move along the racks, stretching across the book trolley to transfer returned volumes to their places.

After his bogus efforts at the computer, he decided to test for reciprocation and approached the object of his new-found fascination with a smile.

"I'm looking for some World War Two poetry, could you direct me to it?

"Yes, of course, sir, please follow me."

To the ends of the earth, David thought, as he followed meekly, looking forward to making a complete twonk of himself.

As luck would have it, the World War Two stuff was on the lower shelves, necessitating bending down. The tang of cologne caught David's nose, and his brain tripped out. And what shampoo kept that short hair gleaming? Something with herbs, with a conditioner, he guessed, leaning down towards it.

"Ah, here's something." The librarian rose suddenly, smiting David on the chin with the aforesaid tresses. I'll never wash that chin again, he decided, though possibly the one underneath it. He was suddenly conscious of being unfit, and determined to get to the gym, to throw a few weights around for all of five minutes.

Then, as his brain turned to mush and threatened to leak through his ears, he decided.

Recklessly, he made his move.

"There's a whole lot more I want to find out about the subject, and you seem to be familiar with it. Shall we discuss it over coffee, when you finish work?"

The shapely eyebrows rose a little. I'll be lucky if I get my face slapped, he thought. But, unbelievably, the response was favourable.

"Half past five, at the Currant Bun."

"Right you are," David replied. "By the way, my name's David; what's yours?"

"Harry," the younger man replied.

MILLENNIUM

The churches were thronged. There was an air of fear, mixed with anticipation. Those who had sinned, or fancied they had, were eager to atone and had surrendered their belongings to the church, even their jewellery. They wished to be in a state of grace when the Judgement fell upon them.

The squire had a clear conscience, though not on account of his having lived a blameless life, but rather because he considered himself above such considerations. Having been born into privilege, he did not see why life, and by extension, afterlife, should not continue to hand him the goodies. He waited calmly to be lifted to Heaven and to a place fit for one of his station. It did not cross his mind that it could be otherwise.

He had given his servants leave to attend church and they, having made their confession and repented, would no doubt join him in Glory, but on a lesser level, of course; they would continue to serve him in the Hereafter.

The squire's wife also looked forward to the next world with some degree of serenity. It could hardly be more tedious than life had been so far. Her father had married her off at sixteen to a boor of a man, who had no conversation, no cultivation and who matched his stock of pigs for gluttony. He thought his only duty towards her was to provide her with fine clothes and servants to scream at; in return for which she was to drop a healthy son every year. That she failed in this was in reality his own weakness, but the fiction had to be kept up that the fault lay within her. This had already been disproven before she met him, when she had given birth to a daughter at the age of fifteen, courtesy of one of her father's stewards, and had had to part with the little one. She felt her life had ended right there, and was indifferent to whatever happened to her after this. Her husband drank copiously, too, though she considered this a blessing, rendering him, as it did, incapable of demanding his conjugal rights. It was with relief each night that she ordered the menservants to carry him to bed, loosen his stock and breeches, remove his boots and leave him there to snore till dawn. She even smiled round at the other ladies in their private pews as she walked past them to take her place; they were scandalised at this show of cheerfulness in the face of the cataclysm to come.

The farmer had told his servants to stay behind. They could pray together in the kitchen and keep a watch for unbelieving thieves. That this attitude betokened a degree of scepticism in his own mind, he chose to ignore. Like the squire, he picked the bits out of the Bible that it suited him to believe, made great play of abiding by them, and depended on the Lord to see him right. Most, though, were in fear of what the scholars had warned them of, and at intervals, overcome with terror, would have to dash out to the middens to purge themselves.

As the sand ran down the hour glasses, as the bells began to mark approaching midnight, the hysteria rose. The priest's incantation and the choir's psalms were drowned out by loud weeping and terrified shrieking.

The last chime rang out. The shrieking rose in volume and continued for a while until realisation began to dawn. They fell silent, looked upwards to see if the roof would yet fall in, then around at each other, abashed at the panic they had shown, knowing that it showed a guilty conscience. They affected nonchalance and a return to piety.

They went back to their homes, to repent, not of their sins, but of having given their valuables to the church. There would begin the tiresome business of exerting pressure on the minister to let them have them back again. Not too difficult for those of influence. Especially those who knew quite well what the minister had been getting up to with the young maidens who went to him for pious instruction.

The squire returned home to find his pigs had been stolen by opportunist infidels; and the farmer, when he got back to the farm, discovered the servants lying drunk in front of a roaring fire, all the coals used up and the cider stores badly depleted.

The squire's wife, meanwhile, sighed in resignation, but smiled dutifully at her husband as she poured him a tankard of wine. She knew that his riotous intemperance would hasten him to his richly deserved reward, and a comfortable widowhood for herself.

"They do say," one was heard to mutter, as the church emptied, "that the scholars believe it's to be *next* year that the Judgement will come, in the year of Our Lord, one thousand and one."

* * *

Well, at least the fireworks hadn't woken him up. Determinedly unimpressed by all the fuss, Tom had retired to bed at half past ten and had put his ear plugs in. He also intended to stay in bed till nine the next morning and not go out all day, if only to avoid being greeted with "Happy New Millennium!" He already knew what the date was; he didn't need aggressively cheerful people to remind him.

He was also irked that knowledgeable people had declared on radio, television and in the press that the real celebration was not until 2001. This led to a flurry of letters to the press pointing out that if this was so, then it must be assumed that the Christian prophet must have been born already one year old. These were replied to with sophistry and shifty figure work, and no satisfactory explanation. This had eventually come, almost casually, from historians, who said that the reason for the confusion was the fact that the ancient Greeks had no zero in their arithmetic. Thanks for telling me, Tom thought. He had been one of the writers to the press and felt he had been made unreasonably to look stupid.

During the night he turned over in bed and looked at the radio clock. Five to twelve. Still half asleep, he slipped easily back into his dreams.

Some three hours later, he woke again and looked sleepily at the clock. Nine o'clock. That time already? Can't be. He got out of bed and drew back the curtain. Pitch black, except for the bonfires and the house lights of the party givers.

Clock must be wrong, of course. The Millennium Bug had started to bite, and electronic gadgetry would be malfunctioning. He didn't care. He had got in a couple of weeks' extra groceries, extra cash and a camping stove. It was up to the clever people now, to get them out of the fix they had got them into in the first place – trying to save money by taking two digits off the date on the computers. The computer programmers, some twenty years previously, had thought the current programming would not last until the end of the century and left the machinery to assume the nineteen as the year date. When it was realised that the programme needed to be changed, it was also realised that this would involve colossal expense. A lot of money was made by a lot of computer nerds to prevent this disaster. This was looked upon sceptically by those who suspected there was little cause for panic and that it was just another money-making exercise. Tom was among the sceptics.

He settled down again, thinking of the superstitions people attached to the date. They expected great things of it. A grand new future, such as children expect the world will offer them as the years open up before them. Or Apocalyptic disaster, something terrible out of Revelations. Either way, he had to admit to himself that, deep down, he was vaguely disappointed. He really wanted life to take an extraordinary turn.

Glancing at the clock again a short while later, he saw it registered twenty to nine. Whatever time it really was, he still felt tired, as if he had been in bed for only five hours.

When day broke at last, he looked through the window and noticed something odd about the dawn. It was on the wrong side of the house. Sunrise in the west? He wasn't back in Australia, was he? Must be still asleep, he thought, and decided to go along with the dream. The sun went behind a cloud, and the overcast day obscured the eerie effect. He got up, plugged the kettle in for a cup of coffee, and while it started to sing, he pottered about, getting dressed. When he came out of the bathroom, he lifted the kettle to pour into his cup. It was stone cold. Yet it had been at boiling point when he had left the room. It should at least be warm. Leaving it, he went to the fridge and helped himself to orange juice, then put two eggs on to boil. At least the gas stove was working.

Coming back into the living room, he glanced out of the window again. The sun was out again, but instead of rising, it appeared to have been sinking. He felt sure it had been above the pear tree when he last looked. He shook his head and blinked; he would wake up soon. Then he turned to the settee, where yesterday's newspaper lay, in disarray. Strange, he thought, I could swear I put that out for recycling last night. Scooping the pages together, he saw the uncompleted crossword. He had finished that yesterday, too. He remembered how easy it had been. Shrugging, he got a pen and filled it in while the eggs boiled.

Except that they didn't. The water was cold, and the gas was out. There was no smell of gas, and the dial indicated that it was off. Perhaps he had absent-mindedly switched it off at some point.

He got the frying pan out, cracked the eggs into it and lit the gas again. They were still runny, so they would fry up all right. Looking through the window again, he watched the golfers out on the course. There was something peculiar about the way the ball was behaving. It seemed to jump out of the hole and run towards the putter, gathering speed until it reached the club. The golfer suddenly swung the putter backwards, slowing his swing until it hovered a few inches to the right of his foot, as if waiting to be struck. A voice farther away called out in the morning air.

"Orf!" It seemed to start on the long vowel, ending abruptly on the F.

Orf! Shouldn't that be 'Fore'?

A ball made its way from over the head of the player on the green, back towards the man who had called the warning, falling to his feet and coming to a halt at his club, which he then lifted backwards and upwards.

Tom looked at the clock again. Twenty past four. A thought came to its frightening conclusion; an apprehension which he had pushed back, not wishing to acknowledge it. He picked up the newspaper once more. The squares in the crossword were blank. He finally acknowledged what was happening. He returned to the kitchen, and realised he was walking backwards.

* * *

After the extraordinary occurrences at the beginning of the third millennium, year 3000 was awaited with trepidation. Records were confused, with various interpretations. The writings and recordings of the time contradicted each other. Some claimed that time ran backwards, finally reaching year One. That the scribes of the time then interposed a year Zero, giving the famous infant his natural birthdate of birth at nine months' gestation and his first birthday after twelve months of life. Superstitions spoke of time lords upset at the clumsy counting methods in AD and desirous of regulating the records.

Others claimed it was the bad dream of a grumpy sceptic who couldn't get his breakfast eggs boiled.

Yet others said it was merely the work of a storyteller with a warped mind and a need to put a resolution to a story.

Whatever the case, the world looked quite different from the way it had in 2000. For a start, there were not many people remaining on earth. Not only crops were genetically modified – people were, too. Owing to the IVF programme running into trouble over mistakes with donated sperm, and sometimes eggs, children got born to couples neither of whom were their natural parents. Many unknowingly married close relations. Surgery with donated organs taken from specially bred animals, who had themselves been modified with human genes, further complicated matters, and disorders and diseases ran rife. There had not been sufficient money or resources to keep up with man-made disasters like this. The scientists had only just managed to rid the world of the HIV virus, when they found themselves faced with the results of their own cleverness.

Then there was global warming. Between 2030 and 2050, the temperature rose to such a level that people died from the heat, leaving only those robust enough to cope with it to breed. The polar icecaps melted, flooding the low countries, drowning millions. Humanity just made it to Alpha Centauri in time, colonising new planets and learning from past mistakes.

MONKEY BUSINESS

Greedy Guts was the alpha male of the troop and took full advantage of his position. He also took the favours of all the adult females. He shoved everyone aside as he rampaged through the jungle and demanded anyone to groom him who wished to get into his good books. But he was bored. He had always had his own way, had always swaggered. There was no novelty in it. Damn it, he was King. It was his job to enjoy life; that of his subjects to suffer and abase themselves. His need to dominate accelerated even as it became stale. But though they accepted his status, they found ways round their acknowledgment of it. They had enough to eat, and had learned to skip neatly out of his way, frustrating his attempts to attack them. He must think up new ways of making a nuisance of himself. He gave it some thought, then slept on it.

He woke well before sunrise and stripped the one remaining bush that bore edible fruit. Once he had gathered it all up into a heap, he sat on it, eating until he was full. As the other members of the troop awoke, they stared at the scene, then moved forward to take the fruit, but Greedy Guts screamed at them and beat them off with a heavy branch. One or two very young monkeys quickly grabbed fruit and ran away with it, but he chased them and tore the fruit from their little hands.

An adult known as Short One protested. "Look, boss, we need this food. You've got more than enough, and we are all hungry. You can't eat any more for the rest of the day, and it will all go rotten. Now share it out and be sensible."

"No chance! I picked them and they're mine. I've worked very hard to get them, and you are not going to steal the fruits of my labour." He looked puzzled for a moment. He had made a pun without meaning to. "Anyway, you lot were lazing around in bed while I was being industrious and entrepreneurial. You mustn't have what you haven't earned. That's only fair."

Slow One spoke up. “But we would have worked for it if you hadn’t taken our livelihoods from us. You’ve monopolised the means of industry and consumerism, and we are all out of a job.” He then looked blank for a moment, then fainted from the unfamiliar rush of intellectual effort.

“Who said life would be fair?” Greedy Guts wanted to know.

“You just did, you moron,” Clever One shouted, “when you claimed your right to take more than your share of the communal stock.”

Greedy Guts had a poor memory for points raised by himself and swiftly abandoned when it suited him, so, to cover his embarrassment, he screamed all the louder, as one does.

Clever One let him have his tantrum and thought about the situation.

“It won’t do you any good. You’ll be in possession of a lot of rotten fruit, and no better off. There’s no point in having surplus goods if you can’t capitalise on them.”

Slow One opened his eyes and spoke. “That’s a grammatical tautology, you know. Surplus goods *are* capital. Their very function is to be capitalised on.” He fainted again.

“You’re just jealous because you’re not prepared to put in the hours of hard graft.” Greedy Guts settled himself more comfortably on the mound of surplus goods, while they held their positions in the stalemate. Eventually, he spoke. “Well, you’ll just have to make a living some other way. I don’t want a lot of scroungers in my troop. It leads to the breakdown of society. You lot will be wanting golden elephants next.”

Clever One was exasperated. “What the hell would we want with golden elephants? Come down off your heap of rotting fruit and stop making stuff up.”

“I’m acting purely on principle. I believe in honour and hard work. That’s why I am top of the heap, and you are not.” He thought a bit more, considering how he could, after all, capitalise on the situation.

“Look, I’ll tell you what I’ll do with you. I’ll let you have one piece of fruit each time you render certain services for me. Make up my bed for me in the tree every night. Bring me the occasional small animal as a snack, when I’m too busy ruling to get these things for myself. My high office brings responsibilities that you lesser beings don’t have to worry about. Or you could collect a pile of heavy branches for me, when I want to attack my enemies.”

"Weapons in exchange for food, eh?" Clever One muttered. "I don't see much future in that."

They left Greedy Guts on his mound of food and moved off to discuss tactics.

Later that day, several females presented themselves to Greedy Guts, and while he was busy with them, the other males crept up behind him, pinioned his limbs and bit him to death. They threw his body to the scared crocodile in the holy river, and everyone held a feast on the mound of fruit.

They all sat about, contentedly belching and scratching. Bold One licked his fingers, one by one.

"We'd better see about picking another leader. They don't grow on trees, you know."

"I don't know whether you've noticed," Clever One pointed out, "but in this neck of the woods, tyrants have a habit of choosing themselves. Besides, I think royalty has had its day. The monarch is supposed to protect the troop from enemy species and lead us into battle, but he always sent us ahead into the fray and stayed at a safe distance; then he stole goods he didn't need and hid them from us. Do you remember how he barricaded the cave with the paintings on the walls and wouldn't let the rest of us see them? I ask you, what good does it do for royalty to hog all the artworks?"

Bold One sighed. "I think he imagined it gave him status, but all it did was to make us a laughing stock."

"Well, let the next one watch he doesn't get too uppity, that's all," warned Slow One, "after all, we are many, he was few, and a random mutation at that." He slid gently to the ground in a coma.

"Meanwhile," Clever One suggested, "I'll act as Leader, *pro tem*."

They all pelted him with fruit.

MOVING SHOT

The bright autumn day was perfect for filming, and although the VIP he hoped to catch on film was not so popular out here in the Bible Belt, those who did admire him would have something for the family album.

As he walked through the spectators lining the route, he noticed he was the only one with a motion camera. His footage would be all the more valuable.

Choosing his spot, he walked over to where the view was most advantageous. At his back was a picket fence, behind which lurked a shadowy figure, apparently a workman, busy with his box of tools. Excited voices were raised, as the limousine turned right, sweeping down into Elm Street. Abraham Zapruder lifted his movie camera to his eye and steadied his footing against the slope of the grassy knoll.

NELLIE'S STORIES

This was the second time in a week that Mrs Wilson had thrown away perfectly good food. The first was a game pie, made for Them Upstairs, and found to be unwanted after all, when the master and mistress were called out on an unexpected dinner date. This most recent waste was a shepherd's pie, made for the staff, but discarded when the fishmonger called with a special gift for the cook: a particularly fine salmon, too good to turn down.

The title of 'Mrs' was an honorary one only, bestowed on the cook as a matter of course and of courtesy. She had never married, but had been in service, first as a kitchen maid, from the age of twelve, and through an astute management of the current cook, she had picked up her trade by a process of flattery and observation, until she was promoted when the cook became too old for the job. Although she came from a family with very little money coming in, she had never, as a child, gone hungry, and when she left home, her employers kept their servants well fed. It meant nothing to her to throw unwanted food in the bin.

Her own kitchen maid, however, had known only too well what it was to wake in the night, chewing the blankets. She had barely escaped the mundane nutritional diseases of the time by stealing food whenever she could. Buns from the baker's cart; fruit from the greengrocers. On rare occasions, milk, when an inattentive maid had left the can on the doorstep, to be filled by the milkman while the maid scurried round, doing the work of five.

Nellie was shocked at the waste, but had learned not to protest. Her protestations were met with scorn. "Don't you presume to criticise your elders and betters, miss," Mrs Wilson had told her. "I've seen more life than you have. I've forgotten more than you'll ever learn." When this tirade of self-serving rubbish came to an end, it was taken up by a stern lecture from the butler, Mr Johnson. Nellie made her face as blank as possible and kept silent. This acted as an even more potent rebuke and did the girl no good at all.

Fortunately, she was not without friends. A daughter of the house, Miss Penny, liked the girl. She saw to it that the sewing was given to her to do, even a little embroidery, which meant that she was allowed to sit in the back parlour on her own. She sang to herself as she worked, occasionally glancing out of the window at the children in the neighbouring gardens. She wondered what life was like for these other creatures, this overclass, and puzzled over how their lives came to be so charmed. The staff talked about their employers, in a mixture of envy, submission and derision. To Mrs Wilson, they were to be taken advantage of. "They've got where they are by taking advantage; we'd be fools not to do the same." Fred, the boot boy, looked on them as gods, to be humoured and whose wrath was to be avoided. Mr Johnson's opinion of them was frequently expressed in the sentence: "They are where they are because they are cleverer than us." That, for him, was an end to it. It had all been set down in tablets of stone at the beginning of Creation. He knew his place, was dignified and obsequious, and helped himself to the best of the wine. "But they were born rich, weren't they?" Nellie said. "They're clever to have held on to it, that's all." If this statement sounded too bold for her to make, she knew that Mrs Wilson agreed with her, though that lady did not encourage the girl to think well of her own opinion, and contented herself with an amused humph. Mr Johnson, in a good mood, merely said, "You'll learn, my dear, how things are, when you are older." He still lived with the certainties of the Victorian era. Even the changes brought by the Great War had passed him by. He believed that he had only to shut his eyes to modern life, to live by traditions no older than himself in any case, and it would all blow over. Flappers, jazz music and moving pictures, they were a passing fancy. Once they were gone, the nation would pull itself together again.

Passing Nellie on the way to the pantry, Fred had whispered to her, "He's not so grand. You know he was supposed to be going to a scientific lecture last night? Well, he didn't, he went to a music hall instead."

"How do you know?"

"I was there myself, sitting further back. And he enjoyed himself, too, laughing at the rude jokes and joining in the singing."

"Did he see you?"

"I made sure he did. I waited for him on the way out."

"Was he put out?"

"Not a bit of it. He nodded to me and said, 'It's an enlightening thing, Fred, to see how the common people amuse themselves. I trust you, too, have learned something from it.' Then he clapped his hat back on his head and strode off, cool as you like."

"What are you two giggling about in there?" Mrs Wilson had thought up a job or two to keep Nellie on the trot.

"Coming, Mrs Wilson."

The shepherd's pie, she had managed to retrieve from the kitchen bin and smuggled it out to her family on an afternoon off. They had made it the means of an entire day's food for the whole family, for her mother, father and five siblings. Nellie, at twenty-five, was the eldest. Her brother had gone into the Navy at sixteen, the next sister down had been killed in a factory accident at the age of fourteen and the youngest girls were still at school.

"Nellie!" Mrs Wilson's voice cut through her thoughts as she sat shelling peas. "Miss Penny wants to see you, right now!" She tried to make it seem as if Nellie was in trouble, and the girl assumed a worried look, to placate her. But she knew it would be, at worst, neutral, and at best, a second-hand frock or gloves.

It was even better.

"Sit down, Nellie, I have a proposition for you," she said. "Mother thinks I ought to have a lady's maid. I don't, but I could do with some amusing company on occasion, and someone to take to the theatre."

"But I've never had the training ..."

"Don't need it. I'll show you the ropes. Just follow instructions in the normal way and you can't go wrong. I'm my own mistress now, anyway, and can give directions to any of the servants."

Nellie wisely held her counsel. If Miss Penny thought her worthy of promotion, she would go along with it and take the chance that she might fail. At worst, she would still have her job as kitchen maid.

When she came out of her mistress's room, Nellie patted her apron pocket, which bulged a little. This did not escape Mrs Wilson's sharp eye as Nellie came into the kitchen. The cook demanded to know what she had in her pocket.

"Silk stockings! Now you take those back straight away. I can see they don't need mending, but I'll back you up to say that you thought they did if you'll return them."

This time, Nellie had no hesitation in showing her indignation. Her innocence had emboldened her.

"How dare you accuse me of stealing! I've just been given these, and I'll have you come with me to Miss Penny to put you right about it."

"You're getting too big for your boots, young woman," Mr Johnson said. "You just mind how to speak to those above you."

"Well, it's not fair; you both know I don't steal, but you took it for granted that I must have done. Besides, that's not all she's given me." She took from the other pocket a small container holding a quantity of emollient cream. "She knows I help with the washing, and how it makes my hands chapped and raw, so she gave me this lotion she got especially for me, from the chemist. Or perhaps you think I've stolen that, too." She went back to shelling the peas, now feeling entitled to bristle at her treatment, and sat at her work, with an injured air.

"It's all right, you silly girl," Mrs Wilson's good nature came to the fore, "it's just that I'm responsible for your good behaviour. If you get into trouble, you get me into hot water, too."

It was while they were sitting at their supper: cold meat for those who wanted it or bread and cheese and the remains of the salad from the lunch, that Nellie dropped her more important bombshell. Not only was she going to be groomed to be a lady's maid, but she was to be taken to the theatre that very next Saturday.

It was quite funny to see the effect this had on them. Even Fred stopped eating to stare at her.

"Well now, you've made an impression and no mistake," Mr Johnson was quite taken by the thought that someone working under him was going to get a little culture. "Make sure you pay attention to the dialogue, in case anyone asks you how you enjoyed it. I wouldn't like you to look naïve or foolish." He had, when young, been to see *Hamlet*. Having been told to listen carefully to the dialogue, he had enquired of the man sitting next to him which bit that was. He had had a vague idea that it was either the bit that came before the play proper or the bit at the end. When told that they were, separately, the prologue and the epilogue, and that the dialogue was the bit in between, he sat, red-faced throughout, hoping no one else had heard him ask the question.

The scullery maid, Winnie, took Nellie's position, and a temporary cleaner was employed from an agency, until Nellie had either made a success of her new job, or had not. This moving about of the staff was unheard of among most families, but these were rich enough and self-confident enough not to conform. Their employer, Mrs Griffiths, with no patience for fashion or style, even made a point of wearing last year's fashions, deliberately to annoy the snobs.

The play was performing at a small but select theatre in the city, and Nellie learned, to her relief, that she would not be sitting among grand people in their finery, but with those who were either earnest and arty or the out-and-out Bohemian, with more on their minds and more in their lives than petty considerations of fashion. They took a taxi, which scandalised Penny's father. He would have preferred the Rolls to have had a showing. Although his money was securely based on trade, a fact which his wife pointedly displayed to the old-fashioned snobs, John Griffiths was not as forward-thinking as his wife and tended to grovel to inherited money. It was to little effect that Lillian lectured him on the honesty of trade and the corruption of land-based wealth. He humoured her, believing she would eventually grow out of her Socialist phase. In this, he was more deluded than ever.

Nellie sat round-eyed throughout, imperfectly understanding the play. The long speeches baffled her; she lost track of what was being conveyed; and found it hard to follow the intricacies of who was unable to marry whom and for what reasons of family closeness. But it was lovely to be able to sit and be entertained; to be waited on in the interval, with coffee and cakes. (The production was a Temperance one, in honour of the playwright, and the snacks themselves were vegetarian.) Most startling of all, Penny introduced Nellie to her friends. "This is my maid, Nellie," she announced to a small group. What the hell do I do now, curtsey? Nellie thought in a panic. But the friends smiled at her, told her their names and chatted to her about the play. She was not asked any awkward questions, only required to nod and smile, and let Penny do the talking. The art lovers had already made their guesses about the set-up; Penny was dressed, as so often, in a man's suit, with a tie. They already knew she had an eye for a pretty girl.

"Well, what did you think, Nell," she was asked, as they sat in the taxi, among the theatre crowds.

"I thought it was wonderful. And have you noticed, when you close your eyes in the dark, you can see the colours and the scenery all over again?"

The rest of the servants had gone to bed, and Winnie was fast asleep, when Nellie slipped in beside her. But the following morning, round the breakfast table in the kitchen, they all wanted to know about it.

"Was it a love story?" asked Winnie.

"Was there a murder?" Fred wanted to know.

"I hope you didn't talk while it was on," Mrs Wilson said.

Mr Johnson tried to look serious and cultured. "What was the play called, and who wrote it?"

Nellie enunciated slowly and carefully. "*Mrs Warren's Profession*, by Bernard Shaw." That, at least, she knew she had got right.

Mrs Wilson, unknowing, nodded wisely. All she knew of Shaw was that shocking play, *Pygmalion*, with the rude word in it. She was relieved to know that the girl had not seen an unsuitable play. Mr Johnson raised his eyebrows and glanced at Fred, wondering how much of a man of the world he was by now. Fred raised his, man to man, but said nothing.

* * *

The Griffiths were to hold a dinner party. Their son, Robert, would be down from Oxford and his parents had managed to get hold of a good-looking girl, the daughter of a friend, with the idea of 'throwing the young people together'. The rest was up to them, and nature.

The girl, Anna, was now the talk of downstairs. Busy as they were all day, with very little time off to get to see the outside world, they looked for the smallest excitement.

"I've seen her before," Mrs Wilson said, "when she was tiny; she was allowed the run of the house. She used to come down to the kitchen a lot and ask if she could have a pastry or other sweet stuffs. A pretty little thing, she was, plump and rosy. Not like some scraggy little articles I could mention." She cast a derisory glance at Winnie.

They were taking their midday meal. Nellie was not needed to wait on Penny. In fact, Penny did not want anybody to hover round her, dancing attendance. She even cleaned her shoes herself. Fred was grateful to her for this.

He now winked across at Winnie.

"Never mind, Win, you'll soon fill out. Besides, it's all the fashion for young girls to be thin. They even strap themselves down at the front to make it look as if they've got no bust."

"That will do, Fred!" Mr Johnson barked at him. "You're not among your disreputable friends now, you know."

"Such talk!" Mrs Wilson felt she had to appear disapproving, though she found the boy amusing.

"Besides, it's not for the likes of us to bother about fashion," Mr Johnson said. "Clean and tidy and respectable, that's all we are called upon to be."

"You'll be waiting on them, you two, Nell and Win," Mrs Wilson said. "Keep an eye out for anything you see developing between them."

* * *

It was to be a light luncheon, chicken, vegetables, with a salad, and strawberry junket to follow.

"I don't know how that is to be enough for the girl," Mrs Wilson said. "She always had a fine healthy appetite. I'd better make some tartlets, and I'll send Winnie to the baker's to get some fresh biscuits in. And she can get some loganberries, too, while she's about it." She babbled happily as she worked. She loved her job; used countless pots and saucepans, letting them all pile up for the skivvy to wash up. She would not have made a successful housewife; she didn't clear up as she went. She had to be a queen bee, surrounded by inferiors.

* * *

Anna was still the picture of good looks and health, but gave the impression, by her manner and speech, of one who was delicate. Her complexion, too, had a pallor that only artificial means could have attained. Nellie made a mental note of this as she stood by, with Winnie, ready to serve.

"Eat up, Anna," Robert urged her. "You've hardly touched anything."

"I really couldn't take anything but a little chicken and a few peas."

"Potatoes? They're new. Dainty little things, ain't they?" Robert helped himself to a generous portion.

"Oh dear no, not potatoes! I'm really not accustomed to taking much to eat."

Mrs Griffiths looked across and raised her eyebrows. You've changed since I last saw you, then, she thought.

The talk was light and inconsequential. The latest gossip among friends and acquaintances. About Flappers and Bright Young Things, and the latest aeroplane flight. Nellie looked on, trying to imagine how these people filled their days, when they had no one but themselves to please; no work to do but dabbling at their education.

When the dessert arrived, Anna waved it aside with a dainty movement of the hand, slowly closing her eyes and opening them languidly.

"I really couldn't, you know. I have a delicate constitution."

I wonder how you keep your fine, strapping figure, then, Nellie thought. The young lady didn't make sense. Was this really a new fad among the idle rich or was it a throwback to the mid-Victorian age? She would make up her mind about it if Anna swooned, fainting over the table. Nellie had a mental picture of her falling, with her face in her soup, and let go a giggle. She quickly turned it into a cough; this did not escape the attention of Robert, who liked his girls as robust as himself.

The servants talked about it at length over the washing-up and the supper.

"It's pretty clear she's trying to impress Mr Robert with her fragile ways," Mrs Wilson said, as they sat at last with their cocoa, round the fire.

"She doesn't know him like I do, then," Mr Johnson said. "I've seen him at many a party – it's the fun-loving girls he seeks out. He won't waste much time on her dripping and drooping all over the place." The talk came to a sudden end, as Miss Anna herself came into the kitchen.

"Hallo, my dear," Mrs Wilson said. "How nice to see you down here again, after so many years. Nellie! Winnie! Get the hot water bottles done for the beds, and quick about it. Fred! You've got plenty to do as well."

"I'm feeling a little stronger, you know," Anna told them all. "Perhaps I could peck at a little chicken and take a drop of wine."

"Certainly, my child; come up to the fire and tell me all about college, while I get you something."

With the younger servants out of the way, and Mr Johnson tactfully withdrawing to his pantry, there was no one to observe Anna and her appetite but the discreet Mrs Wilson. The girl did full justice to a chicken breast, three tartlets, a trifle already made up from the spoils of the tea table, and two glasses of red wine. She was just sitting back, dabbing at her mouth with a table napkin and sighing with satisfaction, when Robert suddenly appeared round the door. He had crept quietly downstairs, hoping to catch Anna in her secret vice, and now the wreckage of the kitchen table announced itself, in all its monstrous depravity.

"What ho, old girl! That's more like it. Thought you were about to fade away back then. Hope it's not the latest thing to pick and peck, as if your hosts are trying to poison you."

"Well, you know how it is – a girl is entitled to have the vapours now and then."

"Not with me around, she ain't. And you'd better be in fine fettle if you're to come with me on a jaunt tomorrow. I'm taking a pack of chaps and girls with me, boating on the Serpentine. I'd just come down to order the tuck basket."

"In that case, I think I'll be able to make it." She still felt she ought to make a show of reluctance, if only to maintain the original fiction for a decent spell further, while fully intending to forgo the chalky complexion the following day.

* * *

Mr Johnson had an eccentric uncle. It was said that he was rich. He had hundreds, tucked away somewhere, so the family gossip went. As a child, he had extracted pennies from schoolmates with one ramp after another. His favourite was to construct a small gift for the teacher at little or no expense to himself, then bully the rest of the class into contributing a halfpenny towards the cost. In a class of fifty, this made him twenty-five pennies; two and a penny was a lot for a schoolboy. He pressurised smaller boys to buy conkers from him, pleading poverty. When the boy protested he could not afford it, Trevor accused him of being mean, selfish and of thinking only ever of himself. As soon as he was old enough, he took jobs as an errand boy, several at a time, hounding out the opposition with his bullying tactics.

At twenty-one, he inherited £50. He immediately banked it and continued in his occupation, as secretary to an accountant. He made his first suit last twenty years, by means of patching and tucking as it began to wear, and by changing into an old suit discarded by his father, as soon as he got home. He never bought slippers, but graciously accepted a pair as a gift. These, too, lasted as long as the suit. As the slippers began to fall apart, he held them together with string picked up here and there, sometimes begging a small piece from a tradesman, casually mentioning that he needed to secure a parcel he was on the way to posting. He had two ties, and as these began to wear out, he had his sister turn them inside out. She silently cursed him as she struggled to do this, inverting each of them in turn over the knife sharpener. Any pilling of material round his cuffs and turn-ups, he carefully removed with scissors or a razor blade.

With his instinct for going where the money was, in his early thirties he went to America, flourished, then brought his riches back to Britain, where the living was cheaper. He sometimes visited the house of his nephew, Andrew Johnson, and it was on the subject of this modern-day miser that Mr Johnson was regaling Mrs Wilson, to her great amusement. The uncle was to visit the below stairs of the Griffiths home, and Mr Johnson thought it well to forewarn the cook; she would have to hide any spare food very well; Uncle Trevor always ate well when he visited, though he stinted himself for food when at home. He would be travelling over from his home in Wales, where the housing was cheap.

When he arrived, he had his pet dog with him. Living alone, he needed company, and so it was that when Winnie glanced through the kitchen window, she saw a large man and a very thin greyhound descending the area steps.

"Well, would you believe it! Even the dog is one that won't eat much." Mrs Wilson believed that greyhounds were thin by nature, rather than by training. Uncle Trevor was out to make money by his pet.

"Hallo, Andrew! How good to see you." He shook hands with his nephew, then said, with a sigh, "My word, I've had a tedious journey. It does sharpen the appetite, don't you think?"

Mrs Wilson gave a quick glance at the butler, then gave in to the hint.

"Come and sit down, Mr Johnson, and I'll see what I can get together for you."

"You'd better call me Trevor, or you'll never know who you're talking to," he said, eyeing the remains of the dinner brought out of the larder.

"The meat is all right cold, but I'll have to heat up the potatoes and beans." Mrs Wilson was apologetic, but Trevor swept this aside.

"No trouble at all. Just give me a little cheese and pickle with the meat, and anything sweet to follow will be splendid."

"I've a few sausages left over from yesterday's lunch," Mrs Wilson said. "I'll put them down for your dog. What do you call him?"

"I haven't thought of a name yet; what would you suggest?"

"Well, Ribcage seems the most appropriate for this skinny little thing."

Uncle Trevor thought this tremendously funny, and had to put down his knife and fork while he gave vent to his mirth.

"By Jove, that's ripe! Tuck in, Ribcage, show 'em what you're made of."

It turned out to be a pretty jolly visit, what with Uncle Trevor's good humour and jokes, and as the evening wore on, he entertained one or other of them, while the rest bustled round on their daily duties. Eventually, they had all finished their work and sat having a cup of tea before going to bed. Uncle Trevor excused himself to see how the dog was doing in the scullery. He hadn't finished the sausages put down for him, and Trevor hated to see good food go to waste, so, thinking no one could see him, he bent down and picked up a sausage, talking loudly to the dog all the time, then popped the sausage into his own mouth.

"That's right, you eat up, like a good dog." He busied himself filling the dog's water bowl, giving himself time to chew. He put the bowl down and scooped up the remaining sausage, stuffing it into his mouth. Then he helped himself to a glass of water. He stood at the sink, chewing and drinking, then wiped his mouth and came back into the kitchen.

What he didn't know was that Mrs Wilson could just see him from where she was, at the fire, his stooped figure reflected in the glass of a free-standing cabinet, an old piece of furniture consigned to the scullery, that now held saucepans.

Time came for Uncle Trevor to leave his nephew and make his way back to Wales. After he had made his farewells, he turned to go. As he went up the area steps with Ribcage, waved for the last time and turned his face towards the streets, they noticed something that had escaped them all evening. He had at some time mended a tear in his trousers. On the seat of his pants was a cobbled-up stitch or seven, covering as many inches. Compounding this was the fact that he had used white cotton. They stared at it unbelievingly, then turned and laughed together at Mr Johnson's preposterous uncle.

"We must have him here again, Mr Johnson," Mrs Wilson said. "He'll cheer us all up no end."

* * *

"Them upstairs are going to their cousins in the country," Mrs Wilson told the rest of the servants, "so we'll have to get used to a different household for a month."

"I shall like being in the country," Nellie said, "but it means plucking the feathers off the game birds; it's so fiddly."

"But it's worth it for Mrs Wilson's game pie," Fred reminded her. "Besides, there will be plenty of dogs and horses this time." Fred knew how Nellie loved animals.

"Horses? What for?"

"They'll be joining the hunt."

"Is Miss Penny going, too?"

"I think so. Why?"

"Well, she doesn't like hunting."

Mrs Wilson looked at her and said, sharply, "How do you come to know so much about them upstairs? I've told you before, don't you concern yourself with what your betters get up to."

Nellie went quiet, and Mrs Wilson's curiosity was stung. She wished the girl was not so obedient, or rather, only when it suited Mrs Wilson, and for her to be more forthcoming when Mrs Wilson found it convenient.

"Anyway," she said, "why shouldn't she like the hunt? The family have always hunted. It's a tradition." The question was thrown open to everyone present, but Nellie knew that she was expected to enlighten them.

"Well, I heard her say it was a bore, and that since foxes are vermin, why didn't they shoot them?" She had everyone's ear now, and in the silence, she went on, "She likes the city more than the countryside, but her doctor told her she should have the fresh air; because she'd spent too much time in smoky cellars, drinking too many cocktails, and her nerves would suffer from too much jazz." This pleased them to hear; it bore out their belief that the rich damaged their health with their indulgence.

"Enough of this," Mr Johnson reprimanded, "I have something to discuss with Mrs Wilson."

As they scuttled off, Fred whispered to Nellie, "Do you think he's going to propose to her at last?"

"Those two are altogether too frivolous, Ivy," Mr Johnson confided, as they sat by the kitchen fire. "Forever giggling together."

"Don't begrudge them that, Andrew. Life is hard enough; let them take their innocent pleasures where they can. Anyway, what was it you were going to tell me?"

"Well, Master Robert had a little chat with me last time he came back from America. The Wall Street Stock Exchange is doing great business, and he is going to invest the inheritance from his grandmother. He suggested I do the same with my life savings. They are buying shares like mad in Wall Street."

"Your entire life savings? Isn't that a bit risky?"

"Not at all. They are extremely cheap."

* * *

August in Worcestershire was lovely, and the servants soon settled to their duties in a different place. Besides, there was plenty to gossip about. Nellie was busy preparing a bedroom for one of the guests when she became aware of a disturbance between a resident maid, Beryl, and her mistress, Lady Redwood. My lady had a pinched look and a permanently sour expression, something to which her husband had become accustomed over the years. It was said that he had not enjoyed conjugal privileges for some thirty years now, and it was not hard to believe. He was generally an amiable man, used to being doted on, and like many a spoilt child, had grown up to be good-natured and to accord to others the kind usage he had been brought up on. Beryl was a large, handsome girl and had taken pity on Lord Redwood when he was banished to a spare bedroom, after his wife complained of feeling rather fragile; these spells happened with increasing regularity nowadays. She had taken a holiday with her sister to Switzerland and had returned in time to welcome the Griffiths. She had forgotten about Beryl, and the girl's rude good looks were the first thing she saw in the hall when she came in from the car. The girl had frequently been impertinent to her mistress, but it was something with which her employer could not be bothered. She would see if the girl had developed better manners.

It was late in the afternoon. Lady Redwood went straight towards the drawing room door. "Bring some tea in here, Beryl, at once," she said, speaking over her shoulder.

She threw her hat and coat over a chair and stretched out in an easy chair. His lordship stood by the window, looking rather glum. He was aware that from this point forward his life was going to be complicated. He lacked subtlety and couldn't see his way.

There were a number of things he couldn't see. His wife saw one of them at once. When Beryl came in with the tray, she stared at the girl hard. Now she need not wait to see if Beryl's manners had improved. Now she could strike back for the girl's cheek. She was a woman without mercy. When Beryl put down the tray, her ladyship said, as coolly as though she were asking for a glass of water: "Beryl, this is not a lying-in hospital. You'd better go and have your baby somewhere else. When are you expecting it?"

On the stairs, Nellie held her breath, expecting to hear the girl throw herself to the floor and beg for mercy. But a silence followed. Perhaps they had all fainted from shock, Nellie thought, but then she heard Lady Redwood say, impatiently, "Well, you don't deny it, do you, when are you expecting it?"

Instead of a broken-voiced confession, the girl's voice rang out strongly. "You'd better ask its father, standing by the window." Then she turned on her heel and left the room. Nellie scuttled back up the stairs, but not before catching a glimpse of Beryl's face, with its grim smile.

Nellie had to repeat, several times, all she had seen and heard. Mrs Wilson, to whom truth was not important in the relating of a juicy scandal, tried to prompt her to embellish the story with colourful additions. Had

Nellie said that Lady Redwood tore her hair, screamed and fainted, she would have been believed by the cook, though not by anyone else.

While they were thus cosily talking over their night-time cocoa, it fell to Mrs Wilson to treat them to a story of her own.

"It was when I was a young housemaid. I was only twelve, and very green. My employer thought herself a grand lady but, believe me, she didn't half give herself airs. Well, it wasn't as if she had a household of regular servants. She only had me, and it was a poky little house. All the same, I had to clean and cook, and do the laundry, and Madame inspected all the linen and lace after I'd done it, and if it wasn't perfect, she'd have me do it again. I had to get up at five o'clock to light the fires and get the range going. Then I'd have to get her breakfast and take it up to her in bed. Well, I was feeling a bit under the weather one morning, and was a bit behind, so I didn't have time to wash after lighting the fires, so when I took her breakfast up, she looked me up and down and then, making sure she'd got her breakfast tray comfortably on the bed, she said: 'Look at yourself, girl, you are a disgrace. I'm ashamed of you, really I am. You're dirty; you're lazy; you have life too easy. I don't know why I don't turn you out on the spot.' She tore into me good and proper; she scarcely gave herself time to swallow a mouthful before she was off again. I just stood there, ready to drop. Anyway, she finally let me go, and I went down to the kitchen and cried. I couldn't eat my own breakfast, I would have choked.

"One evening, when I'd just about finished my work, she rang the kitchen bell, and I dragged myself up into the drawing room. Drawing room! It was little better than a back bedroom. Anyway, my lady says, "Pick up my shawl and pass it to me, Ivy." Well, honest to God! It wasn't three feet away from her chair. She'd had me come all that way up just to hand her her shawl. She must have thought she was the Queen.

"She overdid things though. I'd heard tell, from one of the tradesmen, of a daily cleaning woman she had in before I went there. Madame had been keeping an eye on her, waiting to trip her up in some wrongdoing or other, and she had a nasty little trick for her. She deliberately put a half-crown under a vase that the char had to lift up to do the dusting. She took one look at this half-crown, put it in her apron pocket and waited an hour or so, because there was a man with a barrel organ used to come down the street at a certain time. When he got near to the house, the char went in to see Madame. She knocked on her door and took a deep breath. Madame made her wait for a minute, then called, 'Come in.' Up she strode to the lady's chair (my, I bet her heart didn't half thump!) and she said, 'Excuse me, Madame, did you leave this half-crown deliberately for me to pick up?' 'And what if I did, Mrs Baker? This is my own house. I can leave what I like lying around.' 'You mean you were deliberately trying my honesty?' 'I have the right to do that, too. What are you going to do about it?' 'THIS is what I'm going to do about it.' And she walked over to the window, lifted the sash and threw the coin down to the man with the barrel organ. 'Ta, missus!' she heard the man's voice come floating up, then off she swept, out of the room. I think she left that day; she was working for an agency, and there was plenty of work for her. And I bet she told all the other workers waiting at the agency about this woman, too. They'd soon pass it round, what the old cow was up to."

Winnie went round-eyed with shock and stopped shelling the peas for tomorrow, when she heard Mrs Wilson's vulgar usage. Mrs Wilson let this little thrill subside, until Mr Johnson got impatient and said, "Yes, let's hear the rest of the story."

"Well, she tried something of the sort on me, and it was when I was dusting the banisters one day, that I looked down and saw something stuffed under a stair rod. When I pulled it out, it turned out to be a rolled-up ten-shilling note. Well, no one accidentally stuffs a banknote under a stair rod, and I was wise to her by this time. So, as soon as I had the time, I got all cleaned up and went to confront her. My hair was neatly tucked in my cap; I had a clean apron on. She shouldn't have any excuse to get at me. Fortunately, it was a cold day and there was a fire, so when she told me to come in, I walked up to her and said, almost word for word, what the cleaning woman had said. And Missus repeated her little piece, word for word. 'Right,' I said, 'there's only one place for this,' and I threw the note into the fire and watched it burn. So did Missus. She couldn't believe it. But she didn't dismiss me. Word had got around about her, and she wouldn't easily get a green girl again, to put up with her tricks."

"Pity about the ten-shilling note, though," Fred said, "that would have been about a year's wages for you in them days."

Mrs Wilson sniffed significantly and said nothing. She looked across at the butler, who had heard this story in full, and in confidence. Neither of them would let on to the fact that the young Ivy, before taking the ten-shilling note into her employer, had carefully torn off the serial numbers, front and back, from the note, kept them safe and taken them home to her father to take into a bank, who retrieved them and gave in return four half-crowns.

PANTS ON FIRE

The charming, easy-talking hypnotist landed himself a highly prestigious slot on prime time television. The publicity had been intense, with the promise that: 'This programme will change your life.' Sceptics eagerly tuned in, prepared to be massively disappointed, and looked forward to writing in and telling him so. Dinners were cooked early or delayed; homework was completed; and pub nights were delayed until the following night. As eight o'clock struck, some thirty million viewers settled down for two hours' viewing, with snacks, popcorn, chocolate, hot drinks, cold drinks, lager or cola. Some sat at their evening meal, in an unnatural quiet, their curiosity warring with their appetites. The entertainer had had great success with hundreds of people and their obsessions, fears and addictions, and his fame had spread rapidly and widely. The thirty million, of course, represented about half the population, the other half constituting those too old or too young to be interested, so the bulk of the demographic were sitting in front of their television sets, ready to obey the hypnotist's instructions.

Lined up on the platform were the twenty lucky applicants who were there to display the talents of the hypnotist, to make everything plain and above board. It would be seen that no harm would come to them, nor, by implication, the viewing masses.

He began in the usual way, by telling them that they were not going to go to sleep, but that they would experience a different state of mind, and that, contrary to popular belief, only the strong minded would be successfully hypnotised; also that they would not be made to do anything that would run counter to any ethical choices they would normally make. Twenty pairs of eyes closed in concentration.

"I will bring you back to your usual state of mind by snapping my fingers. But don't forget you will decide what actions to take, nobody else will decide for you."

To reassure them of this, he persuaded one or two of them to take off a shoe and pretend it was a puppy, and they were to play with it, and pet and stroke it. They were told to be sure to forget it, just before the snapping of the fingers to make them open their eyes. In this way, the ice was well and truly broken, amid the laughter and teasing.

He then addressed the rest of his audience, both in the studio and at home, in this way: "I want you to imagine the best way that you could have conducted your life so far. What might have happened, for instance, had you always been true to yourself or never deceived or misled anyone. To think who might have benefited from your generosity of spirit and in material matters. Had never sulked at life, but had set aside your grievances and moved on.

"Most importantly, what effect the telling of truth at all times might have yielded."

He continued in this strain for a while longer, then returned to what was uppermost in his mind. The truth. He had, when young, been subjected to lies, half-truths, deceit, double-dealing, and simple withholding of the truth; an opting-out of the threefold pledge such as is given in a court of law, as his elders indulged in self-serving cherry picking of what benefited themselves to let him know and what to conceal.

He now told his audience that not only would they tell the truth, but the whole truth, and nothing but the truth. He strongly impressed upon them that in this way, they would be sure to achieve the prosperity they craved and, that everything being equal, their health would improve. He included this careful clause to avoid litigation against a claim of quack therapy. Then he told them lightly that they need not remember what he had said, except to feel good about themselves and everyone else. When he snapped his fingers, they opened their eyes, believing that he had been speaking for only a few seconds about positive thinking. He finished off with a few more harmless games, and the show was applauded loudly.

The show took its place around the water cooler, in the canteen, among friends in the coffee houses and pubs in the usual way, with just one unlooked-for effect.

* * *

"Please, Miss, I just can't do long division. Do I really need to learn it? I mean, I don't intend to take a job that involves figures; I'd rather do something that relies on my English."

"Yes, Amy, you are absolutely right. The only reason I take you all through it is because I am directed to do so by the education authorities." The teacher shook her head in sudden bewilderment. How had she come to make such a confession? At breakfast, she had said to her husband that he would have to make his own evening meal, not because she had paperwork to catch up on, but because she had arranged to have a few drinks with colleagues.

* * *

"Please, sir, I haven't got my homework done."

"Why not, Jason? Your dog ate it again, did he?"

"No, sir, I just didn't feel like doing it; I wanted to play games on my computer."

"Are you feeling all right, boy? You look baffled about something."

"As a matter of fact, I do feel rather strange; can I be excused PE?"

The schoolmaster sighed. "Have you brought a note from your mother, if so, let me see it."

"That's just it, sir, I didn't have time to write one."

They both blinked. Such honesty was unusual. But the teacher himself had, that morning, tried to jump the queue, as usual, at the newsagent's. Someone pointed it out to him, and he admitted that he had, indeed, pushed ahead. Another pupil told her mother that, yes, she was perfectly well, but she just didn't feel like going to the class choir practice.

The same teacher who had been truthful to Amy had occasion to call in at a heel bar to get a pair of insoles. She looked through the rack and found the size seven, but it indicated they were a man's size seven.

"Aren't they the same as those for women?" she asked the shopkeeper.

"I'll be with you in a moment, madam."

"Ah yes, here they are. But they *are* the same. Look!" She held the two products together, back to back. They were exactly the same size, thickness and shape. The shopkeeper was put out. He could not deny it, and indeed, was unable to, though he had frequently had arguments with customers, assuring them that there had to be a difference, otherwise the sales directors would not have gone to the bother of pretending there was.

Today, however, no one in the world was able to tell a lie, not even a white one. And now even the common fib was unavailable to those who obsessively exaggerate the differences between the sexes.

"No, madam," the shopkeeper said, "it's all in the minds of the promoters of these products. It's the same with disposable nappies. The blue ones are the same design as the pink ones. I don't know why they do it; it must lose sales for them, but that doesn't seem to matter to them as much as the necessity to flatter men and patronise women." He shook his head and stared into space. What had made him tell the truth so disastrously?

Much else happened, too. Half the viewers and listeners who tuned into *Today in Parliament* were taken aback. Politicians were suddenly telling the truth. Casualties were high. Several vulnerable old people died of shock, and thousands needed counselling. When prime ministers and presidents admitted on television that there were no weapons of mass destruction, apart from those in their own armouries, and that wars had been started for no other reasons than greed and personal ambition, riots broke out and an archbishop came on television to appeal for calm. That he spoiled the effect by blurting out that he had been an atheist all his life, but that he enjoyed the dressing up, did not help.

Lawyers everywhere broke down and explained that, yes, they knew it was collusion, but the pretence must be kept up if they were to make a living. Their secretaries merely raised their eyebrows and carried on typing, though many of them, among themselves at coffee break, let slip the fact that they dyed their hair, had Botox treatment and cheated on their diets.

"Are you going to visit your sick aunt again this afternoon, Miss Jones?" asked Mr Smith, of Smith, Smith and Smith, Commissioners for Oaths.

"No, I'm going home to stuff myself with cream cakes, get legless on cheap wine and bitch about you on the phone to my girlfriends." She left the office, clutching her head.

Cold callers told the people they phoned that they wanted personal details in order to swindle them and get as much money from them as possible, then were heard weeping loudly before ringing off.

Local gossips admitted to their friends that their enemies were not really anorexic or bulimic, that Mrs Thing was not really having it off with Mr Whatsit, and that they had only said so in order to put a gloss on their own reprehensible behaviour. They then supplied details of all their own human failings. Well-meaning people told their friends, "No, that coat looks hideous on you. You need something to hide your knock knees and thick ankles," then became distraught and silent.

Those who were only too addicted to telling the truth about their friends' faults felt no different, but were uneasily aware that what they had to say no longer carried any force.

On the bright side, shopkeepers stopped telling their customers that what they had bought looked well on them and neglected to hope they would have a nice day, and customers did not smile sweetly at them, nor thank them.

When customers chose the best pears from the front display, the greengrocer agreed with them that they were better than the scratty little dried-up ones at the back of the shop, which cost the same. Then they went into the back and had a strong drink.

When callers to the phone-in programmes said, as usual, "How are you?" the presenter wanted to know why. The reply came: "Because I want to give myself time to think, and ingratiate myself with you." When the ninth person had admitted that his reason for not bothering to recycle or give up his 4 x 4 had no bearing on his disbelief in climate change, but because he did not care what kind of world he would leave to his grandchildren, the programme was taken off the air.

Politicians, no longer able to interpret the facts, or rearrange the truth, made in consequence much more entertaining speeches, as they blundered and flustered through Prime Minister's Questions, massively relieved when the call came: "Who goes home?"

When word was passed on to the hypnotised subjects by those who had not 'taken' that the truth tellers had been had, there was great indignation; demonstrations were held. Thousands of marchers filled Trafalgar Square with banners stating: 'We Lost Our Jobs', 'My Wife Ran Away', 'My Husband's Gone To Live In The Shed', 'The Kids

Won't Eat Their Crusts Up', and angry shouts of: "We want our lives back!" "When do we want them? Now!" Activists chained themselves to any available railings, and speakers on Nelson's plinth declared: "It can't go on!"

Finally, the hypnotist was bribed by those in power to hold another show and to debrief everyone of their disastrous truth-telling. Then, as soon as the show was over, he was held in custody until it was clear that the exercise was successful. The last that was heard of him was that he had gone back to juggling and mime.

PENDULUM

The old priest sat dozing in the September sun, letting his thoughts drift pleasantly and intermingling established memories with original ideas. He had always held the view that time spent thinking was not wasted, that thought is a constructive human activity like any other. He compared the present century with the previous one. The twentieth century had been packed with incident, and it was with a sigh of relief that humanity bade farewell to it. That same humanity never did change. Only the focus or the emphasis changed on the sins and virtues of the world. What was tolerated in one era was met with stern disapproval in the following; and, of course, vice versa.

Contrary to what most people felt, for instance, he considered that the present young generation were not as spirited as when he was a boy. But then he judged, as did most people, on the basis of his own experience only. He closed his eyes, remembering.

* * *

The little choirboy loved the drama of the High Mass, and knew, too, that he was lucky to be a part of it. He thought the Santiago Compostela Cathedral was the finest in Spain.

When the grand occasion arrived, he would be within a few feet of the focus of attention to where all eyes turned, including that of the television camera, discreetly placed at the west end of the nave.

The big moment came. The giant censer was lowered, the sandal-wood placed inside, ignited and fanned. Then the big swing was set in motion. Slow and ponderous at first, it gathered speed, and the autumnal tang of garden bonfires began to fill the air; the smoke whirled and eddied. It drifted round pillars and pulpit in wisps and nebulae.

As the censer reached the apogee of each swing, it seemed to hold its breath, before surrendering to gravity, then the grand rush to the altar, pausing in a split second of free fall, before the next long plunge.

The small boy was intoxicated, incensed as if the pot had held the hallucinogens of more primitive religions, as the hypnotic vessel swung over his head. A door opened in his mind and, without reflection, he walked through it. Thoughtless as to the consequences, he did what many a small boy before him had wanted to do (and no doubt, many a sober archbishop). He ran from his place, and as it came hurtling back up the nave, he grabbed the chain and jumped lightly onto the smoking container.

He cared nothing for the shocked gasps and indignant exclamations. All he knew was that he was part of some primaeval pulse. In the few moments before he was brought down to earth, to face both punishment and fame, the boy had gone beyond mere mischief. As he swung suspended above the altar, he felt rarefied, special. Music flowed past him like a river, the pendulum of the Universe took him with it, and he became one with the cosmic heartbeat.

* * *

As the smell of autumn bonfires roused the old man, he stretched, then rose to go in to his tea, wondering if his grand-nieces and -nephews would find their own turning point, and envying them the moment when the mind-expanding experience, of whatever form it took, would reach them, never to be repeated, but to be treasured well into old age.

PHOTO

Jeff combed his thick black hair, parting it on the left. In a decade famous for sport and no-nonsense grooming, the favoured style was to brush it straight back with no parting. Some older men still parted theirs down the centre, but as Jeff applied the Brylcreem, he took a little innocent pleasure from his best feature and pushed it up into a quiff before leaving the mirror.

Gordon's mother was fond of telling people how delicate her son was. "That's why he never married, you know," she would say. She seemed to take a pride in it, as though it quite distinguished him. Gordon was certainly not the marrying kind, but not for the reasons his mother gave. He often wondered if she suspected, but shied away from the troublesome subject. He would be surprised if she didn't. She seemed to know him pretty well in most respects. He had taken risks, once being recognised by an acquaintance in a bohemian bar in Soho. Gordon had his arm placed lightly round another man's waist. But then, as Gordon told himself, something similar had drawn his distant friend to the disreputable place, too. He refused to let it trouble him. It hardly mattered now, anyway. Gordon looked out his best shirt and tie, put on his three-piece suit, adjusted his watch chain and took his lanky frame out into the fresh air.

Bert, too, was a thin man, whose sloping shoulders, thinning hair and gaunt face belied his mischievous sense of humour. It was his liking for surreal antics and silly jokes that had been the saving of his sanity and that of his comrades in the trenches. Once in Civvy Street, his pranks had included the ragging of a very serious young man in the drawing office. This chap used to give himself a good two minutes before home time in the correct placing of his trilby, looking at himself from all angles in the mirror by the hat stand. Bert got together with his mates, one of whom surreptitiously took the hat size when its owner was busy. Bert then went to Burtons and picked out an identical hat, but one size smaller. He swapped it for the real thing when his victim was out at lunch. He still, even now, told the story of how the man had tried to get it on his head and had taken a good five minutes, looking at it and stretching it. He tried jamming it down hard on his head, then finally gave up, put it in his briefcase and went home.

Freddie put on his light grey trousers, believing that they would photograph better than dark ones, slipped on a Fair Isle pullover over his shirt, and a light tie. It took a lot of Brylcreem to tame his curly red hair, and he managed at last to make it fall into waves rather than to stand up in shock. His large, square face viewed the world with stoicism, though he would have preferred to be envied rather than admired.

Harry could never keep his socks up, but in 1933, few men or boys could. The businessman wore sock suspenders, of course, but Harry's most recent job had been general labouring. His wife had been annoyed that he described himself thus on the birth certificate of their youngest child, but Harry had no snobbery in him whatsoever. A job was a job; status, at this level, did not matter to him, though he knew many other working-class people who formed their own levels of social standing. Some took great pride in making their front room a feature to present to the outer world and would never let the children play in it. The rest of the house would be modest to the point of hardship, with lino on the living room floor, bare boards in the bedrooms and a stone floor in the scullery. With no bathroom, Friday night was the occasion for a wash-down in the scullery or a visit during the day to the council slipper baths. The children might be clothed by the British Legion and eat ha'penny dinners at school, but the front room braved the world with its lace curtains, its best table with the heavy green cover and white cloth placed at an angle, its best ornaments over a fireplace that never saw a fire, a glass-fronted cabinet containing crockery that never held a meal, and on the wall, a gas mantle that had been fired only once, protected with the only glass shade in the house. Lacking the money to keep it warm, it was always cold and damp. This was not, however, Harry's way. He flourished his class credentials in a way that puzzled his contemporaries. His attitude was before his time. It would be some forty or fifty years before the world caught up with him, when the comfortable middle classes would try to claim working-class status, redefining it in various ways; sometimes on the basis of their parents having been working class, sometimes merely because they worked for a living.

Jeff was too young to have served in the war, and the veterans he passed on the street, as he made his excuses, telling them he didn't need matches because he didn't smoke, warned him sourly that he wouldn't escape the call-up for the next one. There wouldn't be another one, he thought. Germany had never got its breath back and was in a deep depression. Surely they would never be strong enough to cause trouble again this century?

He sighed. It was all academic for him now, anyway.

Bert had been married, but his wife had soon tired of him and his jokes. Too poor to pay for a divorce, they had separated, and she had gone back to her parents. They had no children, a matter of some regret to Bert. He was full of life and keen to pass it on to the next generation. This looked unlikely now.

Freddie's sturdy good looks belied the increasing tiredness he felt, and now he mostly sat and read the sports pages, thinking of the past and of what might have been.

Bert was at this moment regaling his friends with the story of how he had fooled the chap next door, an expert gardener, into thinking he, Bert, had raised a fine crop of red potatoes, when in fact, Bert didn't so much plant crops as bury them. He had got up in the middle of the night, dug up his plot of pathetic little spuds, put some mature reds in their place and replaced the poor plants on top. The next morning, he had called to his neighbour to say he was going to lift his potatoes this morning. He had now got his friends rolling about at the thought of the old man watching in astonishment as Bert dug up the greengrocer's best, when the summons came.

"Hurry up, lads," Matron called. "You're all beautiful enough, and the photographer wants to make the most of the light before it goes. Arrange yourselves as elegantly as only you know how."

Gordon stood on the left of the picture, Bert on the right, and between them Jeff took his place, leaning his hands on the deckchairs in front. Harry took the one on the left and Freddie on the right.

"Smile, please," the photographer urged. He didn't add the words 'for those who will keep your picture and pass it down for others to make guesses', but that is what was in their minds. Gordon's mother, who wondered about her son's nature; Jeff's favourite niece, who would miss her young uncle; Bert's family and friends who would honour his memory with laughter; Freddie wondered if his wife would remarry, if only for the sake of their son. And Harry thought of his prosperous parents, who had ignored him once he had married and become poor. Who was likely to marry a widow with five kids? he wondered.

The camera caught them, the front two frowning against the sun, the three behind with a light smile politely on their lips as they posed in the garden of the Preston Hall Sanatorium, in Kent, all of them born too soon for streptomycin.

PRIMATES

For a Pleistocene hominid, Moonwatcher was ahead of his time. Like all young primates, he believed that his way of doing things was an improvement on those of his elders, and in general of course, he was right. His parents, too set in their ways to risk doing things differently, continued to do them in the traditional way. This, too, was right. They were unable to learn new tricks. Moonwatcher had learned from them basic lessons in survival, before he was capable of working them out for himself. Now it was his turn, with the freshness of youth to his advantage, to improve more efficient ways.

While the elders of the troop continued to lug branches and dead wood along with their hands, Moonwatcher had figured out a way of entwining vines round them and tugging them along. He co-opted his more submissive kindred to help him, and in return they had his protection from any rogue member with a taste for bullying the young. As he watched the infants playing on a log, he noticed how it rolled when they fell off it. While this only added to the fun for them, Moonwatcher considered the matter. Perhaps if it could so easily be made to move, then it might be employed in moving something else with it, as it had the infants who tumbled off it. Another log, laid across it …

His thoughts were interrupted abruptly by a fight that had broken out between the leader and a younger male with ambitions to lead the troop. Moonwatcher thought this was a waste of energy, but kept a judicious distance from them.

In his more idle moments, he took to tracing with his finger the outline of his shadow. He knew that the shadow was not part of himself, but he also knew that it represented him. As he pondered the possibility of leaving a mark in the soil to show he had been there, the idea of abstract signs to pass other messages came to him. Evolution leapt and moved forward by one tick of the sweep hand.

Tragedy struck the day their leader was attacked by a large animal with sharp teeth and claws; a graceful creature that crept softly and pounced quickly. The primate leader escaped, but was badly injured. The rest of the troop gathered round him, waiting for him to get up again, but he continued to lie there, bleeding, his breath becoming more and more shallow, until it stopped. A youngster made a timid attempt to groom him, hoping this would rouse him. An adult female brushed away the flies that had begun to gather round his head. They all looked on in puzzlement, not daring to help him to his feet; it might be disrespectful.

They eventually left him for the night, expecting him to rejoin them when he was ready.

The following day, however, they discovered he had turned into something else. He looked the same, but now he smelt different. He was quite stiff, and would never move again. They covered him with leaves, to hide the smell, and left him. They knew that he had gone, but he had been so real to them that they believed they would surely see him again, some time. Not in the body he had left behind though; this was rapidly becoming part of the forest and part of the scavengers who carried him away in their stomachs. They put this mystery behind them and turned to other matters.

The up-and-coming male who had challenged the dead leader now ruled the group. Leadership had been suddenly conceded, with no further need for fighting, and it went to his head. He ran through the community, shoving the females aside, looking for confrontation and hitting the less assertive. He overplayed his luck, though, when he grabbed a baby from its mother, swinging it about clumsily and ignoring its squeals of distress. He dropped it and took another infant from its mother's arms and did the same. This was great fun; he'd had no idea that life could be so good. He had not quite decided what other use he was going to make of the infant, when he was suddenly mobbed by screaming females, who hurled themselves at him without any thought for their own safety.

This was a shocking surprise for him. They were usually so submissive, getting out of his way when he rampaged through their midst, never rejecting his advances. The infant was retrieved, and the leader's head bitten repeatedly and savagely, until their anger was vented. They left him bleeding and dizzy, as he lay there, trying to work it all out.

He continued to lie there for two days, wondering if he, too, would turn into that something different, and whether he would begin to smell different and be covered with leaves and abandoned. Would he also become part of those others who ate him? He thought all this as he lay, slowly recovering. Even if he was devoured, he thought, he must go *somewhere*. Maybe, and this seemed to him the most likely, he would go to where he was before he was born; but as his brain was unable to cope with the idea of oblivion, he gave it up and began to crawl back to the group.

He found the females gathered round the remains of a small deer, sharing the choice bits among the infants. At first, they closed ranks and would not let him through, but this was little more than a gesture, and they eventually let him have what they left. He would be welcomed back, but would never again be allowed to seek dominance.

The rising leader was Moonwatcher's own father, whose priority was soon shown to be the protection of the group, not swaggering exploitation. Moonwatcher made a mental note of this, and of the effect that female solidarity had had in voting out a corrupt member.

As he absorbed this new lesson, he settled down for the night with his kindred in the shelter, and as he looked through the gaps in the timbers, he saw the full moon. He was still young enough to wonder about this shiny object. Young enough not to take it for granted. He wanted to touch it, but was not sure how far away it was. Maybe he could reach it when it was low in the sky or dig for it when it went down behind the trees and into the earth.

He once saw it just behind a hill, but when he ran up the hill, it moved away as he ran and rose higher as he got higher up the hill. Perhaps, next time it got caught in the branches of a tree, he could climb the tree and touch it with a stick. Maybe though, it would be better to throw the stick at it first; it might be hostile. He closed his eyes and slept.

* * *

The young chimpanzee regarded the newcomers with curiosity. They had no body fur, except on their heads, but they compensated, by wearing coverings that fitted their bodies, with fastenings down the chest and round the waist. On their feet, they wore sturdy coverings with fastenings that stuck, and opened with a tearing sound. They walked all the time on their hind legs and carried strange tools. One of these, consisting of two black tubes fitted side by side, they sometimes held to their eyes and turned towards the troop of apes. The chimp decided they must be artificial eyes, on stalks, and envied them. He would get hold of them when the creatures put them down. They seemed to know this might happen and kept them hung round their necks.

Although the young chimp did not know it, he had been given a name. The newcomers called him Mo, on account of the way his hair hung round his head in a long fringe, like one of the Three Stooges. They were never seen to be eating, so the apes tolerated them. Clearly, they were not competing with them for food.

They had a big surprise for the apes, when they got upwind of them. Among the welter of scents emanating from them, from insect repellent to aftershave, and which made the young chimp sneeze, was one that startled with its familiarity. These creatures were kindred of some kind, but distanced by time and genetic divergence that only the hairless ones understood. At night, they took their gadgets and retired to the plain. This was too exposed for the apes, so they watched from the trees as their distant cousins made their fires, ate their meals and settled down in their canvas home for the night.

In the morning, they came out again, with another toy. This one they held to one eye, and it made a soft, whirring sound, like an insect. It had a hard round piece on the end, which from certain angles reflected the sky. Mo's curiosity overrode his caution. He approached it slowly, watching the reflection of the sky in the glass disc change to that of the trees. He was near to it now, coming to it sideways. It was swung slowly towards him, bringing him suddenly face to face with his own image. He shrieked in alarm and ran away, his heart thudding. The hairless ones opened their mouths wide, issuing noises like those of hyenas at a kill. What kind of creatures were these, that smelt so like oneself and kept his brother behind a small glass?

One of them took from his pocket a white, square object. In his other hand he held what looked like a twig, straight and shiny black, and with it he began making scratching movements across the white thing. Every now and then, he turned over a sheet and began on a new leaf. Then he turned to his companion; they made soft twittering sounds to each other, then left the clearing and returned to their tents.

When they returned, they brought with them a larger pad and a thicker pen and left them on the ground, for Mo to make of them what he could, then they stood further off. This was clearly a game to which he had been invited. He approached the pad, picked it up, sniffed it, licked it, and did the same with the pen. Finding they were not good for eating, he tried making scratching marks on the white paper. This made a very satisfying black trail, so he scribbled and scrabbled until the page was filled with black trails. After a few false starts, he managed to turn the pages over.

Growing bored with this, he stopped, resting his hand on the pad. He looked at it for a while; it made such a nice contrast: the dark, leathery hand against the dazzling white sheet. Then, taking up the marker again, he took a leap forward several thousand years and began tracing his hand, drawing the marker round each digit, from the little finger to the index finger, round the thumb and down to the wrist.

* * *

Molly sat playing with her toys; though 'toys' would seem an odd word to someone from back at the beginning of the twenty-first century. Her playthings would be categorised by those ancients under 'educational', consisting as they did of mathematical puzzles, intellectual teasers of logic and philosophy, and baffling equations. It must not be assumed that all children born at the tail end of the third millennium were as gifted. Although science and technology had continued to accelerate, people generally were only more knowledgeable, no cleverer, and certainly no wiser. It was simply that the ten-year-old Molly was a bright child, eager to learn and as curious as any young animal.

She looked up from her play and gazed through the thick protective glass of her home, at the black sky. She never tired of looking at the lovely blue planet where her distant ancestors had been born. A battered world that humankind had taken to the brink of destruction, but had saved by emigrating to the moon and to Mars in such numbers that the earth was reprieved by its very desertion. With its remaining air, it seemed to give a sigh of relief and began the slow process of healing.

Molly had been taught all this, and the history of the extraordinary third millennium. There had been no more world wars, for the simple reason that man had not dared to wage them. There would be no advantage in killing themselves just to prove that their weapons were big enough to take everyone out. There remained man's tendency towards civil war and petty squabbles, interrupted only by a short period of peace, following the seepage into the world's water tables of synthetic female hormones. Among other effects, this had rendered the male population subfertile and relatively placid. When this was reversed, just in time to prevent disastrous underpopulation, the normal level of testosterone returned, and with it man's favourite hobby of knocking great lumps out of each other.

Money had by now been abolished, and a complex system of barter and exchange had made an uneasy re-emergence into human affairs. The stock exchanges of the world finally ran out of control, markets fell and luxury industries came to a halt. As ever, natural and man-made disaster forced the people to co-operate in order to survive. And as ever, things changed and stayed as they were. Those whose money had given them power had to find other ways of dominating their fellows, but in time, the most essential industries, medicine, energy and communication, flourished because those who worked for it did so for the love of it, as any National Health nurse could have demonstrated in the time of starvation wages.

With the abolition of money came an end to property crime. There would have been no point. There was sufficient for everyone, but no more than that.

Molly had been instructed in all these things and had taken in the message that people were no worse and no better than they had ever been. The young felt they knew best; the old complained that things had been better in the old days and that civilisation would run down through lack of a moral imperative. Sometimes, both parties stood objectively outside their opinions and conceded that the other had a point.

Like many of her forebears, she had been born and lived on the Sea of Tranquillity, but had never been in the sea, in a real ocean. The simulator, she knew instinctively, was not the same, but only tantalised her with something deep in her nature. She determined to make the journey to earth some day; to get back to the beginnings, before going forward into her own future.

Taking a sheet of paper, since they still had the old technology beside the new, she tried to draw the sea. The naïve waves did not satisfy her, and she sighed and rested her hand on the sheet of paper, thinking. Then thinking turned to reflection, and something else took over. She began to trace the pen round the outline of her hand.

RUBY'S DAY, RECURRING

Ruby woke with the feeling that she had some unfinished business to attend to. She tried to remember what she had been dreaming and came up with a blank. Just the usual frustrating dreams, of trying to get somewhere and being stalled, held up and redirected. She shook it from her and switched on the radio.

"… eight o'clock on the 12th of January, and this is your favourite local radio station. The Mayor of Stafford will be visiting the Tenterbanks Road School today to award prizes for the design of a garden for the blind. A man was nearly run over in Gaol Road last night. 'I was devastated,' he told our reporter. The weather today will begin misty and chill, but will warm up as the day goes on. Later on, we will announce the winner of yesterday's quiz question. The correct answer to the shaggy dog story was, as many will have guessed: 'You can't turn a knight out on a dog like that.' Well done to the clever child who got it." Next door's dog began to bark.

The doorbell rang. That was her friend, Brenda; like Ruby, a pensioner, and finally with time for herself, come to collect her for their Saturday swim, to be followed by Ruby's hair appointment. Ruby was too short-sighted to drive and relied on friends.

"Wake up and smell the carrot juice, Ruby!" Brenda called through the letter box. She could be a bit too enthusiastic sometimes. But Ruby valued her friendship; Brenda was so confident, so positive, and Ruby hoped it would rub off onto her own timid self.

Halfway through their swim, things got boisterous. Some young men had come in, clearly with the intention of causing trouble. One of them grabbed the whistle that one of the female lifeguards had pinned to her top, and blew three times on it. This, he didn't realise, was an emergency signal and brought several lifeguards running onto the poolside. In the ensuing disruption, Ruby and Brenda decided to cut short their exercise.

They sat over coffee in the foyer while they watched the chaos on the poolside.

"Well, let's go round the charity shops," Ruby suggested. "I could do with another big bag to carry my arty farty stuff in."

"Sold anything lately? You'd built up quite a body of work last time I looked round your spare room."

"Only what the public wants. They won't even look at the abstract stuff."

"This town wants shaking up, Rube. It's a pity you can't have an exhibition of all your stuff. The Town Hall would take it all nicely. And do you know what? If they had a security camera trained on your work, you'd find that the pictures that got the most attention would be the abstracts."

"Yes, odd how that happens, isn't it? No matter how people jeer at abstracts, they stand looking at them for quite some time."

"Makes them think, you see. They believe they will find it hard to see anything in them, but secretly I reckon people like to be challenged. Especially those who claim to be most bored by life."

In the charity shop, Ruby saw just the thing she needed. It was a nice wide rucksack, ideal for her paints, in their plastic bottles, with side pockets for brushes and even a bracket for her mahlstick. As she paid for it, an old woman nearby said, "That would have been ideal for me to carry my shopping in." She needed two sticks to walk with, and clearly could not have coped with a shopping trolley. Ruby was about to surrender it to her, when Brenda said, "We'd better make haste, Rubes, we need to get to the hairdresser in a quarter of an hour."

In Delilah's, Ruby sat and waited her turn. Brenda stayed with her for a few minutes, then decided she'd better be off to the new clothes shop. She was a fidget and couldn't sit still for five minutes. "Besides," she said, "I can't stand hairdressers. They patronise you to death and bully you into the wrong colour, then charge you fifty quid for the privilege."

Ruby hadn't thought about that, she was used to doing as she was told; it seemed to be all part of life's tedium, so she tolerated it.

"Right, dear, look at the chart and tell me which colour you want." The hairdresser wanted her to make up her mind, quickly, then she could get back to her conversation with her colleague. Ruby pointed to the lightest of the blondes. “That one, please, definitely, unless you’ve anything lighter.”

“Well, I don’t think that will suit you, dear, how about this one?” She pointed to a mud-coloured tone.

“Well, no, it’s not light enough for me, have you got a lighter shade?”

“I’ve got it already mixed.” The stylist bustled off to get it.

As she waited for the colour to take, she got the usual itchy reaction on her scalp and reached for her comb to give it a little rub with the blunt end.

“No, you mustn’t do that, my dear, you could break the skin.”

“It’s only a plastic comb. It’s not one of your steel curl combs.”

The stylist tutted and sighed, backed up audibly by a customer she had moved on to while Ruby’s colour was taking, and repeated, more forcefully, her disapproval.

When it was done, Ruby didn’t like it much, but was too timid to say so directly.

“Could you get some lighter colours in by the next time I come?”

“Look, dear, we are professionals here. We know better than the customer what is going to look good. Just you trust us.” She turned to her colleague, who began regaling her with an anecdote about a man she knew, at his stag party. Ruby listened in, wanting to be part of the fun.

“So there he was, in the middle of the High Street, with only a shopping bag to cover his modesty.”

Amid the shrieks, Ruby felt emboldened to say: “I bet that would give him something to look back on and laugh at later on.”

They both looked round at her, the smiles fallen from their faces, glaring at her. They looked at each other quizzically, then picked up where they had left off. Ruby felt snubbed.

When her hair was finished, the proprietor got her to part with £50.

Ruby was relieved when Brenda came back and took her off for a coffee. As they sat over hot drinks, Brenda took a good look at Ruby’s hair.

“I don’t like what they’ve done to it, Roo; the colour’s rubbish, and she’s scalped you. Didn’t you tell her you wanted fronds coming round your face?”

“I tried to, but she seemed to know better.”

"You should insist. Stand up for yourself."

"Well, I try, but nobody takes any notice of me."

Brenda's reply was interrupted by a small child at a nearby table, who let out a scream like a whistle. Brenda swirled round on her seat.

"Why don't you scream back at him? It works a treat." The child's mother just looked depressed, but said nothing and carried on drinking her tea.

"I've got a good idea for an invention," Brenda continued, "it consists of a microphone and two earpieces. It fits on the child so that the microphone is at its mouth and the earphones at its ears. Next time it screams, it gets the full blast before anyone else does."

"I think it's just as well that you never had the urge to have children," Ruby murmured, then eyed the chocolate cake on the counter. She steeled herself to turn away from it.

"Go on, girl, treat yourself. It can't add more than half an inch to your waist."

"Better not; we didn't get our half-hour swim today, remember?"

"Right then, onward and upward. Full day today. You've got your art class, and I should be getting home. Gotta get ready for my debating circle."

"What is it this time? Flat earthists, or the man who thinks World War Two didn't happen? There must be someone ready to be taken apart by you."

"Try and stop me."

* * *

The rest of the day ran as normal for Ruby. She went to her art class, putting the final touches to her picture of a local old building. The tutor came over to her.

"If I were you, I'd put some trees behind the building, it will soften the lines." Ruby did not want the lines to be softened; her pleasure in the shapes they made consisted in their being sharp and dramatic, but she complied, putting the fictional trees behind the ancient tiles, sighing with disappointment.

When she got home, she watched *Mastermind*, and as usual, got about a tenth of the answers right, then pottered off to bed.

* * *

Ruby woke with the same feeling of having to finish something begun, but could not think what it was. She switched the radio on.

"... eight o'clock on the 12th of January, and this is your favourite radio station. The Mayor of Stafford will be visiting the Tenterbanks Road School today to award prizes for the design of a garden for the blind ..."

She sat up. They were repeating yesterday's news. That was lazy of them. Besides, she was pretty sure it was the 13th January, not the 12th. She got out of bed and picked up the paper from the mat. No, it said the 12th, and the headlines were exactly the same. She turned to the cross-word. That was the same, too. She went to the kitchen to get breakfast. Next door's dog started barking. But that was a regular feature, anyway. She shook her head. Hoped she was not heading for a breakdown. On past occasions of depressive illness, the problem had lifted immediately she gave up work. And yet, she felt perfectly all right, more than usually optimistic in fact, and looked forward to the day. There was no pressure in her charity work, and she enjoyed it. She looked in the mirror. She still needed a cut and colour. Had she dreamed all of yesterday? She shook the thoughts from her.

The doorbell rang, and she answered it to Brenda.

"Wake up and smell the carrot juice, Ruby, time for our Saturday swim!"

"We had our Saturday swim yesterday," Ruby said as she belted up. But Brenda was not taking much notice, she was concentrating on the road.

On their seventh length, Ruby turned to Brenda and said, "I've got a feeling that big loser making his way to the lifeguard is going to grab her whistle and blow on it." She waited. "Told you so. Now, several lifeguards will come on the poolside and sort things out."

"Nothing unusual about that, Roo. Saturday mornings attract them like flies. Anyway, I've had enough exercise. Let's go somewhere quiet. I want to discuss that tosser next door."

"Brenda, there's something odd about today. All this happened yesterday. It was Saturday, then. I think the day is repeating itself. You know, like in *The Tunnel Under the World*, or *Groundhog Day*. The newspaper headlines were the same, the radio said the same things."

"You've been reading too much science fiction. Anyway, finish your coffee, I want to scour the charity shops."

"Those were *my* lines, when I said them yesterday."

"Don't know what you're talking about. Come on, girl, you need to find a handy bag for your art stuff. By the way, sold anything lately?"

* * *

The day continued, with minor differences. In the charity shop, Ruby held back on picking up the bag she needed, letting the old lady with the walking sticks take it.

At the hairdressers, they sat and chatted for a while until it was Ruby's turn to be subjected to her cut and colour.

"Wait a minute, Brenda, I want to prove to you that today is repeating itself. Stay with me, all day. It will provide you with an entertaining time, if nothing else is achieved." Brenda took little persuading; she was beginning to worry about her friend and her crazy talk.

The day continued to spool itself forward. Once again, Brenda was struck by what she thought were coincidences and found herself half inclined to believe her friend, but to her and to everyone else the day was new again. The world continued to bully Ruby. The hairdresser told her not to rub her scalp with the blunt end of her comb, the art tutor repeated his advice to stick some trees behind her ancient building, with the expected disastrous result, and Ruby managed to remember a few more of the answers on *Mastermind*. Brenda was impressed, especially by *Mastermind*. "Well, let's see what happens tomorrow," she said, not really taking in the implications.

The next day was the same. Brenda had to be told, all over again, what was happening. The trouble was, it was only happening to Ruby. On the way to the pool, Ruby primed Brenda about the day ahead, told her everything that would happen, down to the minutest details of the surrounding people: their clothes, their conversation and the direction in which they went.

"I worry about you, Ruby. You were all right yesterday, but suddenly you've gained some weird ideas."

"I've already told you all this, but your yesterday is not the same as mine, and twenty-four hours afterwards you find the day created anew. I don't know when it will stop, but when it does, you will still know nothing about it. It will be just an ordinary Sunday following Saturday to you."

She saw the youth going for the lifeguard; she jumped out of the pool in time to stop him. She gave him an almighty shove and pushed him in. When they got to the café, she told the waitress to bring her two large slices of the chocolate cake, thinking, what the hell, she might as well enjoy a day in which nobody would remember what she got up to. Judging when the small child would scream, she went up to him, and as soon as the child opened his mouth, she opened hers and screamed right in his ear.

"That's better. Now for that chocolate cake."

"Welcome to the human race, Ruby. I always told you to be more assertive."

* * *

"… eight o'clock on Saturday, the 12th of January, and this is …"

"Come in, Brenda, the door's opened, and I'm ready for my swim."

This time, she told the whistleblower: "Don't blow three blasts, the manager will throw you out and ban you." The youth stared. How did she know what he was going to do?

By the time she had persuaded Brenda to come with her to the art class, rebellion had taken a firm stand.

"If I want clouds instead of trees, that's exactly what I'm going to put," she told the tutor, "and if you try to make me do trees in what passes for tomorrow, I'll throw your own paints all over your canvas. Now go back to your own work and let me get on."

After countless recurring Saturdays, when they found themselves at the hairdressers, Ruby decided to go all out.

"You can take that dye chart away and start on my hair, and if you so much as take one hair more off my head than I've told you to, you will be very interested to see what happens."

She reached for the curl comb and gave a hefty scratch to her head with the sharp end.

When they snubbed her about joining their conversation, she stood up.

"I've had enough of your patronising ignorance. It's time you respected your clients. Do exactly what they ask of you, and apologise if you find you cannot. In fact," she went on, as they stood, transfixed, "I'll give you a little lesson." She grabbed the scissors with one hand and the stylist's hair with the other, and snipped off a great chunk from the back of the stylist's head, following this by smearing the remains of the dye over the mirror. For an encore, she swept all the pots, bottles and implements from the working surface, letting the creams and lotions mingle with the hair on the floor; she pulled off the gown and walked to the door. She turned like Bette Davis.

"Don't worry; things will be back to normal tomorrow, you won't know a thing about it."

"Ruby! That was fantastic. You should have done that years ago. Let's go to your art class and see what fun we can have there." Half an hour later, they left the tutor with green hair, and the parquet floor a tasty shade of purple. That evening, they watched *Mastermind.* Ruby not only got all the answers right, she quoted the questions before the quizmaster got to ask them, pausing only to point out to Brenda that this was not a repeat or a recording, as it was the first programme of a new series.

"How about I stay here till midnight," Brenda suggested. "I want to see if your mad theory is true. At all events, you are worth staying with, since you started being such fun."

* * *

They managed to stay awake, with pots of black coffee. They put the radio on, loud, and as midnight struck, the presenter spoke.

"Good morning, here is the news and weather forecast for Sunday the 13th …"

They both cheered and high-fived. "So *that's* what it was that I had to do. I'd had this feeling every time I woke up that there was something that had to be put right. It took a cosmic freak incident to get me to do it."

Brenda had a sudden thought and gasped, "What about all that mess at the hairdresser's? And the art class? … Oops."

"So what?" Ruby shouted. "Wonderful, isn't it?"

SACRIFICE

The three astronauts had been circling Phobos and Deimos for seven earth days when they developed a fault in the air supply. Adams, Barnett and Chester had been getting along with each other after a fashion and made a special effort to be accommodating towards each other's little quirks and freaks of temperament, but this was now running as thin as the oxygen supply. They had, fortunately, gathered all the data of which their equipment was capable and transmitted it to earth. The only worry they were left with now, was of getting back home.

It became apparent that the craft had been struck by a meteor. It needed to have been no bigger than a grain of sand, but at the speed it had been travelling, the impact was potentially fatal for them all.

As they hurtled silently towards earth, they had time to review their lives and careers. Adams knew that Barnett had been flirting with his wife. In the bustle of training and the tension of lift-off, space travel and making several figures of eight round Phobos and Deimos, their attention was engaged, and they were too busy to think of anything but that which was immediate.

But now that it became uncertain whether or not they would make it back home, they had time to reflect, and to let petty jealousies and not so petty rivalries make their presence felt.

"Don't think I don't know what you and Elaine had been up to when I went off for that special course," Adams sniped at Barnett.

"You have an overactive imagination, Adams. We had nothing between us but a special bond, based on the things we feel passionate about. But I can't expect you to appreciate a genuine platonic friendship. You don't have artistic appreciation, you only have appetites." Barnett was always a cleverer talker than Adams.

This stung Adams. "You needn't try to disguise your own sexual needs as something rarefied. It's nothing more elevated than anything a randy dog feels when he needs a mate. The rest is cultural snobbery."

"Oh, go to your bunk and read one of your westerns, or a bad thriller."

"Don't kid yourself about your fancy education. There's no particular merit in reading about a mother-fixated man going on for page after page about a Madeleine cake, or a day around Dublin by a randy Irishman."

"Oh, you *have* tried to read Proust and Joyce, then." Barnett knew he was showing off, but the conversation had reached the point of bored bickering, and both their responses were becoming automatic.

"OK, you two," Chester broke in. "Just cool it and let's concentrate on getting home. And stop bouncing against the bulkhead like that. It's making me dizzy. We should all try and keep our heads and feet facing the same way as each other. You know what we were told about communication."

The other two men made grudging consent in their own way, and they took stock of the situation.

"We are nearly out of oxygen candles," Barnett reminded them. "We are supposed to keep as still as possible and not get out of breath."

Chester had already done the calculations and knew that there would be oxygen only for two to make it back to base. They all looked at each other. They knew what had to be done.

"So how do we choose?" Adams wanted to know. "Do we base our choice on who is the least valuable to the mission? Or who has the least number of dependants to leave behind? Or maybe, who has achieved less in life compared with the other two?"

"We can't afford to waste time on such philosophical niceties," Chester reminded him. "It must be by drawing straws. It really is as blunt as that. That way, our families will not feel that anyone is discriminated against in not getting their husband, son or father back."

* * *

The choice had been made. The loser took his place in the airlock and prepared for a swift death. He chose to wear his spacesuit, not for any notion of a few last minutes of gasping life, but because he had heard stories of how the human body practically turned itself inside out in the vacuum of deep space. Vanity had always been one of Barnett's weaknesses. He even had time to wonder, before he slipped into unconsciousness, if anyone would see him as he flashed across the night sky, burning up in the atmosphere.

* * *

A mother was walking with her small son, showing him the constellations in the clear winter night.

"Look, Mum, there's a shooting star!"

"Yes, dear, make a wish."

SANDS

They sauntered along in the heat, on their regular Sunday promenade. The promenade itself was dusty and the air stifling. Helen's feet hurt in her best shoes; she would, she felt sure, develop bunions, as her mother had, from wearing elegant shoes, one size too small, as she had insisted Helen herself should. "You will never get a husband if you have large feet. Only pretty girls are able to attract themselves a husband." Helen's own observation of young married women contradicted this statement, but it was not worth her while pointing out the number of plain girls who walked down the aisle to be claimed by a handsome man. She looked enviously across the sands at the antics of working-class children, at their families on their weekly treat, their loud voices ringing across the beach. Aware though she was of the harshness of their lives, sometimes the wish to be one of them overwhelmed her, and she thought it would be worth the sacrifice to give up her prosperous life to be able to romp and play.

Her mother, however, disapproved of romping in children. They were here to be seen and not heard. Helen Douglas, at thirteen, was now beyond romping. She had missed her chance. Before her lay a life of respectability, her duty to her mother, and at best, marriage to a decent man.

She knew enough about the times to know that her mother was at least a generation behind them. This tradition of promenading, for instance, was something that people had stopped doing for the last twenty years; old days that Mrs Douglas still yearned for, before her marriage. Before life had soured her with its disappointments. She now compensated herself with self-sacrifice. She still wore corsets, visited the poor, did good works, suffered headaches and heart pains. She threw her life on this bonfire, an offering to the fates. She had not the imagination to perceive that she was merely sulking at life. Oddly enough, her two daughters were not at all grateful. Not even when she interrupted what jollity they snatched, by elaborately sighing, closing her eyes and complaining of how young people nowadays were thoughtless and carefree.

Helen hated her mother with a desperate sincerity which she was perfectly able to mask. Her elder sister, Jane, had escaped the family as soon as she could ensnare the first presentable young man. She had not yet married him, but nevertheless lived well on his salary in a flat in London. No longer for her the clothes with their great fussy collars and the silly sash round the waist. She now wore a cloche hat, dresses that just touched the knee, and bright lipstick. She had her hair cut short, wore it straight, with a fringe, and she pencilled her eyebrows. She was, of course, according to society, a ruined woman, and her younger sister Helen grew into adolescence with the firm impression that a ruined woman must wear only the best kid gloves and the most stylish shoes, and dine at the most fashionable restaurants. For herself, she accepted as a fact that she would eventually be ground down by her mother's nagging, her bitter diatribes against the absent Jane, and the threats of what would happen to her, Helen, if she took the same path. Her every move was policed, the slightest hint of familiarity towards young men indignantly criticised, and a high moral tone taken towards the threat that the girl might be about to enjoy life.

"Don't dawdle, girl, and stop gaping at the common people," her mother now reprimanded her. "I'm already feeling quite faint." Helen felt somehow that this was her fault, as ever, and turned her gaze forward, walking on to the end of the promenade, with the prospect of a typical Sunday evening: no games, no music, no frivolous reading; only improving books and Bible readings.

Mrs Douglas had only herself to blame for her condition. She dosed herself continually with all the patent medicines, some as a stimulant, some to calm her down, some which claimed to thicken the blood, others to thin it. If she suspected that she was wrecking her constitution, then that was all right with her; it worked to present her as frail and in need of cosseting.

Their father had left them shortly after Helen was born, worn out by his wife's lack of affection, and Helen was now all her mother had got. She would inherit the house and bank balance, a generous settlement by her father made on his escape, in a fit of guilt at not having been able to engage his wife's warmer feelings.

Mrs Douglas' faintness was, to her surprise, a genuine one this time, not just something thought up on the spur of the moment to punish her daughter with, and she sought refuge in the nearest café. It was not even one of the more elegant, but a large, vulgar unit, converted from a warehouse, and that catered for the people on the sands, with trays of tea in thick cups, thick sandwiches, filled with fish paste, and the grosser kind of rock cakes, cut and spread with cheap jam.

The proprietress was sympathetic. Mrs Douglas looked alarmingly pale, she was perspiring slightly, something not wholly attributable to the sun, and as they continued to sit there, she decided to summon help. When the ambulance arrived, there was a medical practitioner in attendance. However, his ministrations had come too late. The stark fact was that, by this time, Mrs Douglas had gone beyond medical help and now needed only the ministrations of an undertaker. She had effected her own demise with drugs of several kinds, some prescribed, overdosages of patent medicines, and others obtainable only from dubious apothecaries.

"Who will break it to the poor child?" the proprietress asked, as the café was quickly emptied, and experts and non-experts bustled about.

Meanwhile, Helen, who had seen all that needed to be seen, wandered out of the café, walked down to the beach, sat down on the sand, took off her shoes and stockings, and made her way towards the water. At first, the sand was dry and hot, her feet unsteady in its bumps and hillocks; she continued past the shouting children, busy with buckets and sandcastles, to where the tide had left the sand wet and firm; she picked her unfamiliar way through the bladderwrack, then, passing on through the unfamiliar landscape, felt the pricking of shell fragments on the soles of her feet. She stepped through cooling rock pools. The sea breeze was stronger, here on more open land, and she breathed in the cool air, savouring it. She reached the part of the beach where the sea had left rippling ridges in the hard sand, impressing themselves against her bare feet. She dropped her shoes and stockings behind her, and stepped into the sea, feeling for the first time in her life, the water rhythmically splashing her feet and legs, standing there among the other children as they squealed and splashed. She lifted her face to the sun and, in the primaeval joy of it, she smiled.

SOLOMON GRUNDY REVISITED

He was aware of being pushed, squeezed, from the warm, comfortable place into a place of brightness. He was not only unaware of who he was but even of *what* he was. He felt himself being dragged out by his head, was held upside down, and a sharp smack delivered to his backside. He let out a yell.

At the age of three, David showed signs of considerable talent. He took his crayons and drew a picture of his mother, with the correct colours for the flesh and hair. By the age of seven, he had depicted the garden, paying minute attention to the trees and bushes. He gave the picture some very realistic clouds, and figures in the background.

At school, he distinguished himself in all academic subjects. This assured him of the attentions of the underachieving bullies. However, it taught him to run fast, and he came top in athletics. He took up boxing and flattened the bullies.

At sixteen, he went to art college and passed all his exams with flying colours, if the pun is excused. At this stage, he also discovered girls. Since he had been successful in so many branches of his life, he confidently expected to succeed in this, too.

However, as he applied conscientious principles of presentation and attainment in himself, he became hypercritical of the young ladies whom he hoped to impress. The result was sulks and flouncings-out from the objects of his desires. He was declared a nerd, a numpty and a dork of the first order. His first failure.

He discovered in himself the fact that Buddhism was to be his philosophy. A sense of detachment was to serve him well through life, and to distance him from its more painful and messy experiences.

By the age of twenty-six, he succeeded in persuading a woman of the same age to marry him. By this time, too, he had become a successful artist, his colourful pieces bringing in a steady income for himself, and an even steadier one for the gallery that sponsored him.

By twenty-seven, his wife had tired of him and took their infant son and decamped to the home of her lover. She settled down with him, and quickly forgot David.

By the time he was forty, his luck had improved. The gallery owner contacted the BBC, and David acquired his own series. He was then invited onto *I'm a Celebrity ... Get Me Out of Here!* He was subjected to the kind of humiliations that addressed all of his phobias. Worse than these was the presence of the other celebrities: a pompous psychic whose only discernible talent was to destroy cutlery; a boxer who believed that a woman's place was at his heel or in his bed; and an otherwise thin young woman with a boyish figure and a pinched face, who had thought fit to wreck the balance of her figure with two enormous silicone implants. These she flaunted as if she had grown them herself, and bored everyone rigid by talking constantly about her life. David began to wish he was dead. However, his suffering was exactly what the licence payers wanted, and he won the title, King of the Jungle, and gained worldwide fame.

At fifty, he reached a midlife crisis. Something was missing. He felt he had contributed as much to art as he was capable of. He had nothing in common with the younger artists, who were applauded excessively, he thought, for displaying in public the contents of their bedrooms, bathrooms and fridges, in all their sordid splendour. While he was thinking of which direction in which to turn his talent, he acquired a cat, a frolicsome kitten which amused him greatly until it turned into a randy great tom, which left home for days and returned, haggard and smelly, having had no more luck with the fair sex than had his owner. David then took him to the vet and brought him back a more passive animal, but with an abiding resentment that it had been cheated of something. The tom glared at him briefly, before loudly demanding food. This was to be the daily pattern for the rest of his life. It crossed David's mind that he wouldn't mind coming back as a cat. A queen cat, that is.

While sifting through the arts to see to which he could now devote his talents, he found himself invited to adjudicate at a story-writing contest. I could do better than this, he thought, and promptly did. His short stories won five prizes in a row, and he decided to branch out. He bought a word processor and wrote a successful novel: a great work devoted to the city of Rome, encompassing its entire history, with fictional stories covering the time from prehistory to the present day. It proved to be both learned and popular. It was reviewed in *The Guardian*, but despite this, it sold well.

His life was proving to be satisfying, but once again he began to feel an emptiness. As was his wont, he found it easiest to think and consider by staring into empty space. He was watching junk TV, which amounted to the same thing. It was showing *Will and Grace*, a sitcom about a straight woman who shares a flat with a gay man. Maybe that was it, then. Perhaps he had been in the closet all his life, without knowing it. He made plans to embark on the softer emotions.

With the same lack of foresight that had dogged his personal life till now, he went in the first gay bar he came to. This happened to be the most disreputable one in the city, and the first good-looking young man he smiled at turned out to be already spoken for, by an insanely jealous roughneck. This charmer caught up with David crossing the car park. The last thing David saw was the knife, and then he knew no more …

... He was aware of being pushed, squeezed, out of the comfortable place into the dimly lit gas cupboard. He was picked up by the scruff of his neck and felt himself being licked all over by a big, furry thing that purred.

STATUES

The old gentleman sat drinking tea, while his granddaughter sipped a cup of black coffee.

"The City isn't what it was in my day. There have been too many changes, too quickly."

"You can't hold back progress, Granddad; things have to change, and you must admit that the City Centre looks a lot better than a hundred years ago." She thought a little. "Or a lot better than fifty years ago."

"We had just got over a terrible war, missy. It took some time to get the colour back into life. What is so hard to get across to anyone who wasn't there in those dark days is how very grey a time it was. We rebuilt it with you in mind."

"And you mustn't think we are ungrateful, Granddad. Now just enjoy it, and stop grumping."

They sat in a café in the pedestrian precinct, looking across at the water sparkling in the sunshine, as it tumbled down the fountain steps.

"We had to work hard in those days. Then, when we came home from work, we had to make our own entertainment."

"What? No cinemas? No dancehalls? And what about the music halls?"

"The music halls were in *my* father's day, you silly girl. You'll be asking me next if we had television. Besides, you know what I mean."

"I know for a fact that you had television in the 1930s, I've seen the photos and the footage."

"That was only for the very rich. Even after the war, not many people had it; and we didn't get our first telly until 1954."

The young woman looked across Victoria Square at the statues, then spoke: "I wonder what the likelihood is for those statues moving – when you consider the atoms and electrons whirling about the stone and metal, I mean. They are already shooting about at random. What is to stop them taking off and making an arm move, in an apparently meaningful gesture?"

The old man sighed. "I knew it was a mistake for you to take Physics. Your aptitude for fantastical nonsense would have been of more purpose in the Arts."

"No, Granddad; one of the rules of nature is that nothing is impossible. Just extremely improbable."

"Well, yes; but no more probable than the balls on a billiard table jumping back up out of the pockets and arranging themselves back on the baize."

"The possibilities of anything occurring in nature are almost infinite." She lifted her cup to her lips then, like everyone else, she froze.

* * *

The traffic came to a stop. Those who constituted it were not aware that they had stopped, but that's all in the nature of time suspension. Subjectively, the people crossing Victoria Square made a smooth progression through the space/time continuum, with only the blink of an eye in which they imagined they had stumbled.

Matthew Boulton, James Watt and William Murdock made their way among the suspended animation, along Broad Street to the square, their gold leaf glinting in the afternoon sun.

Robert Peel had come from outside the police training college in Pershore Road, and was proceeding in an orderly manner up the steps by the side of the fountain, nodding respectfully both to Victoria and the Floozy in the Jacuzzi, lying at her ease at the top of her waterfall. She didn't mind her nickname; she was amused by it.

"Hallo, hallo, hallo," she greeted Robert Peel. He would have raised his hat to her, but the artist who cast him in bronze had not provided one.

"Caught any lawbreakers recently?" the stony one asked him.

"I only *founded* the Police Force, miss; I never served in it," he replied, ducking his head to avoid a pigeon caught in mid-swoop as it hung suspended, a feather just behind and above it following the same trajectory.

"Well, really!" came a disapproving voice from the stone pedestal across the square, "No respectable woman would address a gentleman in such a brazen tone when I was on the throne."

"Who are yo' to call anyone brazen? Standing there, all bronze and granite?"

"Ladies, please!" the founder of law and order protested. "The term was just a metaphor, miss; Victoria was brought up in a much more repressed age, when women were not allowed to express themselves as you have done."

"She was not brought up in it, but she certainly instigated it," came the voice of Joseph Sturge, just arrived from his plinth at Five Ways. "Besides, Your Majesty, I would not boast too much about the age you and I inhabited. It was the most disgraceful era in modern history. The poor starved even while they worked all the hours that they should have been taking healthful recreation."

"But that was their place to do so," Victoria protested. "God made them high and lowly, you know. And as long as they were virtuous, they would get their reward in Heaven."

"You seem to know more about the intentions of the Almighty than the rest of us, then," said the Quaker. "If there were any justice, they should have got their reward in this life, not the next. Besides, man is no more sinful now than he has ever been. There was as much human weakness then as there is now."

"Like little girls on the game," put in the lady on the fountain, as she dabbled her toes in the water.

"The common man brought about his downfall by means of drink," Victoria thundered. "He could have fed his family quite adequately had he abstained."

"He drank to blot out his misery," a voice from the bottom of the square spoke up. The others looked over to the Iron Man, surrounded by tourists, frozen where they stood, some with cameras to their eye, one leaning against the Iron Man, forming a malformed letter A, as he leaned where the sculptor had placed him. Another with his eyes caught in a blink, not looking where he was walking.

The Iron Man had no limbs and no features, apart from eyebrows that drooped rather sadly – he was not regarded as being representative of a real person at all. The sculptor had simply followed what ideas his material gave him, and it was up to the beholder to make what he or she could of it.

"Well, stone me," a lugubrious voice declared, as a hand snatched the suspended feather and placed it on the nose of a passing city gent, who had been striding along when time stopped and was now on the point of a protracted sneeze, his face caught in a foolish expression as his eyes automatically shut.

"They've made some changes round here since I was alive," continued Tony Hancock, who had just come from his memorial in the Old Square. He raised his homburg to the Floozy. "This used to be Galloway's Corner; and what happened to Lyon's Corner House?"

"I think you'll find much has changed for the better," said Joseph Sturge, who was even now trying to make sense of the poetry inscribed round the top of the fountain. "Hmm, it sounds pretty, but a bit modern for me to understand."

"What's so good about modern times?" persisted the former tenant of 23 Railway Cuttings. "And what genius couldn't even spell palisades properly?"

"If you had been around when I was here," said Josiah Mason, who had come over from Erdington, "you would not criticise modern times. If I had not set up an almshouse for twenty women and fifty orphans, they would have died on the streets – or worse," he added, in an undertone, "fallen into a life of crime and prostitution."

"But you only took in children under ten," said the Nymph, "and they could only have visitors twice a year. And how much education did the girls get? And another thing ..."

"Yes, yes, miss, but you must understand these things in the context of the times," protested the benefactor. "Besides, one could only do so much."

"After all," muttered the Iron Man, "all that money swilling about had to go somewhere; there are only so many gold-plated taps the rich can buy."

"Are you some kind of Socialist?" Victoria demanded, suspiciously.

"I have no idea what I am," came the retort, "I am what people make of me."

"Josiah was, after all, a hard-working man," said Robert Peel, defending his contemporary. "He made his fortune out of his own talent and ingenuity; it was he who founded the science college in Edmund

Street. Besides, if it were not for rich philanthropists, many of the poor would have been condemned to the workhouse."

"Here come two recipients of such charity," said the Iron Man, as two children in eighteenth-century dress came into the square. They were stone figures from the Blue Coat School in Harborne, and had a tale to tell of stern treatment at the charitable institution that took them in. They were working children, bound apprentices and domestic servants. Parents and friends, they said, resigned their children 'to the sole management of the subscribers and shall submit the children to be chastised for their faults and forbear coming to the school on such occasion that the master and mistress may not be discouraged in the performance of their duty'.

"So no family life for them," said the Iron Man, "business came first in the good old days."

"I heard from first hand, in the 1940s, what treatment was meted out to them," came a disembodied voice. "In the early years of the twentieth century, children were beaten on the whim of the teachers, and dosed with castor oil, whether their constitutions needed it or not. They grew up with the results of having their insides thus insulted every day." This was the Author, who could not resist putting in her contribution to the conversation.

"Thank you, madam," said the brilliant comedian of the 1950s, "but kindly return to your word processor.

"I notice," he continued, "that the Central Library has gone and a new one put in the place where the old university stood. There was no need to destroy those fine old buildings. The new concert hall could have been built on the spare land opposite the Odeon. I was in Australia at the time, or I would have had something to say about it, depend on that. As it was, it was about that time that I considered that Life had had about enough of me, or vice versa."

"The loss was the world's," Joseph Priestley said, gallantly. "It always could do with a laugh. And thank you for your kind words about the old library. I modelled it on that of Leeds, you know, before I went to America."

"I don't doubt your talents, Sir Josiah," the Iron Man said, reverting to an earlier point interrupted in mid-flow. "But once you had a toehold on the monetary system, what you acquired was profit, produced by those who worked for you."

"You *are* a Socialist!" declared Victoria, scandalised.

"I just want to see a little democracy in action …"

"Democracy! That is something to which I would never have submitted. I said so at the time. And to think that it has now become a respectable concept."

"A lot of things have changed since your time, missus," the Floozy announced, "including your own descendants. But at least, they are more open about it."

"But the way people dress nowadays!" the Queen said, querulously. "Rings through their noses indeed!"

"That's nothink, lady; some of them even have a Prince Albert inserted through their …"

"I know very well where a Prince Albert is inserted, miss. It was a matter known only to me, my consort and his physician."

"Ladies, please!" Robert Peel exclaimed. "There are children present, you know." He turned to them. "And what do you make of the way things are now?" he beamed at them.

"It is beyond our understanding," the boy said. "After all, when we left the Bluecoat School, we were encouraged to join the Grateful Society …"

"Dear God!" said the Iron Man.

"… and the True Blues. Once we had made good ourselves, we gave donations for the school. We were always conscious that our gratitude was demanded of us."

"I never understood what need people had of our gratitude," said the girl, quietly. "We were taught at church that virtue is its own reward, and that one should do good by stealth and blush to have it named."

"Hallo," said Tony Hancock, "here come the workers!"

And here indeed they did come. From their stand in Centenary Square, they had descended, laughing and chattering; leaving behind their miniature factories, pouring artificial smoke. They came in their diminishing sizes, the smaller ones running on their little legs to keep up with the Stakhanovite leader, as he strode out heroically. Immediately behind him was the hussy with her skirt lifted and a saucy leer on her face. Keeping pace with them was the swell in the motor car, who gave a lift to Thomas Atwood, woken out of his reverie as he lounged on the steps of Chamberlain Square.

As they gathered all together, their different materials marking the mood of the age in which they were created: the stone of the ancient spirits of water nymph and sphinx; the bronze of the respectable moneymakers and matriarch; the Iron Man's ferrous metal; Hancock's half metal, half glass, seen at his best with the sun behind him; and the custard-coloured resin of the workers, time got bored with waiting and began to send a warning. So slowly, that its bells sounded like a slowed-down record, Big Brum geared up in a deep, swishing, rushing sound, gradually taking its pace up the register. The statues, alarmed, made haste to return to their original places, but time and speed being relative, they were able to make it before the world came to life again. Birmingham's first MP, back to recline on the steps in front of the new library, surrounded by his bronze pamphlets and stone soapbox; the stone children returned to Harborne; and Tony Hancock to his two-dimensional cup of tea in Old Square. As the first bong rang out, the businessman completed his sneeze and disturbed the feather that the clown had placed on his nose. He brushed it away with some surprise, as the pigeon who had shed it continued on its swoop. The man who had blinked opened his eyes to the world again; the man with the camera clicked the shutter on his friend; they both strolled off into the crowds together, as the water rushed down the fountain steps once more.

* * *

"That's an oxymoron, my dear girl."

"What is?" asked his granddaughter, completing the action she had begun an infinity of time ago and setting down her cup.

"That phrase you just used – 'almost infinite'. Something is either infinite or it's not. There is no point at which it is 'almost'. That implies a beginning to infinity, and with it, an end. And you can't have an end to infinity. That's the point."

"You're too smart for me, Granddad. Anyway, you brought me into the City to show me the sights, remember? The new exhibition at the Ikon? You also told me you had tickets for the new play at the Rep. And weren't we going to go on to a jazz club in Broad Street afterwards?"

"So we are. But you waylaid me by some nonsense about moving statues. If these statues could speak, young lady, they would have a tale to tell you about Birmingham." He carried on talking as they walked down Pinfold Street. "That's the point I was trying to get across; it's a mistake to think of time in terms of then and now, breaking it up into chunks. It's more of a continuation. From the days when drovers took their stock down this little street, Birmingham has *always* been a modern city. The Industrial Revolution started here … everything from a pin to a steamroller …"

THE BLONDE

She put one in mind of an ice cream. Her blonde hair had once looked like one of those soft, swirly ones but, paradoxically, had created an impression of creamy warmth rather than the ice-maiden effect so often striven for. She was in London and had taken time out from a busy schedule to walk the streets incognito. She had, of course, to have an escort, or rather, two. She was far too well-known to take chances with her fame.

The hair had begun, over these last ten years, to lose its softness. It had been bleached almost to straw, without being allowed to grow out and recover. As, indeed, had happened to herself. Her studio would not let their money machine relax for a moment. "I'm being nibbled away by these people," she told her analyst. "Like a buzz saw; it comes at me, slicing pieces off me, bzzzz, like that." They were welcome to the money she brought in; it had no importance for her. Having battled her way to prosperity, all she wanted now, at the age of thirty-six, was stability and affection. Since this came to her only in mass adulation of her glamour, she had no choice but to play up to it. The camera, turned to her, brought her alive, and she responded to it like an infant to a smiling mother. The co-star of their last film together had died of a heart attack, and it was said, unkindly, that it was her fault, with her poor time-keeping, fragile health and the frequently forgotten lines. She was now part way through her latest film, a poignant tale of motherhood abandoned and meetings with children who did not know she was their mother. It had faint echoes of her own life, with its hints of termination and failure.

The three of them slipped out of a side door, the star with a brown wig over her hair, a drab headscarf tied under her chin and a pair of dark glasses to hide her distinctive eyebrows. Where would she like to go? her escorts asked her. Just to walk the streets like a Londoner, she told them. A shapeless coat hid the famous figure and gait, as she strode out in flat heels, between her protectors.

Suddenly she said, "I want to eat a bag of chips. No, not potato chips; they call those crisps over here. And not fries, either. I want the real thing, big, soggy English chips in a paper bag and wrapped over in a newspaper."

"We won't get them in this part of town, honey. Are you sure you wouldn't prefer a proper meal: roast beef and Yorkshire pudding? It doesn't have to be a swell place. Just a little joint in Soho."

She was adamant. English chips were what she wanted, and she would at last have them. They decided to take a cab and ask the driver's advice.

"You want the East End, mate," the cabbie told them, and took them to a small street in the heart of the Docklands. He was wise enough not to remark on the woman's resemblance to the blonde icon. He would have lost his fare. He, like the rest of the developed world, knew all about her disastrous early life, her sudden fame, her failed marriages, an early one at fifteen: the one to the famous baseball player, then the intellectual playwright, and her perilous state of mind, and her walk.

As they stood by the chip van, sprinkling salt and vinegar, blowing on their burnt fingers and sucking in the cool air on each mouthful, Norma Jean felt that, for a brief while, life had relented. She had taken a few magic hours from her tormented existence and returned to the simplicity of early childhood. Whatever life brought her in the future, and for however long or short a time she had left to live, for now, she was happy.

THE CHERRY TREE

Bernard had the block; badly this time, but he couldn't find anything in particular to blame it on. He was under pressure from his publishers; they wanted to build on his recent success and felt he could become the second Saki – Hector Hugh Munro with a modern touch. He had no money worries, though he would not have objected to a bigger pension. His family were all established in careers and families of their own, and at sixty-nine, Bernard considered that he had, on the whole, managed to get it right. He stood at the window, looking out at the old cherry tree, which had a block of its own. This year it had not flowered, let alone borne fruit. Perhaps it, like Bernard, was under the weather.

"Where do you want your coffee, Bernard?"

"In the studio."

"OK. The spare room it is."

He had begun calling the loft the studio when he had resumed oil painting, and Elaine always pulled his leg about it. He didn't mind. When he stacked all his books in the tiny box room, it was all his wife could do to stop him calling it the library.

He had only recently discovered a talent for writing. He had decided on the spur of the moment to write down a lifetime's accumulation of knowledge concerning his favourite subject, astronomy. Like some of the best practitioners, he was an amateur and sent in his drawings and reports of the autumnal meteor showers to *The Sky at Night*. Since these collected pieces would make only a slim volume, he filled the rest of the book with anecdotes of his years as a schoolteacher. It was these that gained him his reputation for wit and satire, and from which he went on further to write fiction, with a slant towards fantasy. The reviewers compared him favourably with the great Edwardian wit who bridged the literary gap between Oscar Wilde and Noel Coward.

But here he was, staring through the window, without a plot, a theme or an idea to commit to his word processor. He decided not to agonise about it, and to ignore the empty screen and the beep. He switched off the WP and went in search of a book. When you can't write, read, he had been told, and most times, it worked.

An unruly cell, deep within the soft tissue of his body, split and began to multiply.

It was when he found he could not leave the house unless he had had nothing to eat that day that he was persuaded to see the doctor. The urgent need to find a loo, complete with water closet and toilet paper, made him almost permanently housebound.

"I wouldn't recommend a barium enema to my worst enemy," he told Elaine, when he rejoined her in the hospital waiting room.

"Well, perhaps this will show us what it is, and it can be tackled," she said, as they left the hospital.

The rogue cells spread further, spies creeping round the citadel, planning their attack.

At least his staying indoors so much encouraged him to write. Working on a piece of good advice from friends who also wrote, he set himself to write anything, even if it wasn't very good. He wrote to friends: chatty letters, asking them about themselves, hoping as a by-product to find material. There were, too, letters to the press and to politicians. He wrote to radio talk show presenters, asking them, if they were such keen armchair warriors, when they were going to enlist. He was not obsessive about the matters on which he wrote, it was all a literary exercise; fodder for tales of wit, spite, love or revenge. His publishers wrote to him, pressing upon him the necessity to provide a few potboilers, just enough to keep him in the public eye.

The results came back from the lab, but did not show anything sinister. In fact, they didn't show anything at all. Meanwhile, the cells quietly multiplied, gradually taking over his body, unknown to him or the experts.

"Why am I agonising over my literary output, when I should be counting my blessings?" he said. "My health is the important thing. It's time I sat back and appreciated the simple things."

Elaine said nothing. He was looking thinner, and his colour was not good. It had a yellowish tinge. She must find an excuse to get him to the doctor again.

The yellowish tinge proved to be mild jaundice. "It's probably a side effect of the medication we left for you to take," the consultant told him. "We'll have you in for tests."

Once Elaine had left him to his hospital bed, he looked around him. Men's Medical, all ages. Young men walking about with fitments attached to their waists, slow-feeding the chemicals into their systems, or old men, who had to leave their beds fifteen times in a night.

"You have just the two choices," the consultant said. "Chemotherapy will give you another twelve months or so, if it works. It might make no impact on the cancer at all. We can't be sure of that. What we can be sure of is the fact that you will get nausea, vomiting and diarrhoea. We'll let you think it over for a fortnight."

Bernard had already made up his mind. He couldn't bear protracted sickness and opted to go home, and stay there. When Elaine called at visiting time, he had already packed his things.

"You're coming home? I understood you were going to have some pretty lengthy treatment." As Bernard did not answer, Elaine came straight to the point that she had been trying to evade.

"What's the prognosis?"

"Don't ask me. I don't want to upset anyone."

"We're going to be upset anyway." After a pause, she asked, "Is it a matter of years?"

"Good Lord, no."

"Twelve months?"

"No. Let's get going."

Elaine was amazed at how calm she felt. The reaction would come later.

During the journey home, Bernard looked around at the traffic. At the shoppers taking home their luxury goods from the city; housewives driving back from the supermarkets; parents collecting small children from school. All this would shortly be coming to an end for him.

He had already had an intimation of his mortality. When he was twelve, he was just drifting off to sleep one night, when the thought suddenly struck him. That one day he would have to die. He had sat bolt upright in bed, his heart thumping. There would come a day when every mundane thing he did, he would do for the last time. He would get up, clean his teeth, for the last time. Have breakfast, go to work, have his evening meal, and it would be the last time. He gave the matter all of three minutes' thought, then set it aside. Since life was so short, he had decided to make every minute of it mean something.

And now it had come. The final deadline; for real this time.

"I've always resented the fact that, one day, I would have to die. Some people picture it as falling off the edge of the conveyor belt or getting off the roundabout. But to me, it's as if I have to leave the party. It's my turn to go, but I'm having too much fun. I'd rather stay on; see what the next thing is. The next natural wonder; the next human achievement. Even the next disaster. Try and make a contribution and a change. And now I won't be able to."

"The only thing we can do," said Elaine, "is to carry on as usual. There isn't time to do anything else." Her bluntness pleased him. The last thing he wanted was for anyone to weep and droop, and to speak in hushed tones.

"I know," he said, "let's do the garden over. It's looking a mess. We haven't touched it since last autumn. If you mow the lawn and sweep up, I'll prune that useless cherry tree. Cut it right down. It's clearly not going to blossom ever again."

It proved beneficial to them both. Every day for a week they cut and mowed, dug and weeded, raked and sowed. That Bernard would not see the result of the sowing was the very point. He would leave it on a promise.

The elation he had been told to expect would not in any case have taken him unawares. He was accustomed to surprising feelings, that descended without motive or warning. He had always adjusted to them, either riding out the bad ones, or enjoying the good ones while he could. What did surprise him was the fact that the expected kickback into despair and terror did not arrive. He continued to see the world in the vivid colours and the intensity of the condemned man.

"The publishers have just phoned you again," Elaine said one afternoon when Bernard had been working in the garden. "Shall you tell them you can't meet the … er …"

"Deadline?" Bernard said, in a matter-of-fact way. "No. I've got one or two ideas. They've been coming to me while I've been lying awake at night. I'll tackle them now. Bring me my coffee, please, to the spare room."

"The studio," said Elaine. Then wished she hadn't. He wouldn't want to be humoured. Just carry on as normal, including the mocking remarks.

As the weeks went by, they made adjustments. Bernard spent longer in the bedroom, looking out at Elaine pottering round the garden. Later, propped up in bed, he worked at a laptop, and Elaine connected the results to the WP.

The ideas were coming thick and fast now. Stories of mystery, wonder and jollity. Tales of intrigue and revenge, ghosts and strangeness. He found himself composing in styles he had never dared try, thinking they were not within his range: love stories, children's adventures, elegiac narratives, streams of consciousness that swept the reader into another world, opening doors in the mind. Speculation and fantasy, wild and whirling words; in phrases that bounced along on their own momentum. So absorbed was he that, despite his weakening state, he did not stop; did not even think to wonder where this tidal wave of creativity had come from. Until, that is, he looked out at the garden one day and saw the cherry tree. The old tree that had been pruned to within an inch of its life. As the secateurs attacked its limbs, it did what many a threatened creature did. Knowing that death might be near, it had put forth buds, had forced out of itself its next generation. It was a Dennis Potter moment. The tree bore the blossomiest blossom he had ever seen. Its whiteness filled the world. The snowy tree celebrated its existence. And, in the same way, so had Bernard. Like the tree, the storyteller, feeling the end coming, would leave behind him delight and fascination.

THE CREATURE

The creature roamed the terrain. He had no specific purpose in moving among the rocks and bleak hills, but he was in search of something; something he could not fix upon, but that would perhaps present itself to him, when his cranial synapses linked up the messages that were coming over the ether. He lifted his triangular proboscis and tested the atmosphere. It moved about in a way pleasing to him, as he absorbed its molecules into his aerobic system, translating them into psychosomatic images. His civilisation, ancient and highly sophisticated, was currently in turmoil, one major group against another, with alliances formed between lesser groups against the greater. He therefore needed time to find peace, and this was the motive that drove him to the wilderness. His pedal extremities chafed against their coverings, rendering them moist and clammy, but he ignored this discomfort, anticipating what he felt sure lay ahead.

His planet was old. It had swung round its parent star many billions of times on its elliptical orbit and had been much abused by its dominant species, but there was beauty still on its battered face. Its natural satellite often appeared in the sky at the same time as the star itself. As he looked at it now, it was a pale wafer. It appeared the same size as the parent sun, one of those astronomical coincidences that prompt the illogical mind to look for pattern and purpose where none exist. Its day was as long as its year, so it always showed its same side to its parent planet.

The creature decided not to rest just yet. He felt that if he did so, he might never rise again. Besides, shelter might yet be within travelling distance before dark.

Rounding a bend in the track, he heard sounds of others approaching. Most of them were of his own species, and he signalled with his head in greeting. One of them raised a freckled paw, its red talons gleaming in the sun, and boldly bared her bicuspids at him. His instincts prompted him to do the same in response. This gesture was not lost on her mate, a large specimen of the genus, with a red mane and facial covering of the same colour fur. He glared at our hero, who immediately lowered his gaze, and fixed his binocular vision on the small, furry creature with them, but not without a furtive look at the female and the spongy appurtenances on her thoracic cage. The small furry one merely glanced up at the lone traveller, then lost interest and resumed searching the ground with its pointed muzzle.

The traveller moved on, the need in him growing stronger. He hoped he would reach his goal before he became too weak to fulfil it. He was already cold, when a stinging precipitation of oxygen and hydrogen began to fall on him from the murky skies. He huddled his coverings closer round him and hurried forward. He eventually passed a building which he thought might hold the possibility of shelter, until he heard signs of the youngest of his species. It was suffering pain or frustration, he knew, because it expressed itself by means of glottal vibration, in turn disturbing the atmosphere, and conveying its message in one long vowel.

Skirting round this unhappy dwelling, he moved on, expelling air forcefully through his oracular orifice. After two more miles, he was just deciding to lie in the lee of a rock for the night, when he saw, on turning a bend in the track, what he sought. There it was, a square dwelling, with the welcoming sign: Bed and Breakfast – Vacancies.

THE DESK

Liz rather liked the look of the old desk. She had picked it up at a car boot sale, and while it was not exactly antique, just a piece of Second World War utility furniture, she suspected that it might for that reason be collectible.

When she opened the roll-top, she found several small drawers: tiny compartments to take small items of stationery. In one of these she found the remains of a rubber band, long perished and useless, one or two rusted pins and a Post Office pen – that is, a well-worn, ink-stained piece of wood, the size and shape of a pencil, with a rusted nib still attached. The initials D. W. had been carved into the wood, in an evidently idle moment, such as an inattentive schoolboy might do. She left these items undisturbed and examined the lower drawers, finding only a newspaper dated 20th January 1943. It was a local paper and carried on the front a group photo of a young aircrew. One of them immediately took her eye. He had the lean good looks considered handsome at the time, long before the chunky hunk became favourable. He held a pipe between his teeth and was evidently cultivating an RAF moustache. The hair on top of his head, as if in defiance of the short back and sides inflicted by the barber, sprang upright in a mass of dark curls. Reading the caption, she saw his name was David Wheatley.

On the inner pages she found advertisements for ladies' gowns, Carter's Little Liver Pills and the Fifty-Shilling Tailors. A man's suit for two pounds fifty, she thought, translating immediately. She was fascinated by such ephemera and decided that these old photos, adverts and price lists might also become collectible. Briskly dumping her stationery in the desk, she closed it and went to bed, to dream of young war heroes who looked like Guy Rolfe.

Insomniac at 3 a.m. as usual, her mind racing like a rat in a wheel, she gave up the attempt to sleep and wandered about. She drew back the curtain on to a brilliant full moon. This had a calming effect, as she stood there, tracing the terminator, the boundary between light and dark, where men had stood. As this tranquil mood gradually came to her, she turned to the desk, sat down and took a sheet of A4 paper and a ballpoint pen. Then, lit only by the Bombers' Moon, she wrote:

> Dear David Wheatley,
> If you survived the war, you will be an old man by now, but I like the way you used to look. I wish I knew more about you: whether you have a wife or girlfriend; what your fellow crewmen are like; how old you are in the photo; and how many tours you have been on. As a twenty-four-year-old legal secretary, born after thirty years of peace, it's clear to me that your life was far more eventful than mine.
>
> Whatever lies ahead of you in 1943, I send my best wishes.
>
> Liz Franklin, London, 14th February 1999.

Leaving the letter there, she closed the lid and went back to bed.

At daybreak, taking her morning coffee with her, she went to the desk to set out her stationery in some kind of order. The desk had an odd look of newness about it. Cheap, but factory fresh. She opened the top and stared. Alongside her stack of A4 paper, there lay a Basildon Bond pad, a bottle of Stephens Ink and the Post Office pen with D. W. carved in the wood. This, too, was brand new, as were the rubber band and pins, exactly where she had left them. The writing pad bore a letter on the top sheet:

> Dear Miss Franklin,
> Either this is a leg-pull by our American comrades or my favourite fantasy has come true. I dearly hope it is the latter, and that H. G. Wells had the right idea.
>
> This desk was bought a few weeks ago, and stands in the corner of the Mess Hall. We are meant to take turns to use it, but so far I have been the only one to do so. When I opened it this morning, I thought all the new stationery had come from

our rich transatlantic friends. And what stationery! Correcting fluid; absorbent marker pens; a pen with a tiny ball in the tip to control the flow of ink; but most marvellous of all, a miniature comptometer, like a tiny Babbage machine. I'd get Sparks to take a look to see how it works, but I might get run in as a spy, with such sophisticated gadgetry about me.

As for telling you about myself: I was born in 1915; I'm a bachelor, and will remain so for the duration of the war. My friends are a fine bunch of chaps. I'd go through Hell with them, and have. But please don't ask for operational details. I feel sure you will understand.

T.T.F.N. David Wheatley, WADDINGTON, 21st July 1943.

PS. Our new desk looks strangely battered and old.

Dear David,

It's a sign of the times, and the imminent end of the century, that I can accept what is happening as easily as I accepted the fact of man walking on the moon and space travel beyond the Solar System by robot. I was born sixty years after you, yet in relative terms I am only four years younger. The best brains are at work on the concept of time travel, and it's been all the rage since the beginning of the Space Age.

I see you have a fine crop of curls, but what a pity they have to be cut so short at the back and sides. Without your cap on, your hair springs up like George Cole's in his younger days.

Best wishes, Liz. 15th February 1999.

PS. What does T.T.F.N. mean?

My Dear Liz,
I hope it is acceptable to return the familiar form of greeting; you must guide me in the etiquette of the late twentieth century.

I get my leg pulled about my girly curls. It's true, we are ordered to keep our hair short, but only that which shows when the cap is worn. There is great competition to see how much long hair we can get away with. We let it grow as long as possible on top and stuff the rest under the cap.

There are many big questions I find myself dwelling on nowadays, but those immediate and relating to my own time, I try not to give too much thought to. So it's a relief and an escape to ponder the far future. While we are on Ops, my mind is fully occupied, and in between, we live it up as much as we can. But it's in the quieter times like this that fear begins to seep through. The men in the Fighter Squadrons often go under, not only from fear, but from sheer exhaustion. They keep going, on booze and Benzedrine, until their constitutions break down, or until they get killed or captured. I would not think of confiding my own fears to my contemporaries. It simply isn't done.

The Space Age! When does that happen? I've looked forward to it since a boy – that's why I chose the RAF. What will we find on the moon, or rather, what did we find on it? How time travel does play havoc with the tenses.

Ta Ta For Now – David. 20th August 1943.

Dear David,
How curious that, among all the thousands of questions you could have asked me, you have not asked the one most pertinent to your time. The answer is, Yes, we did win the war, or rather, you did, for which I can only say, Thank You.

Liz, 16th February 1999.

PS. Sorry about George Cole. I expect he is still only in rep in your time, but look out for him in the Ealing films.

Dear Liz,
I didn't need to ask you who will win the war. I had determined the outcome as soon as I was called up. But it's good to be proven right. Now tell me lots of things about future inventions, ideas, fashions, even; and could I have a photograph of you, please?

With growing affection, David. 20th September 1943.

Dear David,
I leave you a definitive list on several separate sheets. Hope you like the photo.

Must dash, Liz. 17th February 1999.

PS. Do something for me, please. Stop smoking.

Dear Liz,
I've only just finished reading the reams of information you sent with your short note. What can I say? I'm glad about the new medicines, of course, but you hint at some unease in their application. I'll certainly stop smoking. If it's going to kill the King, then it can certainly do the same to less privileged mortals. Can't say I'm surprised at what happens to television. We need only look at the way cinema has developed. Nevertheless, the studios are turning out good stuff, too. So maybe television has much to recommend it as well. No one is obliged to watch it, after all, and there are always books.

But the bit I was eager to learn about was a man in space – a Russian, I see. Good to see they will get back on their feet after all they are going through.

Instant coffee? We've already got that. It's a sticky brown liquid by the brand name of Camp. Nothing like the real thing, of course. I await the granules with interest. Blu Tack sounds a splendid idea, as does Velcro. I could do with such a quick fastener on my flying jacket. By the way, the ballpoint pen you left me has run out of ink. Could you order me a refill, please?

I settle down to sleep these days – sometimes nights – my head filled with notions of microwave ovens, camcorders, computers small enough to put on a desk, and television programmes you can run on a tape, ex-broadcast. It is with mixed feelings that I learn that the Japanese are responsible for these wonders.

Just what do you mean by 'listen out for the beetles'? You won't catch me with my ear to the wainscot. Anyway, you've misspelled beetles, so there.

I like the photo. I see the short hair has come back into fashion. It reminds me of the Eton crop my mother used to have.

Two eggs on my plate, I see. I'll explain what that means next time.

Yours in a jolly mood, David. 20th October 1943.

Dear David,

I can see I shall have to leave you to discover some things for yourself. I will only say, if you have any nieces or nephews with a talent for popular music, tell them to get themselves up to Liverpool by the early 1960s. They could become seriously rich.

I haven't told you about the century's second wave of feminism yet. Brace yourself for the Seventies.

Best of luck, Liz. 18th February 1999.

PS. Looking at the dates on our letters, I notice that, whereas I've been writing one every day, you've written only one a month – yet I find one from you in the desk every day. Your time is telescoping against mine. I wonder if we will ever meet, and in whose time.

* * *

A sudden, dull thud under the aircraft, then the pilot lost control of the flight. For a short time, the crew were thrown around, and the intercom was cut. Both wings were on fire. Flight Sergeant Wheatley unplugged his electrically heated seat, unstrapped himself from the mid-turret and went to investigate.

"We're baling out, Flight; tell the rear gunner to jump," shouted the pilot, by this time holding the plane in a steady decline. When David got to the rear turret, the gunner had already rotated it, undone the doors and fallen out backwards, as procedure.

"He's already gone ..."

"OK. Bale out with the rest."

The plane had now levelled off into a very shallow dive. The bomb aimer, observer, wireless operator and the engineer had all gone. David would be the last to go before the pilot, who, before he left, would set the automatic pilot, 'George', on a course towards open farmland, then let himself out.

Lowering himself through the escape hatch, David braced himself against the slipstream. As soon as he let go, he was whipped away by both the slipstream and the force of the propellers. He had no time to think about what was happening, and was whirled about in free fall for an eternity until he pulled the ripcord. He continued to plunge for a way, until he felt a reassuringly tight jerk as the silk billowed out.

After the noise and heat of a few moments ago, he was suddenly aware of an eerie stillness. All he could see were the stars overhead and the cloud cover under his feet. Falling through the cloud, not knowing where he would land, he felt the cold droplets against his face. Down and down he went through the stillness, hoping he would not fall into a tree or astride a fence, then, as he got to within fifteen feet of the ground, the chute no longer had enough air to support it, and his legs were knocked from under him by a ploughed field.

He heard the plane crash at the same moment as he landed, about three miles away. It exploded immediately, then he heard the small machine gun bullets going off. He rapidly picked himself up, gathered up the parachute, walked about a hundred yards to a hedgerow and stuffed the chute under it. Not knowing which country he was in, he walked quickly for about ten minutes, found some thick bushes, lay down and immediately fell asleep.

Waking at dawn, he felt inside his flying jacket for his maps, but they had fallen out as he hit the ground. His iron rations were still there though, so he breakfasted on Horlicks tablets and concentrated chocolate.

Coming upon a rubbish dump, he rummaged for clues. Just a lot of old envelopes addressed to German soldiers, and an empty Vim container. The label was in Dutch, but since the Germans confiscated whatever they could, it was possible he was still in Germany.

More walking, more bushes to hide in and rest. Three children came by, two boys and a girl, about nine to twelve years old, wearing wooden clogs. He decided to take this as evidence that he was in Holland, and to chance it. He indicated to them his RAF insignia and dog tag. He showed them the phrase book and the question: "Is this a safe way?" They shook their heads. To the question: "Is the enemy nearby?" they replied by pointing all around them. "Where are the English soldiers?" They pointed in the direction of the heavy artillery fire. "How far is it?" They motioned on the dial of his wristwatch, about ten or fifteen hours' walking time.

For all their sakes, he left the area quickly, hiding his flying suit and helmet under a bush. The flying boots were made in such a way that the leggings could be severed from the foot with a penknife, to make an ordinary pair of shoes, and since all civilian men had turn-ups to their trousers, he improvised these by turning up the bottoms and securing them as best he could with wet mud. He loosened the belt to let the trousers drop to cover his shoes; then, with his battledress jacket under his arm, his RAF insignia concealed, and with his heavy black polo-necked sweater he would pass as a civilian.

* * *

Liz opened the desk and found nothing. Stopped in her tracks like this, her mind raced on, on its own momentum. Had she broken some kind of golden rule, by mentioning in her last letter the fact of their separate times shifting out of synch, yet moving towards each other? Then she remembered the phrase 'two eggs on my plate', and she guessed he was on operations.

* * *

During the next nine days, he made his heavy way across muddy fields, encountering helpful Dutch citizens, people who risked their lives by harbouring him in barns, hay ricks and cow sheds, and who brought him coffee and sandwiches. He staggered into streams in the dark, getting wet through, battled against exhaustion and danger. He met with a bizarre piece of luck when he came across a scarecrow wearing a waterproof coat. He shrugged this on, leaving the scarecrow with just a hat. In view of his dark hair, in this land of fair-skinned blonds, he thought: Why not? then he whipped the hat off the remains of the scarecrow and settled it as jauntily as he could on his head. Not exactly a wide boy, he thought, more like a spiv who's hit hard times.

As evening drew on, he neared a group of houses and found to his joy that there was an orchard attached to one of them. He helped himself to fruit, sat against a tree and slaked his thirst and took the edge off his hunger with several apples, stuffing several more into his pockets.

Clambering to his feet once more, he was about to leave the orchard, when a figure came out of the house. In the dusk, he could just determine that it was a German soldier, and flung himself down into a shallow depression, holding his breath. Moving slowly through the trees, the soldier sought the biggest and rosiest specimen. He came to within a few feet of where David lay and stopped.

* * *

"Imperial War Museum; can I help you?"

"I'm trying to trace the whereabouts of a World War Two airman. He was stationed at Waddington ..."

"I'm sorry; we don't deal with records. You might try the Public Records Office, or possibly St Catherine's House."

"I see. Thank you."

Liz sighed. All right then, the desk, provenance of. If this were the plot of a Dickens novel, she thought, it could be solved by some highly improbable coincidence or an expert on the *Antiques Roadshow* tracing its ancestry, maybe.

Of course. An advert in the local paper perhaps, to track down the vendor at the car boot sale. Worth a try.

* * *

The German solider looked back up into the tree, helped himself to an apple, then went back into the house.

Walking on, as it seemed to him, for ever, David's tired brain began to play tricks. He had the fanciful notion that he was, like some earth-bound Flying Dutchman, travelling wearily on for ever, like Wagner's hero, and would do so until he found the love of a good woman. An unlikely warrior, he was much given to analysing his way through any situation, and as he trudged on across the muddy field, his mood was sharply broken by the sound of a barking dog from a nearby farm.

I hope I'm well downwind of the brute, he thought, I must be pretty ripe by now.

Guided by spasmodic gunfire, he continued through the night until he reached another farm. The thought of a cup of hot coffee drew him on like a magnet. He deliberately made what noise he dared, to see if there was a dog at large. Nothing barked or scuffled at a chain, so he made for the farmhouse door. A figure came out to wash his face at the pump. David dropped flat on his face. Raising his head cautiously, he saw it was a German soldier.

He cursed briefly. Now he would have to make a detour of a mile or so. He trudged on, having by now reached that state of wide-eyed exhaustion in which he felt he could go on for ever, and would never sleep again. Eventually, a small hayrick presented itself so, taking off his shoes, he peeled off his sodden socks and wrung them out. The water poured through his fists and formed a puddle. Completely wretched, cold and tired, he clambered onto the hayrick and, against all the odds, slept.

When he woke the next morning, still cold, still tired, he ate the last of his Horlicks tablets and looked about him. For a few treacherous seconds, he seriously considered surrendering himself to the next German soldier he saw and sitting out the remainder of the war in an *Oflag*. Realising that this would not suit his temperament one bit, he shook the thought from him, sighed again and walked on.

* * *

"Hallo, my name is Tom Wheatley. I understand you want to know about my great-uncle's old desk."

"Yes, but I also want to know what happened to him during the war. Did he survive it?"

"Nobody knows. His bomber was shot down over Holland. The pilot saw him bale out, and the rest of the crew got back. But Great-uncle David was never traced. He seems to have vanished into thin air."

"What happened to the desk from the time he vanished?"

"Well, it appears that at some point during the war, he bought it from the station. It seemed to be important to him, judging from the fact that he presented the mess with a superior model."

"How did it come into your possession?"

"Well, it was just always there. It was given to me to do my homework at. I grew up with it, and I put it in the boot sale because I'm refurbishing my place. I had no use for it, really."

When they met face to face, Tom looked at her quite thoroughly, trying to think where he had seen her before. He said as much.

"You may have seen my photograph," Liz told him. "If so, it will make it easier for me to explain things."

When Liz had told him her extraordinary story, Tom sat taking it in without speaking. Eventually, he said, "Well, the photo would seem to clinch it. It's been in the family album for over fifty years. And it was pretty smart of you to keep another print, as proof. This is definitely one for Stephen Hawking."

"Our next step is to check with the Public Records Office," Liz suggested.

All they got from there was the information that Flight Sergeant Wheatley had vanished without trace. No body was found, no uniform or possessions.

* * *

He saw the shell coming towards him, but in his demoralised state, he couldn't be bothered to take shelter. This is it, he thought, too tired even to be distressed at imminent death … And then it was as if it had never happened. He looked up, disbelieving in his survival. He looked around. The hayrick was gone; the farm was gone; even the windmills had vanished. He found himself on some sort of concrete verge, at the side of what he took to be an autobahn. Vehicles flashed by: sleek, streamlined cars; motor caravans; a transporter carrying a consignment of cars, and the portmanteau name, Volkswagen, painted on its side. Was he in Germany, then? He remembered the People's Car, Hitler's pride and joy, and went cold. Had the unthinkable happened after all, and Germany had won this time? He began walking in the direction of the traffic.

It was not long before a police car picked him up. To his further surprise, the policeman in the passenger seat addressed him in English, but with a Dutch accent.

"Do you realise you are breaking the law, by walking on the motorway?"

"I … er … don't quite know how to put this, but I'm a sort of time traveller."

"Of course you are. Get in."

The other officer asked him where his vehicle was.

"I left it flying over the Dutch fields in 1943. I wouldn't bother searching for it if I were you."

The police officers conferred in Dutch as they drove on.

"We should have searched him. He could be a dangerous nutter."

"I don't think so. He's just confused. Look at the way he's looking around him. You'd think he'd never seen anything like it before. The sooner we can dump him with Immigration Control, the better."

"He's looking really rough … Hey, mad Englishman, when did you last have a proper meal?"

"Fifty-six years ago – plus nine days."

* * *

Liz saw the item in the Strange But True page on the Internet:

A young Englishman was picked up by the Dutch highway police on a motorway twenty miles from Amsterdam. He was wearing an old raincoat, a trilby and the remains of a vintage RAF uniform. The only possessions of note were a uniform button that concealed a compass; a silk handkerchief that bore a map of north-west Europe, circa 1943; and the remains of a packet that held Horlicks tablets …

* * *

He need not have worried that the other passengers on the ferry would stare at him. Even with his uniform jacket on, they assumed he was part of a nostalgia party; they were quite the thing now. Forties parties, Sixties hippies.

"What next? Eighties groups, dressed as Yuppies?"

David nodded and smiled at the garrulous old man commenting on the antics of the young. Then the thought struck him …

He managed to get from the old chap his address and phone number. Not difficult – it would have been harder not to have got his life story. You never knew when you might need such a friend, especially one from your own era; certainly in the present circumstances, when you had no idea where you would be staying, or what you could use for money or identity.

* * *

As he walked towards the building where Liz lived, he saw her coming out. At the same time, a woman crossed the road with a pram, and a car came to rest a few yards further on. He ran towards where Liz was, calling her name. She ignored him, even when he stood in her path, waving his arms and yelling at her. They collided …

… The Universe lurched, twisted itself inside out, then settled. Liz had vanished, only to reappear, walking exactly as she had, out of the building, with the same searching look on her face. The woman with the pram crossed the road again, as before, and the car materialised, to come to rest once more. Liz walked towards him with a welcoming smile.

"It is you, isn't it?" they both said at the same time and laughed at themselves.

"Well, I'm glad to see you at last," David said, "I had begun to think we had lost the war after all."

"You wait till I tell you how we beat the Germans again in 1966."

"Not another war?"

"Relax, this was only football. Now to get you cleaned up and a hot meal inside you."

"By the way," he asked her, "how did you know I would be here? Once I'd checked out where you live, I was going to telephone you."

"Well, I don't want to enter into the complexities of time travel, but you already have."

THE MORE THINGS CHANGE ...

The alarm sounded. Beep-beep, beep-beep. Tracey Chandler, her mind responding to what it was trained to expect, woke immediately, sighed, threw the duvet off and slipped out of bed. She didn't disturb Mr Chandler; she valued having time to herself. After putting yesterday's papers in the recycling box, she switched on the television. This early in the day, she could please herself when she watched, without disapproval from her husband, who had a habit of sighing like an air brake at her dissolute habits. Had he been a Victorian father he would no doubt have disapproved of reading novels in the morning.

She adjusted the thermostat to a higher setting, to make the radiators come on. Until then, she would put the new gas fire on. It had worked perfectly when the man demonstrated it yesterday, but this time, nothing happened. She remembered, fondly, the old tiled fireplace, collectible now, that her grandparents had after the war with its differing shades of beige. True, you had to light the fire yourself, but at least it worked.

She had a cup of decaf and a slice of toast then, leaving her husband's breakfast of cereals and tea on a tray, she took two canvas shopping bags and made for the bus stop.

The first call was to the chemist's, to pick up a repeat prescription.

"I'm sorry, Mrs Chandler, but instead of Seroxat tablets, they've given you the Paroxetene, in liquid form. Perhaps you'd like to call round at the surgery and get another prescription." Then, to her disapproval, she was told the Paroxetene would have to be poured away. A terrible waste, but Health and Safety decreed these things.

* * *

The alarm clock woke Beryl Chandler at seven o'clock. The little rod oscillated between the domes like a fire engine, which was why she had to keep it under a cushion across the room every night. She threw back the quilt, pulled out the stone hot water bottle, then went downstairs to the kitchen, took down the blackout and turned the wireless on. She put yesterday's papers on the pile for the Scouts to collect, filled the kettle, switched on the hotplate and placed the kettle on top. She would have to remember not to do this when she eventually got the electric kettle she had been promised. She scalded the pot and got the tea caddy from the shelf.

The Light Programme came gradually to life, playing cheerful music. Ragtime, Cole Porter; a nonsense song by Arthur Askey. George Formby was thought to be a bit too saucy this early in the day.

The fire had been set last night, so all she needed to do was to set a match to the paper and twigs under the coal, and the firelighter did the rest. She would miss the old hob; it was handy for making a milk pudding or for baking potatoes, but Stan wanted a modern tiled grate in various shades of beige. Not to her taste, but he had worked hard on the house and wanted to make it look modern.

She made a list of calls to be made. First the chemist, to pick up the phenobarbitones for Stan, aspirins for herself, for her you-know-whats, and a packet of three to make sure she kept on having her you-know-whats. Two children were plenty in these uncertain times.

Rounding up her shopping bags, shopping basket and ration books, she made for Wimbush's in the High Street. They might have had something nice come in. There was a queue, so perhaps her luck was in. She joined it. Swiss rolls, someone said, only one each.

She hoped there would not be a daytime raid today. It would be too frustrating to have to run for the shelters before she got her Swiss roll. Penge was right in the path of Bomb Alley, which ran all the way from the south-east coast to the capital.

The woman in front of her had a child with her. She saw the woman give the girl sixpence and heard her tell her to stand behind her, as if they were not together. Beryl sniffed. They would get two Swiss rolls for their family; Beryl and Stan would have to manage with one. Then she realised that she would have done the same thing, if the children had still been at home. She swiftly brushed the thought aside. When she thought of Pauline and Geoffrey, she tended to get weepy. They were in the rural North Midlands, and she didn't know when she would next see them. She wondered vaguely why the child in front of her had not been evacuated, but her reverie was broken by the assistant telling them all that the Swiss rolls were running out, and it might not be worth their while to remain in the queue.

As bad luck would have it, the woman in front and her child took the last two Swiss rolls. So they had had the one destined for her and Stan. Bristling with annoyance, she moved on to the butcher's.

"You've had your fats for this week, Mrs Chandler," the butcher told her, then, seeing the tired look on her face, he added, *sotto voce*, "but I've got some spare dripping in the back. You won't mind paying a few more coppers, will you?" He nipped off to get it and came back with a small package.

"Here's that bit of material my wife said you could have," he said, loudly, for the benefit of the queue. This fooled no one, but they said nothing. You never knew when you might want a favour from him yourself.

She took the bus to Bromley library. Only one book per fortnight now, owing either to the paper shortage or half the library staff being directed to war work. She took great care to proffer the exact change on the bus. She had been cheated by the conductress last time, who had given her an Irish florin in her change. Two shillings was a lot to lose when you were on a tight budget.

* * *

The cock crowed and Widow Chandler woke to the sound of birdsong, the clucking of her chickens and the occasional bleat of the nanny goat. She lay in bed for a few more minutes, enjoying the smells of the countryside, no less pleasurable for being familiar and mundane. This was a part of the day she loved best, before the work began. She was one who believed in counting her blessings. She did not pray much, but was given to reflection, and she thought now that, on the whole, life had been good to her. She had had an attentive husband and obedient children; the one now dead, and the others moved on to take up their trades in the nearby town. Having now no family to look after, she had turned her busy nature to making a living in the traditional ways. She delivered babies, laid out the dead, nursed the sick and continued to make the beer. Now she yawned, threw back the blankets and reached for her skirts and smock.

The fire was still in; she had banked it up with some damp wood, which just kept it alive. She had brought her little bed into the kitchen after her husband died, to save fuel and keep warm.

She made her breakfast of an apple, some bread and cheese and some fresh spring water, before picking a few herbs. They would go into some boiling water with a little honey, later in the day. She was glad the winter was over. She had lost ten of her chickens to hungry foxes; the pump had frozen, and she had had the bother of bringing in buckets of snow to thaw before she could make porridge. But some new hen chicks had hatched and were by now busy laying. There had been a good crop of apples last autumn, and they had kept well under straw and old sacking. She was popular, and an essential member of the village. Unlike Old Mother Benton, whom a spiteful neighbour had denounced as a witch, because she had objected to the unruly behaviour of the neighbour's children. She had had nobody to speak up for her, and it hadn't helped that she kept a cat. "So does anybody who wants to keep down the mice," she had told the court. Ah, yes, but hers was a black cat, declared the prosecution. Besides, she was of no use except to herself, and the priest wanted to appear vigilant and to curry favour with the bishop, so the old lady had got hauled off to the bonfire. The burning was watched avidly by the neighbour who had denounced her. She had brought her children with her, too, one of whom became mute on the spot and never spoke again. He was afterwards dismissed as simple, was bullied and chivvied, and used as a drudge.

These were bad times; when had there been any good ones? Widow Chandler thought, and determined to make the most of whatever good fortune came her way.

She bustled about, preparing vegetables for the stew, then put her shawl over her head, took her new purse and tied its strings about her neck this time. She had been robbed by a cutpurse the last time she went to market. Luckily, she had made her few purchases early, and had in it only a few herbs, a stone and a false coin she had picked up in the dust. She cackled quietly to herself. She went to the hen coop, chose a chicken and wrung its neck. She fancied bartering it for a few rabbits.

* * *

Tracey had finished her shopping, local businesses mostly. Use them or lose them, she thought, before the big superstores gobble them all up. She said no thank you to the offer of a plastic bag, keen to save the planet in many tiny ways, and she didn't care if the smart people laughed at her as they drove off in their gas guzzlers. Time for a cup of coffee at the local church, and to buy some Fairtrade goods from them, before she took some items to a charity shop. If she had not worn a particular item of clothing for six months, she passed it on. She remembered just in time to post the letter to British Gas. That's told them, she thought.

* * *

Back from Bromley, Beryl decided on a tea break and called in at the Tea Pot, a café in a small passage off Penge High Street, to chat with friends. To find out whose son was on leave, whose daughter had gone into the Land Army, and who had been directed to war work. It was here that she heard the story of the landlady who opened the letters of one of her lodgers, a man on secret war work. Fortunately the letter was of personal interest only, from an uncle, but the landlady was disinclined to believe her lodger was not a spy and asked him rather sharply why he was not in uniform. He couldn't even tell her that it was secret work. She would have spread it about, with exaggerations, to the entire neighbourhood. He finally told his department, who moved him on. Beryl and her friends didn't, of course, know what happened to the landlady.

Then on to her favourite occupation, a Make Do And Mend session with the Women's Voluntary Service. They had, the week before, learned how to make a batch of butterless, eggless, sugarless rock cakes, and they were to be judged by a committee of fearless ladies who had never quite got used to rationed foods and talked longingly of everything known as Pre-War. Real eggs, real potato mash and refined sugar, instead of the dried egg, the Pom and the ghastly saccharin that drove many to do without sweetened tea altogether.

* * *

Widow Chandler walked through the market until she found the man who caught the rabbits. "I've got a good, plump chicken here," she said, boldly, "easily worth a few of your little rabbits."

"Hmm," he demurred, "but you'll get enough skin to make a pair of mitts though. You couldn't let me have a couple of eggs to go with it, I suppose?"

She looked back at him, shrewdly. She couldn't ever be sure whether he was poacher or gamekeeper. Most likely the one turned the other, if she was any judge.

"I haven't brought eggs with me today, but I'll give you a penny, and the deal is made." They agreed and shook hands. She now had only one call to make. To Crazy Meg, who lived in a cottage near the top of the hill.

"Are you there, Meg?" she called. She didn't want to go searching the hedgerows, to find the village lunatic; she had to get back to milk the goat.

Meg came out of the cottage, and recognising the Widow, called her inside. She was one of the few people Meg trusted.

"I suppose you want the paste I've made up for the rheumatism? Well, come in and have a sup of ale while I get it." She gathered some dock leaves from the garden to wrap round the preparation, which she took from a crock jar.

"Thank you, Meg; that's a farthing, isn't it?"

Meg gave her a look. "I'm only mad, not daft, mistress. You know quite well it's a ha'penny."

The Widow smiled, took the paste and paid for it, then they sat down to pass on what information there was to be exchanged. Meg's nephew had that week made his way to London, on foot, to look for work on the river. He had started before dawn, and reassured his mother that he would be sure to get a ride on a cart along the way and be in town by nightfall.

"It must be some ten to fifteen mile away," the Widow said, "they do say the town is spreading itself, what with all the people coming in to live there to seek their fortune." They both considered this fact in the friendly silence.

"'T'will be needing more highways made, too," she continued, "for folks from the villages to get there." She knew it was all right to talk in this fanciful way to Meg, who had even more fantastical notions herself.

"That's right, my dear. They will have to make tunnels in the earth, with special wagons to carry people. And a great many lanterns, too," she added. Even fantasy bore its own logic. The Widow tried not to laugh at her friend. Her madness, after all, did not take the form of bizarre behaviour, just mad ideas. Her friends humoured her and took care not to let the priest know of her talk of horseless carriages and flying machines.

Eventually the Widow stirred herself, they blessed each other and wished Good Day.

* * *

Tracey decided to walk the rest of the way home. After she had put the washing in, she would sit down in the afternoon and watch *Countdown*, a good reception courtesy of the mast at the top of the Crystal Palace grounds. Not a bad day's work, she thought, as she began the long climb back up Penge High Street and turned right, near the top of the hill, into Kingswood Road.

* * *

Beryl smiled to herself as she walked home. She cherished the looks on the faces of the committee as they struggled to swallow the sample cakes. That would teach them to get us making cakes without even dried fruit to make them palatable. She was also pleased with herself. Her cakes had been judged the best, because she was the only one who remembered to put in the grated carrot, to sweeten them.

I hope Jerry leaves us alone tonight, she thought. I couldn't take another night of those damn rockets on the Crystal Palace grounds. She made a last call at the newsagent's to get the *Daily Herald* for herself and the *Manchester Guardian* for Stan, before making her way up Penge High Street and turning right, into Kingswood Road.

* * *

Widow Chandler had had a profitable day and looked forward to applying Meg's mixture to her aching shoulders, as she made her way up the dusty hill path. She was glad she lived so high up the hill; she at least avoided floods and dampness. Before she turned right, into the lane to her cottage, among the trees in the King's Woods, she took a last look to where the hill went even further up. They do say you can see clear to London from there, she reminded herself.

TIME BOMB

Jessica ran to answer the phone before it rang off and tripped over the sandbag under the window. She lifted the receiver and gave the firm's name …

… Nathan Baxter woke with a start as the dream ended abruptly once again, and he threw aside the duvet. He had had the same vivid dream twice before. He was trying to phone someone with an urgent message. It was not unlike those dreams in which you are trying to read a letter, but you can't follow it. You are just about to grasp the subject matter when the text begins to shift and fade, the letters coalesce and darken, and something intrudes into the dream and breaks it up. He tried to put it out of his head, and got up and went into the bathroom. What was his subconscious trying to tell him?

… the line went dead. Jessica replaced the receiver. This was the third time this had happened. Each time, at five o'clock, someone had phoned, just as she was getting her hat and coat to leave the office; that was why she had tripped each time over the spare sandbag. She had reached for the phone from where the hatstand stood.

"Mind how you go in the blackout," her boss called to her, as she joined the rest of the staff in the exodus for the buses, "and if tonight's raid goes on for more than three hours, you can come in at half past nine tomorrow."

She was grateful for this consideration. Her husband was in the Army, and she had a boy of twelve to care for. She had felt guilty about not having young Frank evacuated, but the boy felt he would prefer to be with her and chance it with the Luftwaffe, than to go and live in dubious safety with strangers. Besides, he felt as protective towards his mother as she did towards him.

Funny about those phone calls, she thought. Probably someone who realised, as they called, that it was five o'clock and decided not to bother after all. But three times? ...

... Nathan determined to ask who it was he was talking to next time and prepared for bed with a cup of chocolate and a Nurofen. He had an odd feeling about her voice. It sounded familiar; a bit like his grandmother, Granny Jess. But she had been dead for some years; what would he need to warn her of?

This time, as Jessica gave the name of the firm, it registered more clearly.

"C. W. S., Penge." (The staff were discouraged from calling it, informally, 'the Co-op'.)

"Who am I addressing, please?"

"Well, I'm only the typist, but my name is Jessica Baxter."

The dream vanished, and he sat bolt upright in bed. Granny Jess had lived in Station Road, in Penge, with her son Frank, Nathan's father, who was twelve at the time. They were bombed out on the 20th January 1943 and went to live with friends in Birmingham. Out of the fire, into the frying pan, you might say. They had had quite a narrow escape, apparently, and there was something odd about the experience. His father was reluctant to discuss it, and Nathan forbore to press him on it, assuming that the trauma of seeing his home in ruins had obscured his memory of the event.

Baxter Senior had lived with his son since Nathan's mother had died and was at this moment in bed himself, sleeping like a log. A creature of habit, he had had a fish and chip supper, bought from a chippie, as ever. Nutritionally incorrect, but he insisted on it. Food is linked very closely to the emotions, Nathan realised, and he allowed him this weakness.

"Very nourishing they are, too," his father maintained, "an absolute lifesaver."

* * *

Nathan had seen a TV series, starring Herbert Lom, who played a psychiatrist. It was he, rather than the patient, who had a recurring dream, and he broke the dream by enacting it. It had involved his trying out alarm clocks in a shop; in the episode, Herbert Lom suddenly had a eureka moment and dashed out of the shop, leaving the bewildered assistant among the jangling timepieces.

Nathan decided to do something similar. He travelled down from Worcestershire to Penge and visited the house, 23 Station Road, now rebuilt some fifty-five years and whose once-new bricks had long since lost their pale colour and had mellowed to the same tone as the surrounding bricks.

While he was in the capital, he went, on an impulse, to the War Museum, still hoping to trigger something in his mind. Then he had a thought; he would ask permission to search the archives – find out about the bomb that missed his father, and how it happened.

"You need the Public Record Office, sir, but you must make an appointment to research," the clerk told him.

At the PRO, he filled in the form and sat at a table to wait for the clerk to bring the books across to him. All this trouble about a fanciful idea. Well, in for a penny, in for a pound.

He riffled through the pages, found the place and the date at last: 'Number 23, Station Road, Penge, SE20. A direct hit. Both occupants killed.'

He felt the blood rushing against his eardrums like a river. He looked closely at the page again, expecting it to blur, expecting then to wake up. But no, there it was. He could hardly point out the error to the clerk. It would seem impertinent, in these august surroundings.

Well, he thought, if this is some kind of time warp, then the Grandfather Paradox was working in reverse. After all, he was here, he had been born – his father had been saved. But he knew that that depended on something that he, Nathan, had to do. But what? Either way, he would follow it through, like Herbert Lom, and rely on his subconscious. He closed the books, swept them up and booked them back in, tactfully declining to point out the mistake.

* * *

When money was decimalised in 1971, he had saved some old coins, a few pennies and threepenny bits, in the hope that they might some day become collectible. He sought them out and placed them on his bedside table before going to bed that night. As soon as he drifted off to sleep, he found himself where he had willed himself to be, in Penge High Street. But was he *when* he wanted to be? He bought an early evening newspaper and was reassured by the date, 19th January 1943.

He found the nearest phone box, looked up the Co-op in the directory, put two pennies in the slot and dialled the number.

As soon as he heard the young Granny Jess give the name, he pressed button A and the money dropped through. Try not to gabble, he told himself.

"You don't know me," he said, "but you will, one day. It's important that neither you nor your son stay in the house tomorrow night."

"Why not?" she asked, curiously unafraid, and struck by something familiar about his voice.

"You wouldn't believe me," he told her, "but you'll just have to trust me."

The dream disintegrated, and he woke. He checked the old money on the bedside table and found that it was short by threepence: the price of a newspaper and a phone call.

The following night, he placed by his bedside a piece of hardboard he had painted black, on which he had chalked the words: SPECIAL TONIGHT, FISH AND CHIP PORTIONS HALF PRICE AFTER NINE O'CLOCK. Then he got into bed.

* * *

On the 20th January 1943, Frank ran into the house to tell his mother about the bargain at the chip shop in the High Street.

"Can I go after nine, please?"

"Certainly not, you'll be in bed by then; and you can straighten up your face and stop sulking. I've got a treat for you – some supplementary oranges came in; you can have one now."

It isn't fair, he thought, making me go to bed early, like some silly kid. At nine o'clock, he said goodnight to his mother and went up to his bedroom. She was listening to *Happidrome* and didn't hear him come down immediately and slip out of the front door with his pocket money. She'll be pleased, really, he told himself, when I come back with extra fish and chips.

There was an irate queue at the chip shop – the proprietor wanted to know who had put the notice outside his shop. Just as Frank arrived, the sirens sounded. Everyone decided to stay put, rather than make their way home.

The strangely dressed man, who had been hanging about for some time, immediately went running down Kingswood Road towards Station Road. He had no idea what he would say when he got there, but he had to get Jessica out of the house.

He need not have worried. She was at that moment dashing out of the door and running to the chip shop, her annoyance with her son over-ridden by her frantic concern for his safety.

The anti-aircraft battery on the Crystal Palace grounds were in full voice by now, and bombs were already falling. Jessica marched her son back towards Station Road, followed at a discreet distance by the strangely dressed man. Slow down, Nathan willed at them. I don't want you killed – and I don't want to vanish into a parallel universe myself, either.

"You silly boy, I was going to get the chips myself. Now let's get into the shelter as soon as we can."

What with all the racket overhead, they hadn't heard the bomb that demolished number twenty-three, Anderson shelter and all. They found the neighbours gathered round, tearing away at the fallen bricks, looking for survivors.

* * *

Nathan slept like a child after this, but something nagged at his mind. He made another appointment at the Public Record Office, ordered the books and apologised for troubling them again as soon. The clerk looked puzzled, as if he had never seen Nathan before in his life. As indeed, he hadn't, in a sense. This in itself told Nathan something he already suspected, and it only needed the last piece in the puzzle.

There it was, on the page: '… direct hit, house unoccupied at the time.' Also in the folder was a human interest story cut from the Daily Mirror. 'Mother and son saved by fish and chip hoax.'

WAITING

The inflatable Donald Duck was a mascot. It had been won by Betty, on the night of the party at Dreamland, after she had won £10 on the pools. This being magic money, and too special to waste on the rent, it was spent on treats, presents, and new shoes for her nieces and nephews. She now patted the duck for luck, as she came into the café kitchen.

"Cheer up, Violet, it might never happen," she called across.

"It already has, you cheeky sod, as you very well know." Violet had fallen pregnant again; this would be her fifth, which she and Bert could ill afford. The trouble was, they did what many couples did who had a large family: on Sunday afternoons they sent them off to Sunday School, leaving themselves with time for what they considered to be free entertainment, though of course, when it resulted in yet another pregnancy, it turned out to be the most expensive.

Ruby pulled at her black satin uniform frock. "I had a feeling you'd have to get the white wool out again, but you know what I'm always telling you. A stitch in time saves nine, said the mother of eight, as she sewed up her husband's pyjamas."

Ivy cackled raucously as she came in. ("You lay 'em, I'll sell 'em," Betty called out.)

"You'll be the death of me, Rube. I don't know where you get these sayings. Do you make them up yourself?"

"Handed down from mother to daughter, Ivy, and the rudest ones are the oldest."

Betty, for one, could always do with light relief and was grateful for Ruby's foolery. Betty's father was terminally ill. No one ever said the word, though they sometimes mouthed it. They spoke instead of resection of the lung and hoped for remission. Betty had a feeling that his heavy smoking was not helping matters, but it had been his only pleasure for some time now, and she didn't discourage him.

It was going to be another hot day on the south-east coast, and though the Depression had slumped to its lowest point, this was not foremost in the minds of women with a living to make. There would always be catering; the perks were not bad, they could all be assured of at least one meal a day, and there were extras to take home to the kids. Besides, during the summer at least, there would always be holidaymakers to be waited on.

They braced themselves for a day bringing swollen ankles and heat exhaustion.

Joan hurried in, five minutes late, with a poorly concealed bruise to the cheek. The others exchanged looks. She never talked about her husband, but put a cheerful face on things. She believed if only she waited long enough, that he would stop. She had two small children to care for and could not afford to leave him. Her workmates, in their turn, waited for her to tell them herself.

Olive was the last to arrive. A quarter of an hour late this time.

"Couldn't you sleep, Olive?" Ruby asked her. The others laughed at the old joke.

Olive bustled about. "You lot wait till you've got to do all the things I've got to do." They all rolled their eyes at this. Olive had two very obedient children, whom she nagged and harassed. Her bustling was a device to give the impression of having matters of great moment and drama to fulfil, rather than of living a life of dull routine and boredom. She had been brought up to please herself in everything, confidently waiting for the world to provide her with glamour and excitement. When it did no such thing, she settled for marriage, flourishing her domesticity like a penitent's sackcloth. She had hovered over her children's breakfast, distractedly lifting each item on the table a few inches, then banging them down again. The milk bottle, the sugar bowl, a cup of dripping, the teapot. She continued this ritual now, lifting things set out for the waitresses to use. The trays, the teapots, the caddies, the milk jugs.

Ruby mimicked Olive's actions with dialogue. "What am I bid for these items at auction, ladies? I have here a teapot, a coffee pot and a pistol. Oh, and by the way, Olive, I've already put tea in the first five, can you find something to do that really needs doing, instead of pithering?"

Most of the women were afraid of Olive. Ruby was not. "And I might remind you that at your age, I'd already had five children."

"More fool you."

The others gasped. "You shouldn't let her talk to you like that," Ivy said.

"You can't stop people talking as they like. For that matter, you can't stop me."

Olive sniffed. "Anyway, how much housework do you ever do?"

Ruby was ready for this one. "As little as I can possibly get away with. It's more efficient that way." At home, she carried a duster around with her, attacking dust and dirt as it occurred to her, in between other activities. If she forgot the duster, she used the hem of her skirt, her sleeve pulled down over her hand, her hankie or the heel of her hand; sometimes she just blew on the dust, shifting it from one place to another. She had had her fifth baby nearly six months ago and had been back at work for a week now, working mornings only, which allowed her time to get back to feed the baby, in between Glaxo feeds. A neighbour took the two oldest to school, and the two toddlers and the baby were being looked after by her husband, whose consumption was not yet sufficiently diagnosed for him to be kept away from his children. He would stay at home until he went into the sanatorium.

Ruby had had just two days in bed with the baby and was virtuously indignant to learn that the Duchess of York had had ten days, after doing her duty to the nation. Fortunately, Ruby always enjoyed being pregnant. It was the actual raising of children which sometimes proved too much. Because of the necessity for her to go out to work, none of her children got too close to her, with the bracing effect of their not becoming too clinging and certainly no danger of their becoming coddled. Also, their immune systems were kept on their toes.

One of the petty irritations of their job was the cap they had to wear. On Violet's fine, silky hair, it had a tendency to slip backwards off her head, so she placed it forward, in the style of some ten years earlier, almost across the forehead. Ivy drew her hair back in a bun, and the cap stood upright on top of her head, with two strong Kirbigrips to keep it from slipping up and off. On Joan, Olive and Ruby, it just about held in place, showing not too much hair in front, but for Betty, her uncontrollable hair, curly and wiry, had its own way, and asserted itself against this badge of service by sliding forward until it showed more hair than cap.

Most of them liked their job, and were very good at it. They enjoyed looking after people and being in charge of the pleasantries of others' lives. Those with children to feed had chosen the job specifically to ensure that their brood had plenty to eat. There was always a modest kitchen surplus, and they were allowed to take home little treats, wrapped in greaseproof paper, though it's true to say that they had not waited for permission. There are fewer instincts so powerful as feeding one's young.

While there was only breakfast to serve, only the undercook was needed for the cooking. The cook proper, who demanded his staff referred to him as Chef – "Yes, Chef," "No, Chef," "Chef says this," "Chef says that," – would make his grand entrance at ten o'clock. The staff had various ways of avoiding giving him his title, sometimes by leaving it out of their replies, and sometimes simply by not saying anything, just giving a non-committal smile and a nod.

Early bathers came out of the sea, went into the bathing huts to change and drifted over to the restaurant. The sands began to fill up with holidaymakers and day trippers. These would not be patronising the restaurant, but would be having trays of tea brought to the sands from the smaller cafés, and those with even fewer financial resources would have brought flasks of tea, and sandwiches, the corned beef or cheese and tomato fillings of which would render the bread flabby and the cheese sweaty. The day became warmer.

Ruby was not feeling very well. She had put the raised temperature down to the hot weather, but her throat was sore, her tongue felt odd, and she was frequently dizzy. She was by nature robust and ignored the impertinence of ill health as something that must not be encouraged. She enjoyed life too much.

Ivy had lost her young man in the Great War, but was still young enough to think of investing her life in raising a family. She would not be one of those natural old maids, who felt their condition had to be explained away by the loss of a man, and that it had put them off marriage for ever; a respectable falsehood that fooled no one. Ivy took life by the scruff of the neck and set about finding herself a husband. That she was fussy about this matter was evinced by the fact that in the fifteen years since the war ended, she still had not found someone to suit. The children she craved would need someone sound, and this was her main consideration.

However, she had not reckoned on falling in love, or infatuation, as she preferred to think of it. This had resulted in her inadvertently making two dates on the same day. At either end of the arcade in which they worked, she would, that evening, have a suitor waiting. One was well set up, in a job he liked, with a decent wage. He was likable, and Ivy liked him, though no more than that. At the other end was an unstable young man who scraped what living he could. He was not particularly good-looking. But he was fun; he generated excitement, and Ivy was convinced that she loved him. There was no other way out of the arcade; she would have to choose. She confided her dilemma in Ruby.

"I think you arranged it to have the two there, Ivy, so that you'd be forced to choose."

"No, honestly, Rube, it was absent-minded. I just made a mistake. I wasn't thinking."

"Not consciously, but subconsciously you wanted to force yourself to make the choice."

Ruby was reading Freud at the time, and she never missed an opportunity to propound his findings. She looked for Freudian slips, unconscious urgings and complexes all the time; sometimes to her friends' amusement, since they were puzzled that a working-class woman with five small children would take the trouble to educate herself like this. When, however, she started going on about sex being the most important instinct of all, they were merely irritated. Ivy herself had had the last word on this.

"It can't be, Ruby, the most important instinct is for food." Ruby had no answer for this. She was very fond of her food, and had to admit to herself that she would rather go without sex than miss a meal.

Once the early breakfasts were over, preparations began for lunch. This was the busiest time. Although Chef gave himself and his restaurant airs of silver service, it was nothing of the kind. Diners were not served at the table, from the tureens, with a tablespoon; they were simply brought the silver, wrapped in a paper napkin, and the meal, already prepared, was brought to the table. The proprietor, it had to be admitted, had once been a chef, but had had a reverse of fortune owing to a distressing case of multiple food poisoning. That he had been one of its victims and that the fault lay with some dubious suppliers did not mitigate judgement, and he had had to move into another town. He also changed his name, to Mario Gopelli, which fooled no one, since he still had the broad Cockney tones from when he had been plain Bill Smith.

By one of those coincidences that give life a false sense of order and pattern, Betty knew of Mario's bad luck, and was just astute enough to let him know that she knew, but humane enough not to take too much advantage of it; only to ensure that he did not bully her nor her colleagues. If he showed signs of abusing his power as an employer, she simply raised her eyebrows and replied, *sotto voce*, "Very well, Mr Smith." He would then leave her alone to get on with her work.

Betty was not of the legion of women who were raising families; she had not lost any children, was not expecting, nor ever had been pregnant. Neither had she ever had a young man. She would not be having children, for the simple reason that she would not want to go through the preliminaries, not even to lying back and thinking of England. Betty was not attracted to men. Had she been of a more exalted class, she might, in the previous generation, have worn a suit and tie, a short haircut and a trilby. Her close friend Rose and she had been companions since school, and Betty had managed to persuade her mother to take Rose in as a lodger. Her mother, all unknowing, and only too glad of the money, was happy to let them share a double bed. In fact, she had been quite apologetic at not being able to provide separate beds. She had herself been in service from the age of twelve, and had never had the luxury of a bed to herself, until now, poignantly, and awaiting widowhood.

The hot day wore on. Customers left; side plates were lifted, hopefully, and tips were picked up and pocketed. Lunch was cleared, and there was a break before preparing tea, when the staff could put their feet up in a tiny staffroom, little more than a large broom cupboard. They sat on stools, upturned boxes and the radiator. For this last, they lifted their black satin frocks, in order not to crease them on the ridges. These were impressed, instead, on their tender bottoms and formed the basis for many a ribald joke. They let Violet sit on the only comfortable chair – a venerable old wooden kitchen armchair, which took up most of the room – as they crowded in. Ivy got her knitting out, took out a skein, placed it on Betty's outstretched hands and began winding a ball. Joan brought their tea in from the kitchen.

Betty opened the tiny transom window, lit a cigarette and directed her smoke out into the quadrangle. "It's good of Mario to let us have ten minutes. The last chap I worked for used to find us something to do all the time, even if it didn't need doing. He couldn't bear not to see us forever on the trot."

Violet blew on her tea. "He's not such a bad old stick, everything considered."

Olive gave a sideways glance at Betty. "He's always got a civil word for you, I notice."

"Must be my big brown eyes." Betty always encouraged them to laugh it off. To denounce Mario would not work well, anyway, since he would then have nothing to lose, except the bother of sacking them all and being obliged to engage six more.

Betty changed the subject. Since Ruby was doing mornings only, they felt free to pass a few sympathetic remarks about her.

"Her husband will be going into the sanatorium any day now. She'll probably lose him," she said. "I wonder how she'll manage."

"He served in the war," Ivy reminded them. "I expect the British Legion will help her out."

They sipped their tea, thoughtfully. "Any hope you'll lose your husband, Joan?" Ivy continued. Only Joan herself gasped. The others had been waiting for this opportunity to give her the support she needed. Ruby's encroaching widowhood had been the trigger.

"We have to put up with these things, don't we?" Joan said now.

"We don't have to do any such thing!" They were surprised to hear Olive express this opinion. They knew her only as a bitter woman, wrapped up in herself. She bridled at their surprise.

"Well, it's true. He won't stop treating you badly unless you make him." She always half apologised for the little humanity that she showed now and then. "You've got to do something. You're just wishing your life away."

There was a pause of half a minute while they sipped tea, drew on cigarettes and wound wool.

"You know what Ruby said to me the other day?" Betty said. "I think it was one of those quotations she keeps coming up with. It went: 'Life is what happens while you're waiting for it to begin.'" They all absorbed the misquotation and thought about this.

Violet nodded. "That just about sums us up. We all spend our lives waiting, one way and another."

Joan expressed the opinion of them all. "The thing about Ruby is she's clever."

Ruby's limitless curiosity about life had always been dismissed in this way. It puzzled those who did not want to make the effort of thinking it through. Among some, this had caused animosity, and she sometimes found herself being victimised. Her present companions, however, liked her; she made them laugh. Besides, she was clearly on the side of the workers, not all of whom support their own class, in any age.

Betty spoke. "The thing is, she looks ahead; she imagines all sorts of things happening and being invented, like machines with a memory or men travelling to the moon." She laughed a little self-consciously, then paused, gently tapping ash from her cigarette, while they all savoured the companionable silence. "She even reckoned we'll have a woman Prime Minister in our lifetime."

"Blimey, give us a chance, girl," Ivy said, "we've not long got the vote."

Joan considered herself more down to earth. "I shouldn't worry about that; a lot of her notions are out there with the fairies, for all she's got some good ideas."

Betty was more prey to superstition. "Oh, I don't know, some of us believe in ghosts."

There was another pause.

Violet voiced an intuition they all had of Betty. "What future do you see for yourself, then, Betty? You don't seem the marrying kind, but you're just the sort to get snapped up."

"Well, I think I'd like to get my own little tea room some day." She veered off the subject of marriage. She and Rose had discussed the idea of a tea room and had begun to save for it.

They all absorbed this thought for a few moments.

Joan suddenly remembered something. "Oh, did anyone remind Ruby to come back for the photo? Mario's brought his box Brownie. He wants a picture of us all." There were, on the wall, photographs of staff going back to the middle of the previous century.

An electric bell summoned them back to the kitchen.

"Put your nice smiles on, girls," Olive said. "And don't forget – always be sincere, especially if you don't mean it."

Betty stubbed out her Woodbine. "I bet you got that off Ruby."

Violet collected up the mugs. "Have a nice time on your date tonight, Ivy, and don't talk to any strange men."

It was Betty who responded. "They're all bloody strange; I'll never figure them out if I live to a hundred and ten."

The photo, when it eventually joined the others on the wall, showed them as they had been. Before Joan finally left her husband and threw herself on the mercy of the church, the parish and her friends. Before Betty went to her father's funeral; before Ruby's scarlet fever disrupted her family's life for the next six months; before Ivy made her choice, and stood by it for life; and before Violet miscarried. It showed them, smiling for the camera, with Ivy at the back on the left, Olive next to her, Joan sitting on the left, next to Betty, who, incidentally, did get the little tea room with Rose, and did live to be a hundred and ten. It showed Ruby, blinking as the shutter opened, and Violet, with the Donald Duck in front. Six women in 1933, all living their ramshackle lives, coping with poverty, disease, violence and bereavement, and living in hope and humour; caught in a snapshot, in the comparative innocence between one crisis and another, waiting.

YULETIDE

The family walked steadily on across the plain. They had been going for several days, trudging through the snow, with very little wildlife showing its face. There were always robins, bold enough to seek titbits of food from the group every time they stopped to make a fire, to set the traps for small rodents and send their terriers in search of rabbits, and the skins of wine and water were welcome refreshment, each time they paused. They had brought with them chickens, eggs and a goat to eat on the journey, and a boar and their best ox for the ceremony. This year, they had set out earlier than usual, to give themselves more time to rest by the way, and had left behind their neighbours, some of them busy preserving and storing food or tending livestock, making and mending farming implements, and generally guarding the homestead while the celebrants went on pilgrimage. Those expecting additions to the family at any time now stayed behind with their midwives, having urged their husbands to go ahead. It was important that they should not miss the ceremony. The health and fortunes of their children would depend upon it.

The young girl walked with her grandmother, conscious of the privilege. Not everyone got so close to the matriarch. The old lady, almost fifty years old now, had earned her place in society, not only because she had had the largest number of children in the group, twelve fat, healthy babies, all of whom had survived, but because of her wisdom and peace-making abilities, and her skill with herbs and potions. She had got through three husbands, not because she was careless of their welfare, but because they were all warriors and had died defending their families. Even now, past childbearing, she did not lack suitors.

This year the girl dared to hope that she would be allowed to carry the mistletoe to the altar. The temple was a new one, the building materials of which had been brought from far away, and this was an added excitement for her. But something in this momentous change had prompted her to think all the more about it. The old temples were something she had regarded as having been there since the world was made. Now she began to realise that humanity could change its surroundings: exert power.

"What would happen if we did not make the journey, Grandmother?" she asked. "Would not the sun rise without our prayers?"

The matriarch had to be diplomatic here; she had long suspected that the spirits would go about their business of their own accord whether or not the observances were undertaken, but she knew how important it was for people to come together to acknowledge the gifts of nature and to believe the spirits had their welfare in mind. She could have said to the group, "We are, after all, puny compared with the forces around us, and all we can do is to till the soil, raise the livestock and provide for our children. The rest is beyond us, and the great Cause is not for us to make appeals to." Had she said all of this, then the result would be despair and disruption. People could not bear to think that nature was indifferent to man.

Now she said, "Continue to think your own thoughts, child, and find your own wisdom, but be careful not to make it too well-known what is in your head." She looked shrewdly at the girl, thinking how fitting a leader she would become in her time.

Since they had left the forests behind, they felt more cheerful. The wintry afternoon sun made their shadows long across the plain. The children looked forward to the following morning. After the ceremonial, there would be feasting and games. There was even a rumour of sweetmeats, but these were always kept secret from the children, to sharpen the pleasure. There would, of course, be much foolery, to remind themselves that they were only mortal, but also to be enjoyed for its own sake.

The girl was twelve; she had, the previous year, come under the influence of the moon goddess and her body obeyed its rhythms. Now that she was fertile, it was time she was married. However, she still had the curiosity of a younger child. She would suddenly ask a disconcerting question, one that would make even her grandmother stop and think.

"Are men more important than women, Grandmother?" she asked her now.

"Whatever gave you that idea, girl?"

"Well, they wear the grandest robes for ceremonies, and they are bigger than us and have more strident voices. It just made me think that the spirits favoured them more and that we were expected to make way for them in everything."

"It is as well to let them *think* they rule us, but to go your own way quietly, without them noticing it."

"Won't that make them angry? I mean, when they discover we have taken our own course, despite them?"

"Not if you distract their attention away from it, and work your magic on them."

There was a pause. "Do they know we have magic powers?"

"They believe we do, and that amounts to the same thing."

"Your herbs and potions, you mean?"

"That's right. But let us be quiet now; the men will see us talking together, and that makes them nervous."

That night's rest was the last one, and it took only half the morning to reach their destination. Darkness had lifted sufficient for them to make out the shape of the new stones, their corners sharp and as yet unweathered, the capstones all still in place. The earth, in its annual wobble, undetectably slow, began to tip its northern hemisphere towards its parent star, bringing the promise of the return of warmth and life, as the sun rose over the heel stone.